CROSSED ODDS

CRYSTAL DYSTOPIA SERIES: BOOK ONE

CAREY BLAKELY

"And then the day came when the risk to remain tight, in a bud, became more painful than the risk it took to blossom."
   —LASSIE BENTON

"The only way out is through."
   —ADAPTED FROM THE ROBERT FROST POEM "A SERVANT TO SERVANTS"

"I think of the self-actualizing man not as an ordinary man with something added, but rather as the ordinary man with nothing taken away."
   —ABRAHAM MASLOW

"We live in a perpetually burning building, and what we must save from it, all the time, is love."
   —TENNESSEE WILLIAMS

CONTENTS

CHAPTER 1
DAILY BREAD

"WHAT IF YOU could shape your future with your thoughts? What if *you* held the keys to your own destiny?" Light shone off his bald head as he smiled; his promise felt as resplendent and unreal as his incredibly white teeth.

Keira sat up in bed, awakened by her alarm. A sideways glance told her it was 06:30 and confirmed that she was alone in bed in the same cramped, uninspiring apartment as yesterday. With the same ache Keira had felt every recent morning, she acknowledged that Blaise was still palpably absent. It had been almost three weeks since she disappeared.

"Clearly, my thoughts didn't change a thing," Keira muttered, getting out of bed.

The shining man and his glittery promises had appeared in her dreams for several nights in a row. His messages were always about the power of thought to change the direction of life. It simultaneously captivated her and seemed like quackery.

As she walked over to the kitchen, her left ankle made a light cracking noise—a running injury from the job. I need to stretch that ankle and focus on healing it, she thought, while at the same time questioning whether there was any purpose in anything anymore.

She opened an aluminum goo pack, her daily bread in the year 2122.

Squeezing the contents into her mouth, she detected a slight hint of chemical strawberry. Issued by the government to all residents of These United States, the goo packs contained the building blocks of life and nutritional requirements to be a healthy human being. But they were a far cry from the enjoyment of real food, a luxury only the uber-rich could afford.

Keira remembered the tart sweetness of an orange, the way juice sprayed up from the pulp as she peeled back the bright rind—the citrus scent an inhalation of pure joy and wonder.

We were so blessed then, she thought as she tossed the goo pack into the recycling receptacle, but we had no idea.

But despair would beget nothing but despair. It was time to get to work and back to the search for Blaise.

It was one of those late October days when the winds blew in hot from the desert, threatening to lick up westward flames of destruction. The air temperatures felt like an unsettling mix of hot and cold, like the season couldn't make up its mind whether to relinquish summer and yield to fall, or to prolong summer and deny fall for a little while longer.

She walked through a sector of the city of inland San Diego that had been revitalized with plantings, unlike most of the oppressively concrete metropolis, and watched the palm fronds bend in the wind as fire alerts buzzed, warning citizens to be extra vigilant.

It was a clear reminder of how tenuous her situation was—caught in a moment of transition—a turning point that could go either way. The air was dry and foreboding, yet also soft and warm as Indian summer should be.

She hoped the planted palm and mesquite trees and birds of paradise would continue to thrive, supplying beauty and inspiration to a city deprived of both, but the chance of fire was nerve-rackingly high.

City employees in yellow fire suits sprayed the greenery with water. The no-flame symbol flashed on every corner of every block; citizens were to refrain from using anything with the ability to spark.

Wildfires were just one of the many dangers threatening These United States, a nation that consisted of forty-eight states after Hawaii and Texas defected in 2075 and the country regrouped under its new name.

In 2122, These United States found itself struggling toward light and life in an effort to lift the country up from the devastation of World War IV, which had ended ten years ago but still left its insidious mark everywhere. It was estimated that about four in ten people worldwide had perished in the war. Plant and animal populations had likewise been decimated.

Yet just as the nation began to nourish hope for the future, the same old mistakes related to power, corruption, shortsightedness, and fear-mongering threatened to undo the progress and send the country hurtling toward a new destruction.

It was a push-pull, a country on the brink.

A similar crossing of worlds played out in Keira's heart. It was quite possible that Blaise was alive, and it was equally possible that she was not. Keira couldn't even bring herself to use the word "dead." Believing there was a chance that Blaise still lived was the motivation Keira needed to put one foot in front of the other and persevere to find her.

KEIRA STEPPED through the door of the Department of Child Abductions: California 4 Division to find her detective partner standing over his desk with a stylus in his mouth, looking antsy. Charlie often exuded nervous energy, leading Keira to nickname him Squirmy, which caught on in the department among the other detectives.

Squirmy could take and deliver a good joke, so he took the ribbing in stride. Besides, he knew he had a powerhouse partner in Keira. The two of them had returned more children and made more arrests than any other detective duo in the department for the past five years in a row—ever since Keira was tapped to join the force.

Keira and Squirmy's skills at returning kidnapped children were in high demand. Very few people could reproduce naturally, which created an unmet desire for children that led to crime and the government's involvement on multiple levels.

"What's up, Squirmy? You're early and on it today."

"Yep, nervous jitters are the new caffeine. Why not just rely on your own frayed nervous system to get you going in the morning?" he asked with a faint smile. "Well, we've got a missing ten-month-old in District South 7 who was just reported stolen from the head of Plant Sustainability, so this one's a Code Red."

Whenever the kidnapping affected a high-ranking government official, the priority and pressure ratcheted up. Because of their track record, Keira and Squirmy were always assigned to the priority cases in California 4.

"Let me strap up. You can brief me during the flight. Thanks," Keira said.

He nodded and began to put on his own weapon straps.

They walked to the elevators and ascended in seconds to the fiftieth floor, where the Departure Portal was located. They approached the closest squad mod, an aircraft powered by electric propellers. To open the gull-wing doors, Keira placed her fingertips on the squad mod's identity sensor on the side rear panel. Once in the pilot's seat, sensors adjusted the seat and mirrors to the optimal position for her body and automatically buckled her in.

She entered the address of the crime scene into the navigation system, which replied to her, "Affirmative, Detective Kincaid. Travel time of two minutes and thirty-four seconds. Cleared for takeoff."

Keira shifted the gear shaft forward, propelling the aircraft out the launch doors into the government airspace. Once clear of the building, the navigation system warned her about oncoming craft from the south. She followed the instructions and soon saw the black jet in question, bearing the insignia of Bank of Commerce California.

She didn't like how select corporations could now use the government airspace, which up to three years ago had been restricted to military, police, and other government officials with special clearance. Corporations worked their hands into whatever they wanted, she thought.

Squirmy cleared his throat. The sound startled Keira slightly, making her realize that she'd been wound tight in her head a bit too long.

"All right, here goes," he said. "The missing is a ten-month-old boy named Liam. The state father is Stephen O'Connor, head of Plant Sustainability. The state mother is Catherine Strauss, a former analyst at Central Budgets. The breeders—seed, egg, and surrogate—have all been rounded up for questioning. We'll get to them upon return."

"Breeder" was the informal name for a fertile person participating in the government program Operation Life Speed, a coordinated attempt to preserve the human population by ramping up the reproductive process. Any person considered highly likely to be fertile based on medical screenings, which were obligatory for all people of prime reproductive age, were recruited. The breeders were wooed with money, occasional real food, and other perks, including being able to keep one child to raise as their own.

Although the breeders lived independently in their own homes and received many benefits from their voluntary participation, the consistent fertility treatments—some of an experimental nature—exacted a harsh psychological and physical toll.

Keira banked right to avoid the high buildings of Skyline Central, the headquarters of the most influential companies located in San Diego.

Squirmy, looking down at his tablet to read the details, continued, "At 06:41, Mr. O'Connor reported the child missing. He said his wife had gone into the baby room to check on Liam and found the crib empty. A window pane had been lasered out and the alarm system disabled, which means we're dealing with at least one sophisticated techie."

Keira nodded while keeping her eyes on the sky. "Did the cameras record anything?"

"No, they disabled the cameras on the outside and inside of the estate, so we've got no eyes on the perp."

That was typically the case in carefully planned kidnappings.

Babies were at a premium. There was no limit to what people would pay or do to get them. While the government used a lottery system to give babies to married couples who wanted them, to be eligible each person had to pass mental and physical assessments, have clean legal records, and be clear of suspicious associations, such as being related to a criminal. The requirements eliminated a significant number of couples.

The rich, like government higher-ups O'Connor and Strauss, could jump the line and pay an exorbitant price for a child, although they were not allowed to buy more than one. The regular people had to wait their turn to get a baby through the lottery, with about a one-in-forty chance their number would be called.

With limited supply came extreme demand. Add in the biological yearning hardwired into human beings to reproduce, and it's not hard to imagine the lengths people would go to in order to acquire a child: kidnapping, bribery, buying from the black market, and falsifying identities, just to name a few.

That's why each major city in These United States had a Department of Child Abductions with detectives like Keira and Squirmy whose main responsibilities were to find and return stolen children and stolen breeders, arrest the perpetrators, infiltrate and break up the black market, and gather intel to stave off planned abductions.

There were days when Keira felt good about returning a baby to a kind couple, but there were days when it was heart-wrenching to arrest a thirty-year-old woman, for example, overcome by the desire to have a child by any means possible. Good people could do bad things. And, furthermore, Keira was uneasy about the government's way of controlling the process.

She understood the state's desire to preserve human life for the future, but she was concerned about the implementation of dictatorial, heavy-handed policies that ran contrary to inalienable human rights.

But like most educated citizens, she had no choice in the job she took. Since the war, the government assigned career paths to university graduates based on their talents and the government's needs.

"Approaching the destination in thirty seconds, Detective Kincaid," the nav announced. "A roof pad has been detected. Prepare to land." The dashboard screen illuminated the house's blueprint and showed the landing coordinates and approach. Keira slowed to a near stop, deployed the landing gear, and descended straight down. She landed softly on the roof pad and opened the gull-wing doors.

"Let's interview the couple together and then get them apart for some less scripted questioning," Keira said. Squirmy agreed.

She often found that couples led separate lives and were unaware, to some extent, of what their spouse was doing. Attempting to hide an affair or gambling problem could occlude leads to the case, so she and Squirmy always tried to assure a parent that their secret was safe while urging them to disclose the truth for the sake of their child. In addition, tensions and disagreements among couples that might offer a clue as to how they got targeted by kidnappers could be better explored by separating the two people.

But Keira knew with a Code Red case like this one, when time was of the essence, that she mostly likely would have to use mind touch.

She took a deep breath and walked with Squirmy toward the roof door. A stone-faced security guard opened it and gestured for them to enter.

CHAPTER 2
RED-TAILED HAWK

THE HOUSE WAS silent other than the sound of their footsteps in the hallway. As the security guard led Keira and Squirmy into the opulent great room, they saw Stephen O'Connor and Catherine Strauss waiting in agitation. Ms. Strauss' face testified to her anguish, while Mr. O'Connor appeared flustered more than anything else. He ran his right hand through his receding salt-and-pepper hair and paced.

When he looked up at Keira, his gaze lingered on her for just a little too long. While she knew that people generally found her attractive and it was human nature to take stock, it seemed incredibly inappropriate at the moment. But a good detective observes everything while revealing nothing. She kept her expression neutral yet warm.

"Mr. O'Connor and Ms. Strauss, I'm Detective Kincaid and this is Detective Watts. We are deeply sorry for your distress."

The couple murmured their thanks. Keira noticed how they stood slightly turned away from each other and avoided eye contact. She sensed it was not a marriage made in heaven and that perhaps there was some distrust over this incident. United couples tended to visibly comfort each other.

"Expedience is important, so it's best that we delve straight in," Keira said. "It was reported, Ms. Strauss, that you were the one who discovered Liam was missing. What time was that?"

"It was right around 6:30 in the morning. I got up to—" she started to cry. "Sorry."

"It's perfectly understandable. Please take your time."

Sniffling and holding back a sob, she continued, "To feed him. I had a creepy feeling as I approached the door. Maybe because I could feel the air from the open window. But, sure enough, he was gone," she said, breaking down again. "His toy elephant that he sleeps with was missing, too."

Keira had found over the years that female kidnappers were more likely to grab something for the baby such as a toy, understanding the soothing aspect of it, while the male kidnappers typically did not.

"Okay, that's very helpful, Ms. Strauss," Keira said. "Did you notice that anything else was missing or that the room had been altered in any way other than the lasered window?"

"There was a yellow smudge that almost looked like paint. It was on the crib sheet near where Liam's head would have been."

Squirmy said, "That's probably narcoline, ma'am, a mild sedative that puts babies almost immediately to sleep."

Ms. Strauss looked panicked.

"It's not toxic for the baby," Squirmy assured her. "He will be fine. It's just a way to keep babies from waking and crying for a short spell."

Keira asked, "Have you had any new service people in your home in the last month or so?"

"No, we haven't," Mr. O'Connor said flatly, his voice devoid of emotion.

Keira did not like his vibe. She asked, "Is the security guard who escorted us a regular employee in your home?"

Mr. O'Connor shook his head. "The Department of Plant Sustainability sent him over as soon as I told human resources this morning that Liam had been kidnapped."

"I see. Well, I'd like Detective Watts to go to the nursery with you, Ms. Strauss. Mr. O'Connor, if you could show me the exterior of the house where the nursery is located, I'd like to take a look around outside."

"Of course," he replied. "Follow me, Detective."

He led her through the impressive great room with its high ceilings and luxury furnishings like a king's table and bronze sculptures, out a side door, and then through a small garden with colorful succulents and manzanita trees. It was very rare for private citizens to have any plants, let alone gardens, that Keira was mesmerized for a moment, remembering back to when she was a little girl who watched birds and butterflies alight in her parents' backyard.

The state was in the process of cleaning up the soil made toxic from bombings during the war. The cost of acquiring clean soil was beyond the reach of most ordinary people, never mind the plants that went with it. The Department of Plant Sustainability, which Mr. O'Connor ran, was charged with growing plants for both the food supply and the carbon-oxygen cycle. She figured he got some freebies for his own home. Lucky bastard, she thought, and then caught herself. His child was missing. He wasn't so lucky today, and she should show sympathy even though there was something off-putting about him.

"That is the window to Liam's room there," Mr. O'Connor said, pointing to a large circular window about twenty feet above them.

Other than the lasered window, there were no obvious signs of a forced entry. Keira wandered the footpath until she saw a partial footprint on the stone walkway. It pointed toward the security wall a few feet away. Shortly after, Keira discovered in the surface of the house's exterior a small chink in the metal, most likely left by electronic climbing equipment.

The perpetrator was quick and light on their feet, Keira thought, because to leave one small footprint and then essentially leap onto the wall without making a loud noise was challenging.

Keira felt uneasy as a gust of wind forced its way down the side yard. The air still had that hot, dry, electric feel to it.

She pulled out her own electronic climbing equipment in order to check the approach to Liam's room from the ground up to the window. After casting the anchoring device into the wall, she let the cable tow her upward. She noticed very small smudges in the façade's surface, most likely from the toes of the kidnapper's shoes tapping against it during the upward and downward climb. The laser job in the window was expertly done with one motion and no shattered glass. This was what law enforcement called a top-dollar criminal.

As Keira hovered by the window, she watched Squirmy talking to a clearly distraught Ms. Strauss, who sat on a small couch clutching a baby blanket.

The contrast between Ms. Strauss' distress and Mr. O'Connor's aloofness bothered Keira. It was time to start shaking him down.

When Keira got back on firm ground, she asked O'Connor if there had been any recent security breaches or suspicious activity at the Department of Plant Sustainability. "Nothing out of the ordinary," he said. "We often detect attempts by foreign hackers to infiltrate our computer systems, but those threats have been contained as far as we can tell. There are also routine protests by the Go Slow Movement that can get out of hand, but that's nothing unusual."

The Go Slow Movement was borne out of the concern that the government, in its attempt to put fish back in the streams and crops back in the fields, was pushing too hard too fast. The protesters were concerned that overtaxing the ecosystem could lead to similar environmental collapses from the past. The state did not agree and attempted to cast the dissenters as kooky, out-of-touch threats to These United States.

"Have you had any new hires at work with direct or digital access to you?"

"No, none of the newly instated employees have had that kind of contact with me. They are primarily planters and harvesters."

"I see." Keira paused before launching into the official spiel. "Please be assured that the Department of Child Abductions does not wish to pry into your personal life, but sometimes actions taken there can lead to security breaches or crimes of this nature. Do I have your permission to ask you some personal questions?"

He sighed. "Sure."

"Are you having or have you had an extramarital affair?"

His face grew red. "Absolutely not."

Keira suspected he was lying. "Do you have any other children?"

"No." That response rang true.

"Have you had any hostile relationships lately with family, friends, colleagues, or anyone else?"

He looked down at his feet. "I'm not particularly close with my siblings, but we don't have any outright grudges. I have a few close friends, though we rarely see each other anymore because of work and family obligations." He made eye contact and appeared to be telling the truth. "As for professional associates, I don't recall or detect any hostilities." That statement had a false ring to it.

With the clock ticking and Mr. O'Connor keeping a tight lid on his life, Keira knew it was time to play the next card.

KEIRA HAD DISCOVERED her strange ability of mind touch when she was six years old and happened to touch foreheads with her friend Jasmine when they leaned in over a board game. She could immediately see in her mind's eye Jasmine's memories as if they were moving images projected onto a screen. She could hear them, too.

Keira saw in those memories that Jasmine had just cheated in their game by taking an extra coin when Keira wasn't looking. She also saw Jasmine's father smack her hard across the face, causing Jasmine to cry loudly and cower on the floor with her hands over her head. Another memory of Jasmine with her brother splashing in gentle ocean waves and giggling played out like a movie of old.

When Keira had reclined into her seat, which pulled her out of physical contact with her friend, the access to Jasmine's memories ended. Shocked, Keira had asked, "What just happened?" Jasmine looked at her like she was being weird.

"It's your turn," was all Jasmine had said, as if nothing extraordinary at all had transpired. Sure enough, there was an extra coin on Jasmine's side, which proved that what Keira had seen was not an illusion—at least in that specific case. Keira didn't confront her about the coin; after watching such a horrible incident in Jasmine's life, she felt it was the least she could do.

The experience spooked but fascinated Keira, who told her mother about it that night. Her mother smiled sadly and patted Keira's hand softly. "My love, you have a tremendous power that must be used carefully. I know because I also have it."

From that conversation and others that grew in complexity as Keira grew older, she learned that mind touch was an extremely rare ability rumored to have been inadvertently created during experiments with electromagnetic fields. However, no one could confirm its exact origin or, for that matter, knew its potential. Her mother taught her that it was invasive to employ mind touch on loved ones and that it should only be used on them in an emergency.

On the job, mind touch could be incredibly useful to Keira because it often revealed key moments that unlocked the mystery of a kidnapping.

But the accessed memories didn't typically appear in the most recent or pertinent order. As a result, Keira would witness awful things that had happened to people that had nothing to do with the case, such as memories from years back of a sexual assault or a family member drowning.

While Keira could somehow use intention to her advantage by thinking about what she wanted to access from the other person before or as she pressed her forehead to theirs, she could not control what she called "the noise." The noise was those other memories she did not wish to see.

Her intention usually allowed her to access at least one memory that gave her insight into a case, but she had no idea how thinking about the information she yearned for actually worked in retrieving those memories. She wished her mother were still alive so that she could ask her about that.

The only living person who knew that Keira possessed this ability was Blaise. Clearly, Squirmy had guessed she had it based on experiences they'd shared on the job, but they never spoke of it directly— both probably understanding the danger it would put them in. The government would most likely make her its pawn, even more than it already had, or, worse yet, secretly wipe her off the books for being a threat to the state. And who knew what would become of Squirmy for just happening to know something unknowable.

Keira considered mind touch to be both a gift and a curse. She carefully and selectively used it in order to try to prevent the curse from overshadowing the gift, but it was never a perfect balance. Her mother had warned her it wouldn't be.

When Keira could solve a case without employing mind touch, she did. She was a talented detective, after all, who could very effectively tap the powers of perception accessible to all yet underutilized by most. Sometimes, however, the situation called for more extreme measures.

~

THE FIRST STEP for stealth mind touch was to ensure that no one was around who could witness it.

O'Connor's security guard had set up post in the downstairs hallway of the house, which was out of sight of the yard. If Keira walked back toward the side entrance, the curve of the house would prevent Ms. Strauss and Squirmy from seeing them if they happened to look out the window.

"Let's head back inside," she said to Mr. O'Connor. "I'd like to quickly see the nursery for myself."

He nodded and began walking at a pace even with hers.

Keira's second step for using mind touch was to make sure she had a clear approach to the person's forehead that wouldn't set off suspicion. While the person would have no recollection of memories being accessed, they would remember what happened immediately prior, which meant that she couldn't just abruptly grab the person's head for no apparent reason.

Typically, then, she either created a distraction, built enough empathy for a hug or caring touch to seem normal, or temporarily stunned the person with a tase. She always tried to avoid the last option.

Since Mr. O'Connor didn't seem to be very physically aware of his surroundings and was about her height, Keira decided to go with distraction. "Is that a red-tailed hawk?" she asked, pointing up to the sky.

He turned slightly toward her and looked up. In an instant she pressed her forehead against his. When she felt his body slacken slightly, she held tightly to his arms to keep him firmly in place. She silently asked the universe, or whatever power granted her the ability of mind touch, to show her clues of Liam's disappearance, Mr. O'Connor's extramarital activities, and any work associations gone sour.

As she figured might be the case, the first memory that emerged was Mr. O'Connor having sex with an attractive woman with large breasts and vivid blue eyes. There was a lot of moaning; Keira could tell that the woman's was fake, but O'Connor's was very real. Since he was on top, Keira got a clear look at the woman's face and upper body, and noticed a small raven tattoo on her left shoulder. That meant she was affiliated with the Chusei, who ran the experience dens and penthouse services on Eighth Avenue.

Wow, it was a pretty dumb move on O'Connor's part to partake of the services offered by the cutthroat Chusei organization, a crime tribe with a reputation for keeping its house in order by any means necessary. Talk about making yourself vulnerable to blackmail and backlash, she thought.

Keira could not control how long or short the memories were. Soon that one disappeared to be replaced by an image of Ms. Strauss rocking a sleeping Liam in her arms and looking at O'Connor as though she despised him. Did she know he was sleeping around, or was he just generally a shit to live with? It could easily be either or both, Keira figured.

That memory lapsed quickly and in came a new one of a crowded city street. O'Connor must have been scanning the street in search of someone or something because the vantage point in the memory kept shifting, taking in the surroundings from various angles. But when he noticed a man in a navy-blue suit carrying a briefcase, his head stopped swiveling as he watched the man approach.

The man gestured to the suitcase and said to him, "I believe this is yours."

O'Connor responded, "I believe you are right."

The man handed him the suitcase, clasped his arm in greeting, and quickly walked away. O'Connor looked up and there saw Blaise!

In his memory Blaise had blonde hair—a wig—but Keira would recognize her delicate profile anywhere. Dressed like a banker, Blaise was looking down at her time piece, possibly feigning indifference to blend in. O'Connor's eyes then continued down the avenue, as he started to walk quickly away with the briefcase in hand.

He had seen Blaise! Had she been surveilling him or someone else, maybe the briefcase carrier? Did O'Connor have anything to do with Blaise's disappearance?

Keira watched his next few memories, but they were from childhood. It wasn't safe to continue in case the security guard or Ms. Strauss came outside.

She backed off his forehead, and the slackening in his body quickly gave way to normal suppleness. He took a quick breath. "I didn't see a bird."

She nodded, and they continued down the path toward the house. Keira was reeling from seeing the memory of Blaise, her girlfriend who had been missing for weeks with no word or trace after going undercover. Her thoughts and pulse raced as she walked beside O'Connor. She realized she needed to gather her composure quickly before it became obvious to him that she suspected something.

Deciding to use one of the oldest tricks in the book, she said, "Sorry, I left my climbing gear on the walkway. I'll be right back."

Pacing back down the walkway toward Liam's window, Keira asked herself what she knew.

First off, it seemed highly likely that Blaise was either surveilling Stephen O'Connor or the man carrying the briefcase. It couldn't be a random coincidence that she was undercover as a federal agent and just happened to be present during the handoff, an exchange that clearly made O'Connor nervous, as evidenced by how rapidly he scanned the street.

What was in that briefcase? Who delivered it? What was O'Connor up to? He didn't seem quite bright enough beyond plant production to be anything other than a useful pawn in someone else's bigger game.

As the head of the Department of Plant Sustainability, O'Connor would have unfettered access to information and procedures related to the food supply—intel of high value to many people within and outside of the country.

He'd also be a tremendous target for blackmail. Having sex with a Chusei was dangerous for someone like O'Connor. They tracked the people who visited their experience dens and penthouses. With O'Connor's high profile and the Chusei links to international crime, it was like putting a mark on your back, she thought. But it was also possible that O'Connor was working some sort of deal with the Chusei and that a session with a trick was an expensive perk.

And then there was the fact that his child was abducted. Did O'Connor mess with the Chusei and pay a great price? But that kidnapping was so clean—not the messy, violent Chusei way of sending a message. It didn't appear, in that way, to be their hit.

Perhaps, worse yet, O'Connor found himself in the crosshairs of multiple organizations with similar aims. Or maybe that's what had happened to Blaise, Keira thought. While looking for one group she may have gotten caught unexpectedly in the net of another. It happened all the time, especially undercover.

Keira looked up at the lasered window and fixed her gaze there. Start with the first step, she told herself. Find the baby. That search will open other windows, pun intended.

The voice of the sparkling man from her dreams reverberated in her head: "What if you could shape your future with your thoughts? What if *you* held the keys to your own destiny?" She still didn't know what his words meant, yet they somehow motivated her.

"I will find you, Liam," she said quietly, with determination. "And then I will find you, Blaise. I am coming."

CHAPTER 3
STRUCK BY LIGHTNING

KEIRA HAD MET Blaise on the job. Keira's work with the Department of Child Abductions was limited to cases within the greater San Diego area, called California 4 by law enforcement. Blaise Richards, on the other hand, served as a detective for the federal Bureau of Abductions and Unauthorized Trade, which tracked the illegal movement and sale of anything from guns to children with the intent to export them out of the country.

These United States found itself in a cold war of sorts. Ever since the end of World War IV, the nation had turned inward, refusing to share intel with countries that had once been allies. During the last world war, it was unclear whether allies Canada and England had brokered deals with Russia and China. Distrust still ran high.

What was clear was that every country faced severe struggles with regrowing and restocking the food supply as well as the human baby supply, and every nation yearned to become less vulnerable. That led to attempts to steal food, plants, weapons, children, breeders, and any intelligence or technology on how to more rapidly cultivate life forms or bolster defenses by pretty much every country on Earth that still existed.

Blaise and her fellow Bureau agents aimed to prevent these types of foreign thefts. They would take over local cases when an international element came into play, which was how Keira and Blaise initially crossed paths.

Keira and Squirmy had cracked a child abduction case in July 2121 that led to the arrest of several people involved in a baby black market. While the perps were fairly small time on the baby front, having just dipped their toe into the illegal sale of children before getting caught, it turns out they were quite experienced in arms sales. Keira found the missing girl in a warehouse filled with guns, grenades, body armor, and even tanks.

That was the treasure trove that the Feds had been searching for and had failed to find up until that point.

Keira was called into an investigation room to be debriefed by the Feds. She walked in to find this slim, gorgeous redhead with green speckled eyes waiting for her. The moment they made eye contact the chemistry between them was palpable.

"Agent Blaise Richards," Blaise had said and extended her arm for a clasp. At Blaise's light touch of her forearm, Keira felt a tingling rush of excitement.

The way Keira saw it, they both kept their guard up during the debriefing like well-trained detectives, while each tried to gain valuable insight into the other. It felt like a chess game with teasing twists.

At the end of the meeting Blaise had said, "Please get in touch if you think of anything else that could be valuable." As she slid her card across the surface of the table, Blaise seemed to purposefully brush her fingertips against Keira's when she reached for the card. Blaise then held Keira's gaze and flashed a sultry half smile. The message was unmistakable.

Keira could barely concentrate for the rest of that afternoon. At the end of her shift, she sent a message to Blaise stating that she had indeed thought of something about the case. Keira suggested a meeting spot near her own apartment. When they met there and sensed that neither had been followed, they quickly walked up to Keira's place.

Blaise had brought a bottle of gin that cost a small fortune, as all alcohol did. "Perks of the job," she explained. Keira wondered if it had been seized but figured she wouldn't ask questions of that variety. She was just happy for the treat and even happier for the beautiful and intriguing company.

As they finished their first drink, Blaise pointed to Keira's guitar case in the corner. "Do you play?"

"From time to time."

"I'd love to hear you."

"It'll take a few more drinks for that to happen."

"I think that can be arranged." Blaise laughed.

After Blaise poured them a second drink, she set the bottle down and leaned toward Keira as they stood in the kitchen, locking lips softly with her. Then they kissed more deeply and then deeper still. Keira ran her hands through Blaise's hair and down her shoulder blades.

Running out of breath, they paused for a second and then laughed, touching noses and kissing again, very gently this time. Keira's body ached to have all of Blaise. She felt as though Blaise was this missing piece she'd been searching for. She had never felt so electrified by anyone.

Blaise pulled back from Keira's lips and said, "I've never been one to believe in the idea of soul mates, but I must say that when you walked into that room this morning, you set my world on fire."

And so their relationship started and then continued in a spectacularly enthralled fashion. They were passionate and inseparable, each bringing the other the closeness and connection they had craved and never quite found elsewhere.

Keira and Blaise had both been with men and women before, with neither one having had much success cultivating long-lasting relationships in either department. Sex, sure. They were both very attractive, a feature they had each learned to capitalize on. But now in their early thirties, they found intense love for the first time.

They chose to be careful. While same-sex relationships were not outright forbidden, during this time when reproduction became the prime directive, same-sex relationships were sometimes cast as frivolous, almost unpatriotic. Although the majority of American people didn't appear to care at all about who slept with whom, the government occasionally made a show of publicly shaming homosexuality through propaganda campaigns. And there were of course the diehards who took up the hateful cause because it made their own lives seem less dim by comparison.

Keira also didn't trust that there was a line the government wouldn't cross. She wondered what rights the government might infringe on next, like her right to a relationship with another woman or her right to vote. She felt it was safer to mostly keep herself to herself.

Furthermore, inter- and intra-agency dating was highly frowned upon in law enforcement—ostensibly because of concerns with nepotism, abuse of rank, protecting sensitive intel, and exposing other officers to unnecessary risk. However, Keira suspected the unofficial policy had more to do with control. Keira and Blaise decided at the outset, for those various reasons, to keep their relationship a secret. As far as they knew, they were the only two people in the world who knew they were together.

But when Blaise disappeared, Keira began to wonder whether she herself was the target and Blaise the bait. It was just a sinking feeling that she could find no evidence for. Other times she figured it was the more likely scenario of an undercover agent's identity getting blown, forcing her at best to go deeper undercover and at worst to be killed.

While Keira knew Blaise had been on an undercover assignment, she didn't know any details about the case. Blaise would only share information with Keira when she felt it was safe or appropriate to do so, like after an investigation had ended and some details were publicly available. The same went for Keira with her own investigations.

Given the nature of their dangerous jobs, they had a few codes they came up with as precautions. So, when Keira awoke one night around 01:00 to the message on her time piece, "The meeting has been moved to SR5," her heart sank. That meant Blaise was in danger and to immediately meet her at a pre-disclosed location, a bunker beneath train tracks on the east side of the city.

Keira rushed to the spot, arriving within ten minutes of receiving the message, but Blaise wasn't there. There was no sign of her having been in the room either. Keira waited a full hour, their pre-agreed time frame. Blaise never arrived and never contacted Keira again.

Her trail went cold. No hints, no leads, no contacts. Keira couldn't reach out to Blaise's colleagues for help because they didn't know that Keira and Blaise were lovers. They might not trust Keira's story, at least not enough to offer unofficial assistance that could get them in trouble, and they certainly wouldn't disclose information about a Bureau agent to a city investigator without an official order. But for that matter, Keira didn't know who at the Bureau was clean or corrupt. She had to be careful about which pots to stir.

Keira had worked as hard as she possibly could behind the scenes to find a clue. She rummaged through Blaise's belongings, tried to remember every detail in the days leading up to the disappearance, read every related file she could access in the government's system on recent abductions, weapons trades, etc. She even employed mind touch on a few Bureau agents she followed after work, but their memories revealed nothing directly useful.

Keira had discovered no promising leads until accessing O'Connor's memories today. There she had found her Blaise, clear as day, floating on a memory. What had happened to her after that? The answer, Keira believed, was drawing closer.

CHAPTER 4
SCENT OF ROSES

BACK AT THE squad mod on the roof of missing baby Liam's home, Squirmy shared his impression that Ms. Strauss appeared to be what you'd expect: an extremely distressed mother who would give anything in the world to get her baby back.

He elaborated, "She painted a picture of a pretty cold marriage. Her husband works, doesn't share much about his daily comings and goings. They met through their government positions. She doesn't seem to miss her old job. I think she just has put all of her love into that child. The kid is all that matters to her."

"That makes sense. I definitely didn't sense any foul play with her either," Keira said, tucking a strand of her long brown hair behind her ear and getting buckled in. They agreed that Strauss could be removed from the unofficial suspect list, at least for now. "Let's see what the forensics team comes up with after they process the scene," Keira said. "I doubt we'll get lucky with a DNA sample, but you never know."

She started up the squad mod, then manually engaged the fan system, which drowned out the audio in the cabin. Knowing that their conversations in the aircraft could be listened to at headquarters, she was being cautious. First off, it was never good to say disparaging things about a government official. Secondly, she shouldn't say anything that hinted at an innate ability to gather hunches and pursue them with accurate precision.

With the fans whirring, Keira shared with Squirmy, "It seems highly likely that Mr. O'Connor has had some dalliances outside the home. So I am wondering if he's been blackmailed or compromised in some way. Given his high-level position and what's at stake with Plant Sustainability, there are many potential suspects who would have motive. I'd like us to look into the Go Slow Movement. They've been staging protests and expressing their frustration on an almost daily basis. Was this a way of getting his attention?"

Keira continued, "For reasons that are hard to explain, I also want to check out the Chusei. I'll go undercover to the penthouses as soon as we return. In the meantime, it would be great if you could interview the breeders of Strauss and O'Connor's child." Breeders always had to be ruled out. It was standard procedure.

Squirmy flexed his fingers nervously. "You be careful, Keira. The Chusei have taken out a couple of cops in the last few months."

"I know. Thanks. I definitely will. On the bright side, in the name of justice I just might get a chance to score," she laughed.

Since Squirmy didn't know about Blaise, she thought it best to pretend to be a typical single person with sexual urges like almost everyone else. Nonetheless, it bothered her to be dishonest with him. She found it hard deciding when to be guarded, even if it meant lying, and when to reveal herself.

He chuckled. "Nothing like sex and drugs to pick up the day."

Keira turned off the fans and made her way smoothly through the sky as her fears and hopes about Blaise crossed each other like the clouds and sunrays before her.

Once at the station, Keira put in an electronic request to go undercover to the penthouses. It was promptly accepted given the do-whatever-it-takes nature of a kidnapping case involving a high-ranking government official.

That was convenient because she could play the expedience card and just move on to the next clue without much explanation. Squirmy was typically diplomatic and convincing in her stead, allowing her to avoid whenever possible her boss' direct questions about how she knew what she knew.

She stripped down completely and stepped into the Impersonator, placing the fingertips of her left hand onto the recognition pad.

"Welcome, Detective Kincaid," the electronic voice said. "Retrieving your dimensions." Sensors did a full-body scan in three seconds to get her height, weight, waist size, and every other applicable measurement.

"Start with the left panel to choose your look."

The Impersonator allowed detectives to select a particular identity type to emulate, with options as wide-ranging as corporate executive to homeless person. Detectives could leave the detailed decisions like wig color up to AI, or they could choose each part of the disguise. Keira had a bit of a fashion sense and liked to put the look together herself.

She knew she'd have an easier time getting to the trick from O'Connor's memory by appearing professional and wealthy. The Chusei did not trust low-class people with their live assets in the penthouses. To get a simulated experience in the experience dens, on the other hand, came down to having the money for it, although those customers were tracked too and could get blacklisted for bad behavior.

The simulated experiences in the dens gave recipients the almost forgotten taste of fresh food, the orgasmic sensations of sex, the bodily high of an adrenaline rush, and almost any other desired sensation one could think of. But like the tangible drugs of old, one hit made a person crave another. Besides, the experience dens were engineered to not quite satisfy the whole urge, which kept some addicts coming back in search for more, a desire that could never be satiated. Junkies blew their wages on teasing pleasure that they could not afford and that was never wholly theirs.

The live assets, however, could blow your mind the old-fashioned way in the bedroom. Alcohol and drugs, which became luxury items after the war, were included in the experience if desired. Not many people could afford that elevated level of real-life pleasure, which was why the area of the Empress Hotel that offered those services was dubbed the penthouses. With the resources of the government, Keira could buy her way in—as long as she did not arouse suspicion by the Chusei.

The Impersonator disguised detectives and provided them with another set of fingerprints matched to an authentic, though fake, identity in the system. Detectives could even go so far as face-shaping, rendering their faces unrecognizable to their real identity, but that took hours to do and then hours to undo, so Keira wouldn't opt for that for this mission.

Despite these techniques, cops' covers still got blown at the Chusei's experience dens and penthouses. Why? Because the cops acted nervous. Their performance was unconvincing.

The Chusei organized crime tribe was of Japanese ancestry and followed an internal code of conduct that remained a mystery to most outsiders. But one thing was very clear: the Chusei had a keen ability to sniff out fakes and snuff them out before anyone even realized they were missing. The Chusei might not figure out that the fakes were cops, although torture had been pretty effective at bringing that to light. They might assume a suspicious person was from a different organized crime tribe attempting to infiltrate their operations.

Anyone who aroused suspicion from any angle—competition, law enforcement, out-of-control junkie, etc.—was dealt with quickly.

To survive during undercover missions to the experience dens and penthouses, Keira had learned the importance of wholeheartedly assuming her fake identity. She tried to inhabit that person's mannerisms, ambitions, needs. Today she would be an intimacy-starved insurance CEO yearning for another woman's touch and absolute discretion.

She selected "corporate executive" from the left panel, followed by "input mode" to indicate she wanted to make the individual selections.

The next screen presented outfit options. Keira chose a tight, long skirt that went halfway down the knees—made it navy in color and a fabric soft to the touch—and a flowy, beige blouse with an asymmetrical tie near the neck. High heels with a slightly conservative style were a must; she went with a classic closed-toe, tapered shape. She added crystal dangling earrings and a mother-of-pearl bracelet, then reddish-auburn lipstick.

The whole vibe said sexy but vulnerable and old-fashioned. She planned to make herself appear as attractive yet unintimidating as possible because she would need to build intimacy and trust in order to get close enough for mind touch—perhaps multiple times over the course of the half hour that she'd have.

She pressed the "complete impersonation" button.

"Close your eyes, Detective Kincaid." She did as prompted. "Initiating impersonation sequence." She heard a whirring sound for about thirty seconds and felt her limbs being gently moved. "Open your eyes. Press 'satisfied' to continue, 'unsatisfied' to start again."

In the reflecting glass Keira liked the look of the outfit she now wore. She pressed "satisfied."

The Impersonator then prompted her to choose an eye color. Keira, who had blue eyes naturally, selected brown. She rested her chin onto the support and tried to relax as the machine gently pulled her eyelids open and inserted a brown lens onto each eyeball. She straightened her slightly wavy hair in the straightener globe. It didn't seem wise to wear a wig for this mission since it could easily fall off in bed.

Next, she had to receive new fingerprints onto the surface of her own, which was akin to wearing extremely thin, translucent coverings over her hands. The added layer had the feeling and appearance of skin. As far as was known, no one outside of the government had come up with the technology to detect or remove the graft.

The last step was to receive her impersonated name and other identifying characteristics. "Detective Kincaid, your assignment name is Sarah Rubin. You're thirty-four years old, divorced three years ago, and have no children. You live on the twenty-first floor of the J Complex and work for Davis & Penfield Incorporated, an insurance firm, as vice president of marketing."

Keira took the time to memorize the information and then had an identity card printed.

"Good luck, Detective Kincaid. If your identity gets compromised, initiate the exit strategy." The exit strategy consisted of sending a code through the network that alerted the department that an officer was in dire straits. The problem was a cop could be abducted before they had time to send the code or killed before help arrived. The Chusei realized that police backup might arrive within minutes, which was plenty of time for them to incinerate a body with the hotel garbage.

Keira certainly didn't relish making this dangerous visit. While she was worried about what the Chusei could do, finding Blaise was all that mattered to her.

"Place your right arm on the injection pad and roll up your sleeve. When ready for the calming agent, say 'ready.'"

"Ready."

A pneumatic hand injected her forearm with triptoline, a drug that kept blood pressure normal for several hours, boosted serotonin levels, and made recipients incredibly focused on their surroundings. This created a strange combination of feeling calm and happy, yet hyper alert. Keira preferred not to take the triptoline boost because it made her feel less in control, but it was now required for penthouse visits after the various undercover deaths.

The effect started to hit almost immediately. Keira felt her vitals settle to a calm hum while becoming aware of everything around her—the colors, the layout, the way her clothes wrapped around her body.

"You have two hours and fifty-nine minutes to complete your assignment, Detective Kincaid. Prepare for the drop. Please report back immediately upon return."

Keira stood in a circular space marked on the floor and waited to be descended to the undercover Departure room. In order to keep undercover investigators in the impersonated headspace, measures were taken to isolate them from other police. She would go straight from the Impersonator to Departure without contacting Squirmy or anyone else.

Once at Departure, Keira stepped forward and looked around at the transportation inventory of motorbikes, manual bikes, and cars. A single corporate executive would most likely use a self-driving motor-bike, which was in the center of the room waiting for her. She sat on the seat and waited for the bike's lever to place the helmet on her head, then retract into the center console.

She put her hands on the grips and feet on the pegs. The motorbike powered on at her command, the hatch doors opened, and out she went onto the street, the bike turning for her and making its way three blocks to the Autoway 5, a highway built about a hundred feet above the ground.

The autoway system was for the wealthy; most people could not afford vehicles or the use fees that came with them. When Keira was off duty, she'd occasionally pay for ride shares, but they were rather expensive. Normally, she would walk, ride her manual bike, or take the metro, which was generally faster at getting around than a motorbike. But for the wealthy it wasn't as much about speed as it was about exclusivity and separation from the masses.

One of Keira's favorite aspects of her job was how it gave her the opportunity to see how the very rich and the very poor—and everyone in between—lived. One moment she'd find herself in a palatial estate being offered champagne, and the next she'd be in a cramped, below-ground apartment that never saw the light of day. The below-ground housing offered residents an energy-efficient respite from rising global temperatures, but it was depressing to not experience natural light. The residents essentially dwelled in darkness like human moles.

The motorbike ascended the ramp onto the autoway, maintaining an automatic distance of ten feet from all other vehicles. It rapidly gained speed until cruising at the speed limit of ninety-five miles per hour. Evenly spaced traffic moved efficiently down the three inbound lanes. A massive wall divided the autoway, keeping the outbound traffic from view.

Ads flashed across the wall, alerting passengers to the opening of an elite restaurant that perhaps five percent of residents could afford, the allure of a new perfume, and the tantalizing taste of Zest—a liquor infused with real lemon flavor.

The motorbike carefully changed lanes before taking a righthand exit. It continued down surface streets past large concrete and glass skyscrapers and the windowless county jail to the Entertainment District, with its 3D immersive theaters, music halls, and casinos.

At the outskirts of the Entertainment District was the Empress Hotel. Below ground one could find the experience dens. On the hotel's highest floors were the penthouses. In between were regular hotel rooms. Getting into the dens was much like going to a speakeasy in that a person needed the code and had to know the location of the entrance, which was a nondescript door down the alley. To get access to the penthouses, pleasantly housed within the grandiosity of the sky-scraping hotel, required more savoir faire.

The government had a tenuous agreement with the Chusei and other organized crime tribes. Since simulated-den and prostitution revenue brought money into city and state coffers, the government allowed both to operate. However, the organized crime tribes had to maintain order by, for example, keeping junkies out of sight.

What wasn't allowed was the illegal trade of drugs and weapons, which all the crime tribes trafficked in but were careful to keep under wraps. The most daring attempted to get into the human trade.

Corruption via bribes of officials and cops facilitated some of the illicit trade, while the clean parts of government aimed to enforce laws across the board. As usual, a checkerboard of justice emerged when payouts and armclasp agreements constantly buttressed against the attempts to ensure order and peace.

As a cop, Keira knew she could find herself on the wrong end of a barrel held by a member of a crime tribe or another cop. She tried to be prepared for anything while also accepting that circumstances could arise outside her control. It wasn't easy to find the balance between being alert and overly anxious.

The motorbike turned into the parking structure of the Empress Hotel. A scanner signaled to the motorbike's control system to pull into spot 108.

After getting off the bike and fixing her hair with her hands, a short elevator ride brought Keira into the lobby with its crystal chandeliers and acrobatic performers.

The scent of roses permeated the air, as a male acrobat slowly flipped a female performer over his shoulders and then spun around to pull her back toward him. They wore red silken armbands that billowed sensuously around each other. Keira caught herself danger-ously drifting into her own thoughts, missing Blaise. The triptoline was engrossing her in her yearnings and surroundings. I need to stay in character and think of the mission, she thought. I am Sarah Rubin today.

While she felt guilty that she was about to have sex with someone other than Blaise, she couldn't think of a more direct way to access the woman from O'Connor's memory. As her conscience tried to lecture her, the serotonin chilled it out. She told herself, "Let your own emotions fade; let Sarah's rise."

She ran her hands down her navy skirt, smoothing and pulling it perfectly into position. Then she walked up to the check-in desk and said to the young man who greeted her, "I'm looking for someone on the 101st floor by the last name Johnson."

Without betraying any surprise or emotion at hearing the code language for hiring a prostitute, the young man in his crisp hotel suit said, "Yes, of course. Let me assist you with that." He handed her a silver e-pad. "Identify your partner when you find them."

The e-pad showed one trick—male, female, or transitioning—at a time in a scroll. All Chusei members, from prostitutes to gangsters to accountants to janitors, had to have at least twenty percent Japanese heritage. They were genetically tested before being officially accepted, or coerced, into the crime tribe. As such, all the tricks were at least partially Japanese, but some looked more White, Black, or Latino than Asian.

The eighth option on the e-pad, who looked of mixed Asian-White descent, was definitely the woman from O'Connor's memory. Keira recognized her facial features, especially her searing blue eyes, and pressed on her image.

The next screen said, "Cost 10,350 beta coins. Tap to proceed." She tapped, marveling how a half hour could run the equivalent of about a week of her salary. But the government made money from the Chusei's operations and could afford to give some of it back to them.

The following screen announced, "Available at 13:00 pending hotel approval."

The young assistant then said, "Please place your fingertips on the pad to your right." She did. "Thank you, Ms. Rubin. Just give me a moment."

Keira knew that Sarah Rubin's identity was being vetted and approved in a separate room out of sight. The Chusei would be able to see where she worked, her relationship status, criminal record, and other details. It helped that Sarah was divorced. The Chusei would reject certain requests if they thought a jilted spouse could prove problematic for their operations.

Keira also knew that cameras were focused on her right now, providing a clear view of her face and demeanor. She acted as demurely as possible.

"Excellent, Ms. Rubin. Tomoko will meet you at 13:00. In the meantime, please proceed to the cocktail lounge on the 101st floor. My colleague will take care of you there." He bowed and turned back to his console.

CHAPTER 5
WHISKEY ON THE ROCKS

KEIRA SIPPED a whiskey on the rocks in a lounge on the 101st floor. She was surrounded by gurgling fountains and enormous fish tanks housing tropical species and corals that were probably made in a lab. Alcohol was out of her budget, so the drink was a rare treat for her. The pleasure and alertness boost from the triptoline shot was peaking now. Keira loved the crisp edges of the whiskey on her tongue and the gorgeous colors and sounds of the aesthetically pleasing lounge.

It was not hard to see why detectives got hooked on triptoline. It made a person feel amazing and completely tuned in, kind of like savoring the moment at its apex. The problem was that a detective could become keenly aware of their pleasure at the expense of vigilance. Keira tried to stay above the drug, to remember she was on it. That was not always easy. Realizing she'd become distracted by the mouth feel of the whiskey and her exotic surroundings, she brought her awareness around again to embodying what Sarah Rubin would appear like to an outsider: reserved, unassuming.

A man in a kimono approached her and bowed. "Tomoko is ready for you, Ms. Rubin. Please follow me." He walked with purpose, but each step landed softly. The golden-hued metal hotel walls glistened and reflected their elongated images back to them.

The man stepped into a receded doorway. He opened the door,

smiled, and bowed quickly. "Have a pleasurable afternoon, Ms. Rubin." I already am, she thought, as she enjoyed her whiskey buzz. Then she reminded herself to pull it together. She took a deep breath.

Keira walked in to find Tomoko wearing green and white silken underwear and a skimpy bra, with a waist-long robe hanging open. She was definitely the beautiful woman with the large breasts from Mr. O'Connor's memory. Keira heard the door close behind her.

Tomoko gave Keira a coy once-over and smiled, appearing to at least appreciate what she saw. "Can I help you to any refreshments?" Tomoko asked, gesturing to a wall stocked with liquor and a bar with joints, cocaine, and pills contained neatly in separate glass tumblers.

"Not right now, but thank you."

"Let me know if you change your mind at any time. They are always on offer." Tomoko approached Keira and rested her hands gently on Keira's hips. She cocked her head and made eye contact with her searing blue eyes. "May I call you Sarah?"

"Yes, please do."

Tomoko grasped Keira's hands with her own and placed them on her bare hips. Tomoko's skin felt soft and warm. "Do you want me to be gentle with you, Sarah?"

"Yes," Keira whispered, as Tomoko moved her hands around to the small of Keira's back and pulled her closer.

Tomoko then touched Keira's cheek, brushing her hair out of her face and kissing her softly on the lips and then again firmer and longer. She ran her hand down Keira's blouse, lightly touching her breasts and then kissed her and let her tongue gently swirl around and against Keira's. She unbuttoned and slowly removed Keira's blouse, and then let her own robe fall to the floor.

Tomoko was certainly talented and gorgeous, Keira thought. The heightened sense perception of triptoline enhanced the pleasure of the touching and teasing, but Keira was still keenly aware of her love for Blaise and how she had a mission to accomplish. She thought of the information she wanted to retrieve as she prepared for mind touch, all the while trying to move gently like she pictured Sarah would.

As she gingerly removed Tomoko's front-snapping bra, she leaned in and pressed her forehead against Tomoko's and continued to caress

Tomoko's body so as not to arouse suspicion in case anyone was actively watching video surveillance of the room.

The first memory appeared to come from riding on the metro. Tomoko watched a young man and woman cry and embrace, as if they'd received bad news that they were trying to process. The train hurtled through the dark tunnel toward whatever awaited them.

In the second memory, Tomoko stroked the cheek of a sleeping baby in a crib, with a stuffed elephant tucked against the child's torso. It must be Liam, Keira thought, because Ms. Strauss said his elephant toy was missing. Given how Tomoko kept her gaze focused on Liam, with his precious soft cheeks, she clearly seemed mesmerized. Did she want him as her own child or just want a baby in general?

In the memory, Tomoko looked up as a petite woman entered the room and asked quietly, "Has he woken up yet?"

Tomoko said no and then kissed her. "He's so beautiful," Tomoko whispered. "Look how peaceful he looks."

The other woman, who had caramel-colored skin and thick black hair that fell to her shoulders, caressed Tomoko's neck. "Sweetheart, one day we'll have our own child. I promise. But for now, try to just see the little guy as the collateral that he is. We can't let our emotions put us in harm's way. He'll be returned to his mother once Victor gets what he wants." She turned to leave and opened the door. In that moment, the sound of cascading water became evident. Were they in a room near the lounge where Keira had just waited?

That memory faded and one of a male client doing a line of blow on Tomoko's stomach came up. Keira pulled back from Tomoko's forehead and kept her hands moving. She hoped she hadn't taken too long.

Coming off mind touch, Tomoko didn't miss a beat. She pulled Keira's skirt and undergarments off and continued caressing her. Then she grasped Keira's hand and walked her toward the bed.

While following along, Keira wondered whether Tomoko's lover was the person who carried out Liam's kidnapping. She was light on her feet, moved nimbly, and conveyed confidence in a high-pressure situation. She also fit the profile of a female kidnapper who would have been more likely than a male to gather a toy as a comfort. Maybe

Liam hadn't woken up yet in the memory due to the narcoline. Who was Victor?

Tomoko guided Keira down onto the bed and then slowly got on top of her. She used her hand to rub Keira's clit at first and then pressed her lips and tongue against it, and suddenly Keira could think of nothing other than how good she felt and how much she wanted to climax. Fucking triptoline, she thought, but gave into it. She wasn't sure how much time had passed before she achieved a mind-blowing orgasm of drug-induced proportions.

When she could control her breathing again and the throbbing of her pleasure-provoked body settled down into a pleasant hum, she gently pulled Tomoko against her, rubbing her cheek against hers and then the tip of her nose against Tomoko's so that they faced each other closely. Keira went in for a kiss so that she could press her forehead against Tomoko's for more mind touch, but Tomoko teasingly pulled back.

"I'd like to hear you moan like that again, Sarah. I think I've got just the thing you're looking for." Tomoko slid down so that her head was on the opposite side of the bed from Keira's and then pressed her pelvis against Keira's—holding Keira's legs as leverage to allow her to rub rhythmically against her. Keira lost herself in the warm, wet delight of their scissoring bodies and wondered if she'd have another chance at mind touch as she gripped the sheets and practically buckled with ecstasy.

They appeared to climax at the same time, or perhaps Tomoko was incredible at faking it. Tomoko made her way back up Keira's body, kissing her legs and stomach and breasts. When she hovered over Keira's face and smiled, Keira slowly reached for her cheeks and pulled her in for a kiss. Lips locked, she turned Tomoko over in a smooth motion so that she was now on top of her. Keira pressed her forehead against Tomoko's.

The memory opened with Tomoko walking out of the same room from the Liam memory, taking a left down a hallway, and then a right into the room that she and Keira were in now. Keira tried to recount the number of steps so that later she could reverse course from this room and find where Liam had been held.

In the memory, a large, muscular man whose forehead bore the tattooed markings of the Chusei bodyguards stood next to a smaller man wearing an expensive suit and holding a glass of what looked like whiskey. They stood at the bar where Tomoko had minutes ago offered Keira a refreshment. Keira could sense Tomoko's fear.

The smaller man said, "Good evening, Tomoko. Remember the government official you entertained a couple of weeks ago? I need you to do the same tonight at 22:00. Give him anything he wants in order to keep him occupied, and be prepared for an interruption." He gave her a look that said he was not playing. Then he downed his drink and set the glass on the bar.

"Of course, Victor. You will not be disappointed."

He nodded, buttoned his suit above the navel, and motioned with his chin for the large bodyguard to follow.

The next memory was the start of a pretty childhood scene in a park with kites flying and kids running and squealing. Keira pulled her head back from Tomoko's forehead.

Tomoko stroked Keira's arm. "Unfortunately, we only have a little bit of time left together, Sarah. How would you like to spend it?"

"How about with a drink?"

"As you wish, my dear." Tomoko took Keira's hand and led her to the bar where Victor and the bodyguard had stood in the memory. "What would you like?"

"I'd love a whiskey on the rocks. Thank you." Then it dawned on her that Sarah would probably prefer vodka with a mixer. Oh well. Roll with it, she thought.

"Surprising choice, but whiskey it is. I like your style." Tomoko selected a bottle of aged Japanese whiskey from the shelf. "You've got fire in the belly and a refined finish, just like this little number," she said with a wink, tapping the bottle. She poured a glass over ice for each of them. "Cheers." They toasted, touching their glasses together with a pleasing crystal ring.

Tomoko took a sip and then set her glass down and began to massage Keira's back and shoulders. "Ooh, those shoulders are tight," she said as she kneaded them with warm hands. "You need to visit me more often. That'll take care of the stress."

Keira laughed in the reserved way she imagined Sarah would. "I think you're right about that."

As Tomoko began to massage Keira's head, Keira noticed the handle of a revolver sticking out ever so slightly under the far side of the bar. It made sense. Some clients, unfortunately, probably got out of control. While the bodyguards would quickly make their way into these monitored rooms, events could unfold in moments. Always better to be prepared to deal with things on your own. She liked Tomoko and sincerely hoped that she was treated well and felt in control as much as possible in her line of work.

Keira then turned her attention to the memories she'd accessed as Tomoko went back to massaging her shoulders. She wondered what the warning meant about an interruption. Maybe they planned to shake down O'Connor while he was naked and vulnerable. Had it already happened?

It's possible the man in the memory referred to a different government official, but her gut told her it was O'Connor. It seems he hadn't fulfilled his end of some sort of bargain. The baby was perhaps the first warning. If so, the lives of father and son would hang in the balance until the Chusei got what they wanted. Of that Keira was certain.

She hoped to get a chance after the session to get near that room, but the Chusei host would probably escort her immediately to the elevator.

She got an idea. "Tomoko, is there a spa I can use after we finish here?"

"Yes! There's a beautiful onsen in the hotel. I'll ask Kenichi to take you there." Tomoko wrapped her arms around Keira from behind and embraced her tightly, whispering, "You take good care of yourself now, okay?"

"You're sweet. I will. Thank you so much for everything." She stuck with the formal but pleasant nature of make-believe Sarah.

"My pleasure."

Keira finished her whiskey and felt incredibly calm and pleasured. She still had the strange triptoline sensation of hyper awareness, which turned toward the sensual gratification throbbing in her body. To attempt to appear like the more restrained Sarah, Keira tried to shift her awareness to non-sexual sensations by doing a quick mind trick of focusing on five things she could see, four things she could hear, three things she could taste, and two things she could smell.

After both getting dressed, Tomoko walked Keira to the door. When Tomoko opened it, the same escort awaited her there and gave a slight bow. Tomoko lightly touched Keira's back and said something to the man in Japanese. Then to Keira she said, "I must go now, my dear, but Kenichi will take care of you." The two women held each other's gaze for a moment, and Keira felt like a certain respect passed between them. Then Tomoko bowed and retreated into the room.

Once out of sight, Kenichi said, "Ms. Rubin, Tomoko said you are interested in spending time at the spa. We would love to have you as our honored guest. Is the cost of 3,500 beta coins agreeable to you?"

Another small fortune. "That would be fine. Thank you, Kenichi."

He smiled. "Then please follow me."

To Keira's luck, he began walking down the hallway from the memory. She started counting steps. Sure enough, the door that corresponded with Liam's room from the memory was guarded by a muscular man. She avoided eye contact with him and kept her gaze straight ahead.

Several paces later, they turned down a different hallway toward the spa, which had an entrance featuring a waterfall and two small fountains. This was probably the water sound from the memory, not the lounge, Keira thought.

Realizing that the place was too heavily monitored to make any kind of bold move, Keira decided she would just work with the new intel she'd received and not try to pull off anything daring now. Since leaving the onsen right after paying would look strange, she figured she'd might as well enjoy the healing hot springs on the government's dime and wait for the triptoline to start wearing off. There were worse things.

∼

BACK AT THE station Keira underwent a reverse impersonation, returning to her own clothes and removing the colored contact lenses and grafted fingerprints. The triptoline had run its full course and her vitals checked out normal, which allowed her to immediately return to duty.

She found Squirmy and caught him up on the latest developments, leaving out the racier details and how she came to acquire such information. At this point, Squirmy seemed to know better than to push Keira to say how she knew what she knew. Plus, she was almost always right with these leads, which allowed her to build trust with him.

She puzzled over how they could get to the room where Liam might be kept. Keira suggested that they watch for O'Connor at the Empress Hotel to see if he'd show up around 22:00 for an appointment with Tomoko. While there was no way for her to know whether the appointment was tonight, she couldn't blow the potential opportunity.

Squirmy then caught Keira up on what he'd looked into. Over the past few hours, he had interviewed the breeders and found them to be completely in the dark about what had happened. The surrogate in particular became increasingly upset—part of the postpartum roller coaster some went through, unable to always detach from the babies they carried or the role they served as the physical lifeline to the world.

The surrogate kept interrupting him to ask if the boy was alive, breaking down in tears, and inquiring what the police were doing to find him.

Squirmy wondered whether she was also afraid that her own child could be taken from her. In order to ensure breeders' compliance once enrolled in Operation Life Speed, government officials made it clear in not so subtle ways that the breeders' ability to continue to own their own child was at the discretion of the state. In other words, how free in reality were the breeders to leave the program if it became too much for them to handle?

While Squirmy was trying to assure the clearly agitated surrogate that the situation was under control, an overseer from the breeding department tranquilized her, and then two strong nurses removed her from the interview room. Squirmy was clearly still feeling lousy about adding to the woman's plight as he updated Keira.

Keira appreciated his empathy and how he tried his best to treat people fairly and with compassion on the job. She shared his belief in acting according to one's own values, not just the authority of the badge.

"I also started pulling up internal reports from Plant Sustainability about Go Slow," Squirmy said. "The movement seems to have tried numerous times this month—more than usual—to infiltrate Plant Sustainability's cyber security system."

"Were they successful?"

Squirmy tilted his head. "That's what's unclear. The internal Plant Sustainability reports say they warded off intrusion, but when I looked closely at the hack attempts, there's one attempt that seems pretty likely to have retrieved something based on its penetration depth. And on social agitation platforms recently, Go Slow has claimed that it knows of an experimental chemical compound that Plant Sustainability plans to use. However, that official decision exists nowhere in the public domain or even in Plant Sustainability's servers."

"So either the hack uncovered information that Plant Sustainability then buried, or this is just a bunch of hysteria intended to get the public riled up," Keira said.

"Bingo."

"Let's round up the usual suspects then. Where did that saying come from?"

"I have no idea."

"Do you want to start with the number-one guy or go lower down the ranks?"

"Travis is always delightful, as you know. Let's start at the top."

Keira used her time piece to search for Travis Hollmeyer. In his latest hologram image, taken during an arrest six months ago, he looked like he'd been through the ringer with a black eye, unshaven chin, and gaunt cheekbones. She requested his home-arrest address, which system photos showed to be a dingy apartment down a seedy alley in Normal Heights. Due to backlogs with the court system, house arrest was used prior to sentencing and in lieu of bail.

Travis Hollmeyer had served as the lead agitator for the Go Slow Movement for the past year, or however long ago it was that the original agitator died in an accident that no one believed was accidental.

Previously in his career, Travis had worked as a journalist reporting on environmental travesties and the impacts on humans of toxins and gene manipulations. Apparently, he'd seen enough to find telling the truth through the news ineffective; he believed it was time to take matters into his and other likeminded people's hands as a social activist or, as some would call him, an anarchist.

He was well-intentioned but could be a real dick, and he hated the police.

Given their law-enforcement credentials and Travis' house-arrest status, Keira and Squirmy would be able to access his place without his permission and without warning. While Keira didn't think that was right, they had a missing baby and a girlfriend to find. Waters were perpetually muddied these days, she thought. It was hard to see the bottom or the top.

Knowing that their unannounced visit would not go over well, they each grabbed an aerosol subduing agent from the Weapons Room.

"Is this day over yet?" Squirmy joked.

"I know. Right?"

CHAPTER 6
FINDING SPIDER'S LAIR

TRAVIS GRABBED a metal pipe and started to charge at them. "Who the fuck are you?"

"Police! Stop!"

Since Travis showed no signs of slowing down, from five feet away Keira sprayed subduing agent in his face and watched him recoil and eventually, after thirty seconds of hacking and swearing, collapse and go unconscious. He would be fine, but she felt bad about causing him temporary harm.

"I see he's still his typically charming self," Squirmy said.

"Absolutely. Hasn't skipped a beat."

They cuffed his hands and feet and then hoisted him into a chair, settling him down as gently as possible given his dead weight. They applied a loose restraint across his shoulders and abdomen and waited for him to wake up.

"You fucking Nazis," Travis said when he opened his eyes and realized his situation. He drooled a little, an effect of the subduing agent.

"You didn't leave us much choice there, buddy, when you came at us with a metal pipe," Squirmy said. "We kind of had to pull the power card."

Travis sneered. "The police pull the power card whether they have to or not."

"Fair enough, fair enough," Squirmy said and crossed his arms against his chest and looked down at Travis strapped into the chair in front of him. "But we didn't come here to discuss the politics of power with you. We have a missing baby on our hands—one associated with a high-ranking government official—and your organization was the last to make threats against his department."

Travis looked genuinely surprised. Keira got the impression he didn't know anything about the kidnapping. But that didn't mean he didn't know something that could be useful.

"I don't mess with children, even the children of douchebags. Go Slow uses other methods."

"Like cyberattacks?" Squirmy ventured.

Travis laughed. "I wouldn't know anything about that."

That was clearly a lie, but Keira wasn't bothered by Go Slow's attempts to infiltrate the government's systems. If anything, these days it was clear to her that the truth often needed to be wrested from the hands of the government, which liked to keep a chokehold on information.

"We don't care about your computer games," Keira said. "What we want to know is whether any of your followers would be bold enough to plan or carry out an act of kidnapping—one that comes with the death penalty, I might add—against a bigwig in Plant Sustainability."

Travis exhaled audibly. "Why would I tell you anything about anyone involved with Go Slow?"

"Well, let's see," Keira said. "Playing the power card that you understandably hate, we could charge you for attempting to assault a police officer, for failing to cooperate with an official investigation, and maybe throw in an extra charge about attempting to harbor a criminal. Just for flair." She looked at Squirmy. "Does that cover it?"

"Yeah, I'd say it does." He turned his attention to Travis again. "And, based on what I recall from your rap sheet, one more misdemeanor sends you to the Labs." Squirmy inhaled through his teeth. "I don't know about you, but I sure as shit wouldn't want to be sent there. I've never seen anyone return with his balls or brains intact. Gosh, and what percentage of them actually return? It seems like fewer and fewer these days."

Travis looked nauseous, which could be a side effect of the subduing agent or the realization that he was boxed in a corner.

The Labs was the unofficial name of the laboratories where experiments were carried out on prisoners and others the state considered undesirable and expendable, such as homeless people and babies born with major deformities. The government tested new drugs, new food formulas, new hormone treatments, and anything and everything else they wanted to on the unfortunate souls sent to Citizen Reform, its official name.

In essence, human experimentation sped up the approval process for food cultivation and drug therapies. The government's thinking went: Why waste time testing a food product on mice when you had real humans in your lab instead? Since ramping up food production was a prime goal, the human rights of some became less important than the human rights of others, according to the way these government officials perceived the current state of humanity.

"To be clear," Keira said, "if you feed us any bullshit, we will come back and levy those charges against you and then personally see you aboard the tram to the Labs." Despite her posturing with Travis, Keira thought the Labs were a despicable perversion of justice.

She had witnessed firsthand convicted criminals in their orange prison robes stand shackled on the platform waiting for the shuttle that would transport them to the Labs to who knows what horrors.

Some pissed themselves on the platform. Others cried and whimpered, pleading for another chance. There was nothing like unknown experimentation to scare the daylights out of a person, which was why some jumped in front of the train. That never worked because of the train's automatic safety mechanisms, however.

Travis groaned and moved his head to get his bangs out of his eyes. "All right, all right. I got it. Look, I don't know anything about a kidnapping or a baby. I swear. We don't use tactics like that. We don't believe in harming the innocent to get our message across."

So far so good. Keira thought he was telling the truth.

Travis continued, "Let's just say that we have 'ways' of getting information. And during one of those ways, my guy realized that another party was also trying to glean information from Plant Sustainability. He stopped the attempt short but doesn't know if he was detected by either Plant Sustainability or the other party."

"I see. What did your guy find before he exited?" Keira asked.

Travis' eyes narrowed in anger. He was thin, pale, and aged beyond his years. "He located documents attesting to the fact that the government plans to use Green-Y, a chemical compound known to cause cancer and birth defects in roughly seven percent of the exposed population, in order to boost plant production. How do you knowingly doom one in fourteen people to malady or death just so that you can grow food faster and in larger amounts? Isn't the point of feeding people to nourish them and keep them alive? This is the same government that you two drones wake up to and serve every day, by the way."

Squirmy and Keira looked at each other. This was the first they'd heard of this plan. While it sickened Keira to hear that her government would accept such odds, it did not surprise her one bit. But at the same time, she remained skeptical. The government ran all kinds of ideas up the flagpole; not many of them actually got implemented.

Squirmy said, "So this is the chemical compound that Go Slow has been alluding to on your social platforms. Why haven't you announced what it is or released the government documents like you often do?"

"Because we don't know who that other interested party might be. China? A spying chemical company? We didn't want to put targets on our backs or hand the death codes to interested parties."

"Who has the downloads?" Keira asked.

"You know I can't tell you that."

"Look, your colleague has information that could get him killed," Keira said. "Obviously, someone is ratcheting up the stakes by stealing a baby from a Plant Sustainability official. This could be directly related to the hacked information about Green-Y. I promise you that we will protect your guy if he cooperates."

Keira could see Travis mulling his options. He seemed reluctant, then resigned. "He goes by Spyder. I don't know his real name. He lives in Apartment C above the Chinese fortune teller on the corner of 37th and Meade Avenue."

"Thank you, Travis. We genuinely appreciate your help and want to keep Spyder safe," Keira said.

"I'm sorry to have to do this to you," Squirmy said, "but we can't run the risk of you tipping him off. I'm going to give you a sedative that will last a few hours. You'll wake up groggy and probably with a headache. Just drink lots of water to flush it from your system, and you'll feel fine by the time you go to bed tonight."

Travis appeared pissed but hopeless. He didn't say another word while Squirmy administered the sedative via injection into his right upper arm. Travis locked eyes with Keira as if to say you'd better be good on your word. She nodded, giving him her silent acknowledgment of the pact, and then he lost consciousness.

Keira uncuffed and unbound Travis while Squirmy held him up in the chair. They lifted him onto a nearby sofa and put a cup of water on the floor near his head.

After they left his apartment, Keira got the feeling that someone was watching her. She looked around but didn't see anyone or anything out of the ordinary. Just to be sure, she changed the access code to Travis' door.

Keira and Squirmy were dressed in plainclothes to blend in. They were also on foot so as to fit in with the poor neighborhood. No one rode a motorbike here. Keira used her time piece to figure out the walking route to Spyder's place. It was about ten blocks away.

She still had the sensation that someone was watching her. Squirmy did, too. They decided to split up to see if anyone followed either of them and to meet in front of a laundromat a few blocks from Spyder's apartment.

As she quickly made her way down the sidewalk, Keira no longer felt like she had eyes on her. That was a relief but also a concern. She worried that someone might try to get to Travis. But his place was a basement apartment with no windows that was only accessible through the door. And only law enforcement could get through that door by keying in the code and passing the fingerprint clearance.

There was always the threat of a crooked cop working deals from the inside to the outside, but now that she'd created a new code with breadcrumbs, she'd be able to see in the system when other officers used it to enter his place.

Minutes later she saw Squirmy on the designated corner in front of the laundromat, pretending to check his time piece while keeping an eye out for her.

When she approached, he said he didn't see anything that tipped him off and that the feeling of being watched also had faded once he walked a few blocks away.

She shared her concerns about access to Travis' place.

"We covered him the best we can, Keira. I wish it felt like it was enough, but I get that it doesn't. Let's see what we find at Spyder's and then we'll go check on Travis again."

CHAPTER 7
SHIPS IN THE HARBOR

NO ONE ANSWERED their repeated knocking, so Squirmy and Keira forced their way into Spyder's apartment.

They immediately gagged at the horrid stench. At first glance, the apartment looked neat and cared for, which made Keira's heart sink.

Sure enough, in the living room on the floor was a dead man lying on his back in blood. His throat had been slit cleanly—execution style. Squirmy dry-heaved from the putrid scene and stench. Keira had to walk away for a moment to steady herself.

There were several computers set up on a long table in the living room. She tried accessing each one, but they were all password protected. No surprise there.

Attempting to ignore the slowly decomposing body at the center of the living room, they searched the apartment for information. Keira knew their efforts were probably futile. A systems hacker wouldn't have printed documents sitting around or have left behind an obvious information trail. He probably lived wrapped in the cloak of mystery and, at least from her perspective, died in the same manner.

There was no sign of a struggle, so the assassin might have snuck up on Spyder and slit his throat with a wire. If that were the case, which was speculation at this point, that would mean that there was no confrontation or demanding of answers. Someone just wanted Spyder dead. Contain the threat and move on.

"We'll see if forensics finds any DNA here. I doubt it because this hit was done cleanly by someone who seems to know what they were doing," Keira said. "I'd guess he's been dead for at least a week. This building looks abandoned, which is probably why no one reported the stench." She sighed.

"Yeah, the poor bastard." Squirmy shook his head, still nauseous, and called the station to report the murder.

Keira looked down at Spyder's body and stared at the spider tattoo on his left forearm. Lengthwise, the abdomen of the spider contained the word "veritas," Latin for truth. The eight legs extended from there and appeared to wrap around his arm.

A loud buzzing sound made her jump. She realized it was Spyder's time piece vibrating aggressively against the hard floor.

With a glove on, she moved Spyder's right arm in order to see his screen. The message read: "Ships still can't leave the harbor. Have you set sail yet?" Harper was the name of the sender.

She touched the face of Spyder's time piece, hoping to respond to the message, but it instantly shut off. He had it programmed to his own touch, an option most time-piece wearers employed.

The message seemed fairly clear, in that the organization or individual sensed danger and was waiting to act. Spyder must have had a mission to execute. Did he take care of it before he died? Probably not, Keira figured, if someone was asking about the status now.

Squirmy cross-checked the name Harper with the Go Slow Movement, but he came up empty.

Keira said, "We need to look into Green-Y. Plant Sustainability obviously buried it by removing any mention of Green-Y from their servers, although please check again to be double sure, especially now that we have the product name. Once we've gone through any digital record we can find, we should talk to O'Connor again. See what he knows about it."

Her own time piece buzzed. It was an alert that Travis' apartment had been accessed. The officer on the record was a Jude Henshaw from Cybersecurity. The timing seemed awfully suspicious. Someone dropped in on Travis within a half hour of their visit, just by coincidence?

"Shit, let's get over there," Keira said.

They took a drone rideshare in order to arrive faster. When they entered Travis' place, he was nowhere to be found. The glass of water was still sitting where they'd left it. There were no obvious signs of a struggle, like overturned furniture, but perhaps that was because Travis had been unconscious.

Keira contacted the station to inquire about Officer Henshaw. She waited on hold while the AI attendant retrieved information.

"Detective Kincaid, this is a Code 4," the AI attendant announced. That meant someone was impersonating a police officer. "Officer Jude Henshaw has been deceased for four years, two months, and six days. Security has been breached. Proceed with caution. An alert has been issued."

How were a dead officer's fingerprints still capable of receiving access to an arrested man? Either the computer programmer who set up the system made a huge mistake or someone was able to hack the system and rewrite the codes and permissions.

Keira thought in horror of Travis waking up to find himself about to be tortured for information. She doubted he would be kept alive. For his sake, she hoped he'd be spared the agony by instead being killed while unconscious from the sedative. Keira felt like she was going to puke. They had inadvertently put a hit on Travis just by visiting him.

Travis had tried to protect the environment and the public, and make the government more accountable for its actions. While she didn't always agree with his methods, she admired his altruism. It took courage to stand for moral principles in this overly intrusive society clawing its way back to life by any means necessary. These United States could lose the integrity and purpose that the country was founded on if people like Travis didn't risk their lives to remind the nation's residents of what matters, of human rights, and simply of what's right.

As she stood there reeling from the latest discovery in a day that had been so intense and now overwhelming, Squirmy suggested that they go underground until they could make more sense of what was happening. Keira agreed.

Given that someone might be monitoring their movements through official police channels, they decided to go rogue—underground on their own without police protection. It was the only code officially unwritten in the police system so that it couldn't be hacked, the one to issue when all other alternatives seemed doomed to fail.

Keira dictated 0-2-0, which meant that they had zero regular options to pursue (zero to zero), and sent it.

"Confirmed, Detective Kincaid. Good luck and Godspeed."

CHAPTER 8
RAVEN'S WATCH

IT WAS dark and windy as they walked down the street toward The Hive, a bizarre concrete structure built to look like a beehive. There were a few apartments within The Hive that were set aside as hotel accommodations. Given they accepted cash payments and did not require registration information, such as names or time-piece numbers, Keira figured it was a safe place to anonymously stay. She and Squirmy would need rest before paying a visit to the Empress Hotel later in the evening.

After paying for a room with two beds, they walked up the winding ramp that wound through the interior of The Hive, modeled after the now perished Guggenheim in New York City. Very little remained of Manhattan as a result of the war and sea-level rise. Besides, it was thought to be too toxic for human habitation after all the nuclear bombings. The city was being rebuilt inland with the aim to achieve another state of glory. Leave it to New Yorkers to have grit and determination, Keira thought.

As she wound around the ramp, she was reminded of the last time she had been there with Blaise when their apartment was being fumigated. They had giggled on the way up the walkway before stopping to look at the historical photographs of San Diego adorning the walls. The images of carefree revelers from decades past toasting the new year along the waterfront and of boats racing in the bay had made both of them quiet with longing for better, freer times.

Later, Keira had held Blaise in the room and had kissed the crown of her head as they gazed out the window at the skyline and talked about their day. She remembered the warmth of Blaise's body and the slight lavender scent of lotion on her skin.

Every once in a while, the recollection of such moments could make Keira feel like she was split in two, lopped off from an essential half of herself. It felt painful to breath as she walked along the ramp. At least the photographs had been swapped out for abstract paintings.

She thought of an old movie she had once watched called *Blade Runner*, when a dying replicant declares of his lived experiences, "All those moments will be lost in time, like tears in rain." She was afraid of losing her own precious memories—of Blaise being washed away from her mind's grip if the weeks dragged on into years—because what would she have then?

She and Squirmy walked in the room. Luckily, it faced a different direction from the room she'd last shared with Blaise. She didn't want to gaze in longing at the view they'd gazed upon together and think of all that was now gone. Instead, the large picture window looked toward the distant glittery lights of the Entertainment District.

Keira turned her thoughts to Tomoko and Liam. How could she get into the room where he was being held? With the rapid developments of the day, she hadn't had the presence of mind to come up with a viable plan.

It was 18:37. If they were going to tail O'Connor and see if he showed up at the penthouses for a 22:00 appointment, she didn't have much time to figure it out. They each ate a goo pack and decided to take a power nap in order to gear up for the evening's detective work.

The beds hung from the ceiling, appearing to float above the floor —a popular design trend in the hospitality industry. It seemed to be a psychological attempt to get visitors to feel as if they were floating above it all, letting go of their worldly worries. Keira was too exhausted at the moment to give her worries further thought and quickly fell sleep.

~

When Keira's alarm woke her at 20:00, she glanced over to see Squirmy seated at the table, with a hologram image from his time piece casting an eerie glow over his face. He looked haggard and in need of a shave.

"Did you sleep?" she asked.

"Nah, too much mind chatter."

"Yeah, there's a lot to think about."

"Seriously. Well, I've been looking into Green-Y. I confirmed there's no mention of it anywhere on Plant Sustainability's servers. They must have wiped it clean after the cyber breach."

"That doesn't surprise me." Keira reached her left arm up over her head and leaned out, stretching her side. She felt stiff and groggy.

"There's almost no information about Green-Y online," Squirmy added. "I found a link to a clinical trial of it, but there was nothing actually at that site—just a blank page with a systems error warning. Someone is working hard to keep it guarded. The only information I was able to access was an article from a German newspaper from April of this year."

The Germans were some of the best internet architects in the world, known for their ability to create cyber systems nearly impossible to penetrate.

Squirmy said, "I ran it through translation. The general gist: From early testing, Green-Y seemed capable of boosting wheat and other plant production in two ways. One, speed up the time between planting and harvesting. Two, create higher crop yields. As you can imagine, tampering with nature has its downsides. The researchers estimated that the chemical compound would lead to greater rates of cancer and birth defects. As Travis said, they concluded that Green-Y could affect seven percent of the population in that way."

He sighed and shook his head before continuing, "Apparently caring more about their people than our government does about ours, the Germans officially banned Green-Y. You know how they are. They experiment with everything, but they only take what is safe. And efficient. And cost-effective."

"Was Green-Y created by the German government or a private entity?"

"The article didn't say. Another German trait: secrecy."

Keira laughed. "So true. One thing we definitely have to figure out soon is what Stephen O'Connor knows about Green-Y, or what someone thinks he knows. Our best bet tonight is to get close enough to him to plant a wire. If we can get ears on what he's saying when he doesn't know we're listening, then we can start to break this mystery open. And if we can't plant the wire, I say we resort to confronting him after he leaves the hotel. He'll know the optics are bad, which could be a bargaining chip for us."

Squirmy agreed and offered to be the one to plant the wire. He was good at blending in and continuing on his way unnoticed.

They left the hotel on foot shortly after. The air was still hot and dry, but fortunately no fires had flared up. Anti-spark warning signs still flashed on street corners.

They found a cheap clothing store where Squirmy could buy a hat to at least partially conceal his face.

He emerged from the store wearing the new hat pulled down low and a construction worker's shirt.

"I almost didn't recognize you," Keira joked.

He chuckled.

THEY STOOD a block from the Empress Hotel watching junkies quietly come and go from the alley connected to the experience dens.

What a waste of wages and hope, Keira thought. They got a high that left them feeling low as soon as they exited the dens and found themselves back in 2122's dreary reality.

While she could relate to wanting to live in a dreamscape, the sensory simulations of tasting food and seeing lush expanses of greenery made it hard to fight the good fight in real life, especially because the simulations never quite scratched the itch.

She'd visited the experience dens a few times, and they always made her feel depressed and unmotivated the next day. Her body had also ached. She wondered if that had something to do with the electrical signals sent through wires into the skin during the experience and the way that the peak of pleasure got cut off just before it could be fully realized. Each session, in that way, was like a painful tease. The emptiness of real life and the frustration of not having fully escaped it led to a terrible aftereffect.

During her more optimistic moments, Keira believed the country was making progress in returning to the ideal it had once squandered and that the war had practically finished off. In her lifetime she believed the experience dens would become unnecessary because reality would offer those sensations to all once again. But she recognized that might be a long time coming or, worse yet, just a pretty dream to help pass the time.

Go Slow posited that society remained trapped in a collective depression brought on by the widespread loss of life from the war and subsequent lack of hope for the future. From bleakness to brightness, they encouraged, but one step at a time. The government censored their messages, driving them underground, and instead broadcast state propaganda to the masses. Progress was real and unparalleled, officials promised. It was hard to see, the government spokespeople conceded, but patience would be rewarded.

Limbo, however, was the unbearable lull of existence. No one wanted to wait, but few believed the government's hype. And, of course, there was no going backwards. The dead were dead. Life as people had known it was indeed gone. And so was Blaise. If Keira could just at least find her. The yearning pulled Keira's attention back to the mission at hand.

Squirmy and Keira monitored the hotel entrance and the parking lot exit from their corner, where they could be inconspicuous among the crowd of people spilling onto the walkway as a nearby carnival let out.

While Keira's gut told her the 22:00 meeting with O'Connor would happen tonight, she worried that she was wrong, that it had already occurred, and they wouldn't get access or intel. Only time would tell.

A couple of teenagers walked by holding hands and smiling at each other. The girl carried in her free hand a souvenir from the carnival, a glass globe of delightfully swirling colors that the boy probably bought for her based on the proud way he regarded it and her. They looked for all the world like they were the only two people in it. Keira missed that feeling.

Just as a wave of sadness began its familiar rise, she spotted O'Connor emerging from a parking lot. He wiped his balding head with his right hand and looked around.

She nudged Squirmy, who immediately started walking toward the pedestrian bridge. She stayed put and observed from a distance. From the way O'Connor looked around, he appeared worried that he was being followed.

As O'Connor made his way toward the hotel entrance, Keira watched as Squirmy bumped him and kept walking. O'Connor turned around appearing irritated, but he didn't seem to suspect anything other than someone being rude or clumsy. He turned back around and headed into the lobby.

Shortly after, Keira got a message on her time piece from Squirmy with an address. The hologram mapping system showed her the fastest way to get to what was a kids' playground nearby, empty this time of night. That would be a quiet place to listen to the audio.

When she got to the park, she sat next to Squirmy on a play pod made to look like a whale that could be spun around and rocked up and down.

Squirmy said, "All I've heard so far is O'Connor talking to the check-in clerk. He's on his way upstairs." He handed her a pair of wireless listening devices that she inserted into her ears.

She heard the elevator door open and a host greet O'Connor. His voice was different from Kenichi's, who had escorted her earlier today. The host exchanged a few pleasantries and then asked O'Connor to follow him. You could hear them walking down the hall.

Then Tomoko greeted O'Connor. "It's nice to see you again, sir."

"You as well," O'Connor responded. The host left them.

"Can I get you a drink, a joint? Anything else that suits your pleasure?"

O'Connor asked for a double vodka. He sounded weary.

Keira could hear the sound of ice clinking in a glass. Tomoko carried on with small talk as O'Connor drank his drink and spoke the bare minimum. As Tomoko apparently attempted to take his clothes off, he asked her to wait.

It didn't seem like he was expecting to relish this visit like the one she'd accessed from his memory. As far as Keira could tell, he was freaked out and had only shown up because he knew he had to. No one ignores a demand from the Chusei and expects to carry on with all their body parts or family members intact.

He asked for another double vodka. Keira could hear Tomoko preparing it and humming softly.

There was silence followed by a soft thudding noise. Maybe he had downed the drink and set it on the bar.

O'Connor then said in a soft voice, perhaps hoping to elude the audio detectors in the room, "Could you please ask Victor to come in here already? I do not plan on stripping down and then having him ambush me."

Tomoko whispered back, "I don't recommend that, sir. Victor will be angry."

"I think we both know he's already livid." He laughed like a desperate man who found any sort of logical advice hysterical.

O'Connor then shouted, "Just come and get me already for fuck's sake!" Keira was shocked by his brazenness and turned toward Squirmy, whose eyes widened with incredulity.

O'Connor ordered Tomoko to make him another drink.

Within moments, Keira could hear a door open and close.

"Mr. O'Connor, you're even more of a fool than I could have imagined." It was the calm voice of the short man, Victor, from Tomoko's memory. "You do not demand my presence. Do you understand me?"

"Well, it appears that I just did." Keira and Squirmy made eye contact, dumbfounded by O'Connor's behavior. Instead of meeting fear with courage, he seemed to have chosen foolish bravado.

"Yes, and there are consequences for that."

Keira listened to what sounded like a physical struggle, followed by stifled screams.

"Yas can continue breaking the rest of your fingers, or you can nod to let me know that the childish games are over." There was a pause.

"Good, I'm glad to see you're not a complete idiot." He then politely asked Tomoko to leave the room.

O'Connor's whimpering and ragged breathing became much louder all of a sudden. He must have had a gag removed.

The crime boss continued, "We had a deal, Mr. O'Connor, one that you have not upheld. We Chusei take loyalty very seriously. As you have seen through the disappearance in the middle of the night of a certain little baby boy, there are consequences for your lack of follow-through. You may think you're clever or one step ahead of us, but you should know we are like ravens flying overhead and seeing your every movement. We just choose when to soar and when to swoop down."

There was another muffled scream. The bodyguard probably broke another of O'Connor's fingers with a gag in his mouth.

When he could seemingly breathe again, O'Connor asked, his voice infused with pain, where his son was and if he was okay.

"He's being well taken care of. I can assure you that we are not baby killers. We will, however, sell him to the highest bidder—gosh, babies are so profitable these days—if you don't make good on our arrangement." He paused, letting the message sink in. "So, let's back up a bit. Why didn't you make the drop-off? You approached the location and then left. Since then, you've spent all your time at work and at home. It appears your favorite part to play is the role of good husband, which we both know is an act."

"I was being followed! I couldn't risk it, but the information is in a very safe place. I assure you."

"Of course you were being followed. We were following you."

"I think others were, too."

"That's not your concern, Mr. O'Connor. Let us handle any attempts at interference. That's something we're quite good at."

"I don't think your client knows the extent of what's at stake. Green-Y would be incredibly dangerous to actually implement. Look, I'll return the money! I haven't spent it. And I'll give you the briefcase with the files." He sounded desperate and on the verge of tears.

"So now you find a conscience after your baby is stolen from you and a couple of your fingers are broken. Suddenly, you care about other people." Victor laughed. "While I'll be the first to admit this is a dirty business, we've all made promises that must be kept. My client is growing impatient from cleaning up all the messes you keep creating."

O'Connor started sobbing. "I'm sorry. I got in over my head." He sounded like he was trying to catch his breath. "Can I see my son?"

"Only after you've made the drop, which you *will do* tonight. I have arranged for a car to take you to your office to retrieve the briefcase. Then you will immediately go to the drop-off location and follow all the instructions I send." He inhaled audibly. "If you do not do as asked, Mr. O'Connor, you'll never see your son again. We'll also send video footage of your fun here to your boss. That will probably not go over well. Lastly, everyone you've ever cared about will become a potential target of our vast resources. We like having options. It feeds the creative problem-solving process."

"I'll do it." O'Connor's voice was shaky.

"Ice your hands and pull yourself together. Yas will escort you to the car in fifteen minutes."

There was a sound of a door closing, followed by nervous breathing from O'Connor.

Keira hadn't expected to intercept such time-sensitive intel. The revelations were incredibly helpful, but the timing was problematic.

"We picked a hard time to go 0-2-0," she said. "Now we have no vehicles to tail O'Connor with. We can't exactly ask a cabbie to follow a car from spot to spot without arousing suspicion." A new rule implemented in California required all hired cars after 21:00 to have drivers. There had been too many stalking complaints and disorderly charges late at night; anonymity through driverless vehicles apparently brought out the creep in people .

Squirmy bit his lip, looking pensive. Then his eyes lit up. "I'll have my buddy from Securities Fraud give us a lift. He loves a bit of excitement after being stuck behind the desk looking at financial reports all day."

"Can we trust him?"

"Hell yeah. I know how he is. He won't want to lose his connection to the danger of playing detective by running his mouth. I'll dial him up."

As Squirmy stepped away to make the call, Keira stood up and put her hands on her hips. O'Connor hadn't spoken since Victor left the room. She had only heard sounds of water running from a sink, ice being rummaged through, and labored breathing.

He sure was out of his league, she thought. One thing she'd discovered from working in law enforcement was that the people who attempted to dabble in crime after only knowing the world of rule-following and regular employment often ended up getting caught or killed. They just lacked the street smarts and ruthlessness for it.

She wondered why the crime boss, Victor, insisted that O'Connor do the drop. Clearly, the Chusei could get the briefcase from O'Connor and make the handoff themselves, so why were they making O'Connor do it?

As she mulled that question, only two scenarios seemed likely: the Chusei feared that another crime tribe or law enforcement would try to intercept the deal, and they'd rather have O'Connor take the direct hit while they contained the threat from a distance. Alternatively, the Chusei or their client planned to kill O'Connor as soon as the transaction was done. Or maybe it was both.

O'Connor was certainly a liability in that he knew too much and had shown himself to be untrustworthy. The Chusei had no tolerance for the disloyal. He would certainly pay a price beyond his kidnapped baby and broken fingers for the predicament he'd seemingly created for them.

Keira inhaled deeply and let her breath out slowly, realizing they'd have to be very careful in this tail. The Chusei would be monitoring O'Connor closely. It was still unclear who the client was who wanted the information on Green-Y and what that person or organization might be capable of. Who gave O'Connor the briefcase, and what specifically did it contain? O'Connor certainly knew insider information about Green-Y that seemed to have been wiped clean from government servers. What did the government plan to do with Green-Y?

Keira felt overwhelmed by all the unanswered questions. She was also frustrated that tonight's surveillance hadn't revealed any further connections between Blaise and O'Connor. Blaise had obviously been monitoring O'Connor or the person who handed him the briefcase, but without knowing the identity of the Chusei client who wanted the information on Green-Y, Keira was at a bit of a roadblock.

Unfortunately, she and Squirmy had planted that wire on O'Connor without a warrant, meaning no charges would be admissible in court. For a government that could be so corrupt in some ways, judges were still sticklers about warrants. Keira suspected that was due to their own desire for controlling who got searched and surveilled and who did not. Furthermore, Keira and Squirmy couldn't step in to make an arrest tonight without actually witnessing firsthand a crime being committed. Handing a briefcase over was not a crime unless there was admissible proof of what it contained.

They could stop going rogue and ask for police backup, but Keira felt that might be like lighting a match near an open gas tank. Plus, there was still the risk of their plan being tipped off by someone monitoring the police system.

Would the Chusei make good on their promise to return Liam? While it was likely they'd take out O'Connor, Keira believed they'd return the boy to his mother if O'Connor did what he was told. The Chusei were known for being true to their word, making them reliable to do business with. Brutal, but honest in their brutality. She decided to take that gamble because it seemed more important to follow O'Connor with Squirmy than to try to get Liam on her own, which seemed unlikely to succeed.

After finishing his call, Squirmy walked toward Keira. "Jim's on his way. Let's get back to the Empress to get eyes on O'Connor. I told Jim to pull up one block south of the lobby. He's got a black Mercedes that looks like a limo, so it won't attract attention."

Keira could hear O'Connor's nervous breathing and the sound of people in the lobby. He was on the move.

CHAPTER 9
BULL'S EYE

THEY TAILED the car carrying O'Connor, a luxury sedan with retractable doors. As expected, it stopped at O'Connor's office for several minutes while he went inside.

He emerged clutching the briefcase that Keira had seen in his memory and walking fast as if afraid someone might try to seize it before he got back to the car. He looked around before stepping into the backseat. The door closed, sealing him inside a space Keira assumed he found suffocating. Every space feels too small, she thought, when you know you could be attacked at any moment.

Luckily, the wire hadn't fallen off his shirt. So far O'Connor had barely spoken, only communicating with the driver through short responses.

She hadn't noticed any other vehicles following him. Still, she figured the Chusei were monitoring the car from a distance and could have people waiting near the destination.

Keira, Squirmy, and Jim followed at a distance of about fifty yards on the autoway. O'Connor's sedan exited into the Textiles District, a seedy sector of the city comprised of warehouses and tenement housing.

After also exiting there, Squirmy told Jim to turn down a different street from the sedan so as to avoid notice. Squirmy and Keira monitored the sedan's movement on Squirmy's e-screen. The Chusei car, illuminated in neon green on the screen, proceeded almost all the way toward the aqueduct before turning right into a warehouse lot. Then it appeared to enter a warehouse and stop.

They parked three blocks away in the lot of a 100 Dollar Store and told Jim to wait in the car. "Do you have a gun?" Squirmy asked him.

"Yep, my hottie is under the driver's seat and ready for a night on the town."

Squirmy rolled his eyes and told Jim to have the gun out and ready but not visible. "I doubt anyone caught our tail, but you never know. Keep a cool head and only use that gun if absolutely necessary. You hear me?"

Jim nodded. "Aye aye, captain."

Squirmy looked his characteristically skittish self, but Keira preferred that a partner be nervous rather than cocky. She pulled her hood over her head and adjusted her firearm against her hip belt.

Over the wire, a voice they hadn't heard before told O'Connor to wait. The man had a foreign accent that she couldn't quite place.

To try to look like a normal couple in the neighborhood instead of undercover detectives or burglars, Keira and Squirmy clasped hands. They walked quietly and quickly in the dark toward the warehouse. Squirmy's hand was slightly damp.

O'Connor's breathing was labored, like he was struggling to maintain his composure. From the light thumping sounds that ensued, she figured he was getting patted down.

Keira's own pulse quickened as she realized the guard could find the wire and then flip out about O'Connor being tracked. Although it was extremely light and probably wouldn't make a detectable sound if it struck the floor, a thorough visual inspection could spot it.

"This way," she heard, followed by footsteps. By the way the footsteps grew fainter and fainter, Keira realized that the wire had fallen off. Relieved it hadn't been discovered, she was now concerned they wouldn't have ears on O'Connor anymore.

They were now only twenty feet from the warehouse. It was surrounded by a high metal fence. The only audio they heard was echoing footsteps and occasional bursts of conversation in a foreign language.

"Russians," Squirmy said.

The realization struck Keira forcefully: The Feds were always on the lookout for Russian, Chinese, and Mexican crime within These United States. Blaise might have been called in to take a deeper look, especially if it had been discovered that a high-ranking American official intended to commit treason. A clue to Blaise's whereabouts could be in this warehouse, Keira thought, and suddenly their mission was more important to her than anything else in the world.

The fence was high and would certainly be monitored by security cameras. They didn't have ears on the place, at least not in an ideal way anymore, nor did they have eyes on it.

Keira scanned the block, seeking a solution, as she and Squirmy stood there on the sidewalk holding hands and trying to look like they were waiting for a ride or, more likely in this neighborhood, a purchase of cheap street drugs with high overdose odds.

The warehouse next door, with a sign on its street-facing wall that read "Smith's Fabrics" in big block letters, had a shorter chain-link fence that would be relatively easy to climb over plus a roofline that was about the same height as the one they wanted to access. All of a sudden, she saw her approach with crystal clarity.

She pulled Squirmy's hand to follow her. Not a fan of heights, he wasn't thrilled by the plan she shared, but he couldn't think of anything better.

They walked to the end of the fence line of the Smith's Fabrics warehouse in order to be as far as possible from the warehouse occupied by the Russians and hopefully out of direct sight of its cameras. They climbed up and over the fence and just barely cleared the metal leg traps at the base of the other side—inexpensive security features that would leave any trespasser maimed and howling.

They ran along the far side of the Smith's fence until they were about at the halfway point of the building. Keira grabbed her electronic climbing equipment off her torso belt and shot the grounding device up toward the roof, which was about thirty feet high. The grounding device had sensors that allowed it to locate the best anchoring spot nearby, either by wedging itself against a ledge or burrowing down into the surface until firmly implanted.

The green flash on the device alerted her that the anchor was in place. She expanded the handles outward for maximum grip, raised them over her head, and squeezed to signal that she was ready. The cord pulled her upwards. Once on top of the roof, she sent the levers down to Squirmy. He rode up, looking like he might vomit.

Once he was on his feet on top of the roof, she said, "You're not going to like this part."

She walked to the distant edge and cast the grounding device onto the roof of the warehouse where the Russians and O'Connor were. Once it was anchored, she also attached it to the roof they stood on. This created a tightrope of sorts between the two roofs. She planned to traverse it by riding the levers and letting her legs hang down.

"I can't," Squirmy said, who avoided even peering over the edge.

"That's okay. I'll go across, and you be backup." She gripped the handles and sped across, her feet dangling down into the darkness.

Once safely on the other roof, she crept quietly along it hoping to find a skylight or other opening. If not, she'd have to laser one, which would take longer. There had still only been brief bits of conversation in Russian as well as footsteps picked up by the wire.

She located a skylight toward the roof's center. She approached it carefully, squatted low, and peered down.

Below her she saw O'Connor standing with his hands tied behind his back. He was flanked by two stocky guards. Another man sat a table looking at documents from O'Connor's briefcase. Keira couldn't see the man's face clearly from her angle, but he appeared small, almost frail.

She turned the wire's signal off and instead turned on an audio-enhancer tool, which allowed users to better hear their immediate surroundings even through glass and walls. Fortunately, the audio enhancer signaled that she was within working range. The sound in the room below came to life in her ears. A guard coughed and cleared his throat. In the background it sounded like heavy items were being moved.

No one spoke as the man methodically read through the paperwork. It looked as though he was studying a report.

O'Connor shifted weight between his feet and put his head down. Then the seated man set the documents in a neat pile and said something in Russian. Another man walked into view from behind a large shelving rack, responding to him. The seated man got up and walked away, as if he'd been dismissed.

The new man said, "Mr. O'Connor, everything is there as was promised." He had a thick accent and short black hair that glistened in the artificial light. "But there is one thing I need you to do for me before I let you go." He said something to the two guards, who quickly walked away and out of Keira's view.

O'Connor didn't speak, appearing terrified.

Seconds later, the two guards returned walking a hooded person between them.

The man who had been speaking to O'Connor said something to the guards. One nodded and removed the hood, revealing Blaise's face!

Keira's heart hammered in her chest as she peered down, shocked, at her love below. She was immensely relieved to find Blaise alive and equally horrified to find her in this precarious position.

Blaise squinted at the light and put her head down defensively, as if expecting a blow. One guard grabbed her by the chin and forced her to look at O'Connor.

She did not appear injured—just thin and pale. Blaise's gaze was intensely defiant. Clearly, her spirit had not been broken, Keira thought.

Keira felt powerless to make a move. It was too dangerous to shoot downward on all the Russians, as that would put Blaise in the line of fire.

The man seemingly in charge asked, "Do you know this woman, Mr. O'Connor?"

"No, I-I don't," O'Connor stammered. "I've never seen her before, as far as I know."

"We believe she was following you, which means she's probably either with the Bureau or a crime tribe trying to get in on our action. I was hoping you would solve our little predicament by identifying her."

"Sorry," O'Connor said, looking nervous. "I don't know her."

"Fine. In that case, you'll just have to be the cleanup crew." The man pulled a gun from the back of his pants.

Keira's pulse walloped in her ears as she pulled her own gun and released the safety. She pressed it against the surface of the skylight and aimed at the man's head. He was in her sights.

"Get rid of her," the man said to O'Connor. He addressed the guards in Russian, who then began to untie O'Connor's hands.

Keira radioed Squirmy. "There's a hostage. A Bureau agent. I'm waiting for a clear shot. Prepare for a messy exit on all fronts. Clear."

The man tried to hand the gun to O'Connor, who did not reach for it.

As Keira felt panicked looking down at this rapidly evolving scene, Blaise looked strangely calm as if resigned to her fate. No Bureau agent expects to make it out of captivity alive. They're trained to protect country above self, to accept the ultimate sacrifice without revealing national intelligence—a soldier until the end.

Squirmy radioed. "10-4. Clear."

Keira's pulse was practically deafening as she kept the man, who now had his back to her, trained in her sights. Aiming for the head was higher risk; she moved the target down to strike the heart. At that angle, the shot would just barely miss Blaise on the ricochet and might take down a guard. After that she could hopefully get a couple more shots off before the Russians fired back. It was her best bet.

"Take the gun."

"Me?" O'Connor sounded dumbfounded. "I've never killed anyone in my life. I don't even know her. And I already did what you asked of me!"

"There's always a first time, Mr. O'Connor. Take the gun!"

Keira fired. Glass shattered. She kept her weight back to keep from falling through the now obliterated skylight. The bullet hit the leader's back at the bull's eye. He tumbled forward, dropping the gun he had tried to hand to O'Connor. The ricochet from Keira's bullet struck one guard in the stomach, and he fell. The other kept his grip on Blaise and began to drag her out of the room with him. Keira didn't have a clear shot. Shit!

Two new guards wielding large guns appeared from behind the shelving racks and started to aim at Keira. She had no choice but to retreat.

She kept low to the roof's surface, scrambling on all fours toward the climbing cable as bullets whizzed through the air. She grabbed the levers and zipped across to the Smith's warehouse roof. Keira could see Squirmy monitoring the perimeter, his gun at the ready.

As she got to her feet on the Smith's roof, she heard vehicle tires peeling out. Squirmy ran to the front of the warehouse, and she followed close behind.

Two black armored vehicles with no license plates sped out of the warehouse. She and Squirmy shot at the tires, but the vehicles kept going, disappearing quickly out of sight.

Blaise was gone. Into the dark night.

Keira slumped down exhausted and overwhelmed. She couldn't believe she had failed to take down the other guard and safely extract Blaise. Keira thought she might throw up.

Squirmy made an urgent radio request for drones or live personnel to follow the exiting vehicles.

There wouldn't be much time left to save Blaise. The Russians figured she was a Fed or from a competing crime syndicate. Since they couldn't get their answer or cooperation from O'Connor, they'd probably still want her dead and her body dumped. Then it dawned on Keira that they might have already executed her in the warehouse. The urge to throw up grew stronger.

"Are you okay?" Squirmy asked.

"No, not at all. I'll explain later, but first we need to quickly comb the warehouse while a tail follows those vehicles. We're too far behind them now to catch up. Please ask Jim to bring the car around. We'll coordinate with the tail as soon as we take stock of what's in the warehouse. Maybe there will be some kind of clue about the next part of their plan."

He nodded, concern for her showing plainly in his eyes.

After they rappelled down the Smith's Fabrics warehouse, they could see light spilling from the opened port where Blaise had been held.

Keira peered around the corner but didn't see any movement. She grabbed a discarded tire rim that was near her foot and tossed it into the cavernous room. It landed with a clatter, but no footsteps or gunfire ensued. The warehouse appeared empty.

Keira slowly made her way in, scanning the room. She headed back to the scene of the shooting. The bodies of the boss and the guard were splayed on the floor, their blood pooling on the concrete. The guard had a bullet hole in his head. It must have been a mercy killing because it wasn't her shot.

The gun that the boss had tried to hand to O'Connor sat propped up in blood like a shipwreck at low tide. The table where the seated man had reviewed the documents was clear, which meant the Russians had grabbed the briefcase during the pandemonium. Glass bits from the blown skylight were scattered along the floor. They crunched under Keira's boots. She made her way to the very back of the warehouse but didn't see any other bodies.

She sighed with relief knowing that Blaise hadn't been killed in the warehouse. But Keira feared she would run out of time or perhaps already had. She had to move fast.

"Let's check these side rooms," she said to Squirmy. "Maybe the Russians left something behind that could be useful in locating them or understanding their plan."

She started to step again, gun raised to her shoulder height with both arms extended. Out of her peripheral vision, she saw motion to her right.

A woman's voice called out, "Bureau agent! Don't shoot."

As Keira swiveled her shoulders to the right, she could see Blaise emerging cautiously from around a doorway.

"Blaise!"

"Keira! By God, it is you." Blaise then began to collapse against the doorframe.

Keira sprinted over to her. She grabbed a slumping Blaise around the hips to help her stand and then cut off her hand restraints. Not seeing any wounds, she wrapped her arms around Blaise's back, pulling her into a tight embrace. She kissed Blaise's neck tenderly and tried to steady her own breath. She felt like her heart was going to burst. Keira whispered, "I'm so relieved and grateful you're alive. I was broken without you." She felt Blaise squeeze back as much as she could but could tell she was physically weak.

Squirmy, standing about ten feet away, froze in place with his mouth slightly open. Keira gave him a head motion to continue searching the warehouse. He quickly walked off, probably glad to be out of view of their private moment.

Keira pulled back a little so that she could look at Blaise's face. She choked up as she gazed into Blaise's gorgeous green eyes and touched the lips that she feared would never utter her name again. "Are you okay, my love?"

Blaise smiled wanly. "Yes, but it feels like I ran two marathons in a row. I could probably sleep for a month." Keira tucked Blaise against her body again and caressed her back and head gently.

"Are you injured?" she asked softly.

"No, just exhausted," Blaise said, nestling her face into the crook of Keira's neck. Her breath felt warm against Keira's skin. "You kept me alive. Thoughts of you kept me alive." Blaise began to cry, her body heaving up and down with the sobs.

Keira cradled Blaise's head and kissed her hair softly, holding her close. They clung to each other for a long time. Blaise's body relaxed, and the tears stopped.

"Nice shot, by the way," Blaise said, wiping her eyes and laughing. "You've always had the best aim. I should have known right away that was you." Then she kissed Keira on the lips with all the energy she had left.

CHAPTER 10
BREADCRUMBS

AS IT TURNED OUT, the man who reviewed the documents from O'Connor's briefcase at the warehouse was a Russian scientist who ended up saving Blaise.

Blaise explained that after Keira had shot the Russian crime boss and one guard, the other guard grabbed her and started dragging her away. But he immediately was summoned to load the vehicles and told the scientist to finish Blaise off instead.

The scientist had nodded, Blaise said, and pushed her into a side room. She figured it was over—so close to being rescued but now beyond hope. As she tried to prepare herself for the inevitable with her mind racing over what had just happened and what was about to go down, the scientist said to her quietly in English, "Do as I say, and you will live."

He then had loudly ordered her up against the wall and told her to be still. She wondered if he was messing with her, but sure enough he aimed the gun away from her and fired at the adjoining wall. After whispering, "Get down and pretend to be dead," he walked out. Blaise got on her stomach and splayed her legs out on the floor, completely dumbfounded by her unexpected fortune.

She heard the vehicles drive away but stayed down in case any

Russians remained. Shortly after, she heard Keira and Squirmy enter the warehouse. She stayed put, unsure of who was there.

When Blaise heard what she thought was Keira's voice, she figured she was loopy from the intense stress and lack of sleep. After she got up, which was hard to do with her hands restrained behind her back, and peered out into the main part of the warehouse, she could see from the way Keira and Squirmy moved in formation that they were law enforcement, so she called out to them. It wasn't until Keira turned toward her that Blaise knew it was really her.

O'Connor hadn't been as lucky. Police drones tracked the Russians to an abandoned lot six miles from the warehouse, where two choppers waited.

The police drones engaged fire, killing two men. One of the remaining Russians shot O'Connor point-blank as the rest of the group loaded into the helicopters.

O'Connor's murder could be seen clearly from the drone footage. Seconds later, missile launchers from the choppers shot down the police drones, and all eyes on the Russians were lost. It's unclear where the Russians went from there. They probably kept their flight short and low so as to avoid detection in the monitored airspace. The Feds didn't know whether they still remained in the country.

Liam was returned to his mother, delivered in the middle of the night in much the same manner that he'd disappeared. The Chusei had apparently made good on their word, but there had been no tangible sign of their involvement. Keira and Squirmy weren't sure what had happened to the Chusei car that dropped O'Connor off at the warehouse. Did the Chusei see, directly or through recordings, the events that unfolded in the warehouse? While some investigative pieces had started to come together, many pressing questions kept the puzzle far from finished.

Keira obviously had to come clean with Squirmy about her relationship with Blaise. He didn't ask much and said he was happy for her. He also vowed to keep it a secret in order to keep their colleagues from gossiping and sniping. Good ol' Squirmy.

Their boss, of course, took accolades and granted interviews with the media for saving a Bureau agent and aiding in the return of a kidnapped child. It was just as well for Keira and Squirmy since both of them hated talking to reporters or being in the limelight.

~

FROM BOTH OFFICIAL debriefings and conversations with Blaise, Keira and Squirmy began to get a fuller sense of what had happened and what was still at stake for all of them.

Blaise had been pulled in to investigate the potential sale of government assets after the Bureau's cyber trackers flagged activity traced to O'Connor's computer system at Plant Sustainability. From ensuing intelligence it became clear that O'Connor had hired a computer programmer to recover the deleted files about Green-Y from government servers. That was the information carried in the briefcase.

Blaise's mission was to stop O'Connor before he could deliver the documents to the Russians and to bring him in for questioning. She was unsure of the depth of his involvement or what he specifically knew about the Russian buyers. Blaise had wondered if he was a bumbling middleman or more fully informed.

She had tailed O'Connor to and from the handoff point and followed every precaution about distance and approach. But the next thing Blaise knew—as she followed O'Connor down the street with the suitcase in his hand—she was jostled, a hood went over her head, and a needle was jabbed in her arm. Immediately the world went black.

She briefly came to in a transport vehicle, where she heard what sounded like Americans talking. Then she lost consciousness and awoke again in the warehouse where Keira would eventually find her almost three weeks later.

From what Blaise could gather in snippets of Russian conversation during her stint as a prisoner, O'Connor had gotten spooked and not delivered on his promises. Neither the Chusei nor the Russians had tried to apprehend him due to his close government ties, which meant he was frequently under government surveillance and, in this case, protected by its watchful eye. Blaise surmised that the kidnapping was what got his attention and got him to go rogue—forgoing government security in order to get his son back.

Assuming early on in captivity that her own days were numbered, she had found a rough part of the wall to work her rudimentary hand restraint against and eventually broke it apart one night after hours of effort. She grabbed her time piece off the table where the guard sat dozing and made it about fifty yards outside the warehouse door before sending the message to Keira to meet at the bunker. Just as she thought she had truly broken free, she heard shouting and turned around to see three men converging on her. She was dragged back inside, devastated.

From that point forward, Blaise was restrained more tightly and monitored more closely. Although she was frequently yelled at and subjected to sleep deprivation, she got the impression that they were uncomfortable pushing the envelope with her. They made efforts to get information from her, but when it was clear she wouldn't break easily, they seemed to prefer a wait-and-see approach.

Blaise wasn't sure why the Russians hadn't killed her. She had overheard intense debate about whether to keep her alive, but it was in muffled fragments that gave her an incomplete story.

The last she heard, the crime boss seemed to be waiting for word on what to do with her by someone he referred to as Ivan. Perhaps Ivan had given the order to press O'Connor to identify her and then take her out. But that was just speculation.

Before she got scooped, Blaise knew that Russia was experiencing famine and starvation on a widespread level, a fact unknown to the general public of These United States. To her it made sense that the Russians would be desperate enough to use a substance like Green-Y, despite the toll it would exact on a significant portion of the population, in order to do whatever it took to get food production ramped up.

But it wasn't the theft of Green-Y's blueprints that had the Feds worried, Blaise explained. They were not overly concerned about Green-Y's use halfway across the world, especially since it was not a substance that These United States planned to implement. Nonetheless, the government did not want the American public to be aware that its officials had run in-depth analysis of the risk-benefit factors of Green-Y and had seriously considered using it knowing that it could cause cancer or birth defects in an estimated seven percent of the population.

However, keeping that information a state secret was only a minor concern. What really drew the Feds was the fact that Green-Y and weapons production shared a common chemical connection, a compound called eritrune that required both naturally occurring and synthetic materials to make.

Clandestine drone footage in Russia showed what appeared to be a fast-paced creation of labs and warehouses that did not seem consistent with the food supply exclusively. Nitrogen production and phosphate mining, both needed to create eritrune, had accelerated, but so had the extraction of uranium, which indicated nuclear endeavors might also be in the works.

It was believed that the Russians would attempt a one-two punch of increased plant production plus increased weapons production of various types. Based on the materials mined and the Russians' existing weapons technology, it appeared possible that they could somewhat quickly create weapons of mass destruction capable of wiping out entire cities if deployed properly.

Green-Y, essentially then, was like a breadcrumb leading to evidence of a much higher-level threat. Where that would go from here remained to be seen, but the pressure was on Blaise and other agents to figure out a way forward to thwart those plans within These United States. The Feds were to act in coordination with American spies embedded in Russia to share intel and attempt to contain the threat.

On a related note, Keira learned that the other party trying to access Plant Sustainability's servers at the same time as Spyder was a Chinese hacker network that routinely attempted to gain access to information across These United States' government computer systems. As such, that was considered just another day at the office for the Chinese group, who did not appear to recover any information during the attempt in question.

That left Spyder's murder and Travis' abduction still a mystery. Did the Chusei or Russians take out Spyder and Travis for knowing about Green-Y? Unfortunately, adult abduction fell outside of Keira and Squirmy's jurisdiction at the Department of Child Abductions, and

Spyder's murder was assigned to Homicide. Instead, they were told to continue aggressively pursuing the O'Connor kidnapping, mainly because their boss for public-relations purposes wanted someone to hang for it.

While it was clear from their wiretap and other surveillance that the Chusei had at least orchestrated the kidnapping, nothing that Keira and Squirmy had gathered would hold up in court. Evidence collected via mind touch certainly would not get them anywhere in the legal process. Furthermore, the wiretap was done without a warrant.

Keira suspected that the Chusei had pulled in an outside party for the actual act of kidnapping, which definitely did not resemble their brutal crime-scene style. Tomoko's lover from the accessed memory was light on her feet and certainly knew about the kidnapping. Had she carried it out? Was she a Chusei member or a hired gun?

Unsurprisingly, the murders of O'Connor and Spyder received inaccurate media coverage. It seemed as though the government was keeping the real circumstances around their deaths hidden by feeding reporters fake news. O'Connor was depicted as a victim of attempted bribery and kidnapping rather than a traitor who sold state secrets. Spyder's death was explained away as a drug deal gone wrong. That announcement barely broke into the news cycle. Travis' abduction was never publicly reported.

As far as Keira could tell, no journalists seemed to be aware of the connection between Go Slow and Plant Sustainability, although she hoped that someone would investigate it before the government buried information surrounding Green-Y, Spyder, and Travis completely beyond public reach.

While Keira felt grave concern about the state of the world and particularly about what the Russians might do next, she had learned to live with existential uncertainty. Almost everyone had. It was a byproduct of cataclysmic war, climate change, corruption, and government overreach.

But a yearning to unearth the truth, protect the innocent, and safeguard the country for future generations motivated Keira. That, plus her newly reignited relationship with Blaise, kept her pushing forward. Truth and love. What else really mattered? Everything else had pretty much been taken away.

~

IN THE DAYS immediately following the warehouse incident, Keira found herself floating in a mixed state of relief and disbelief. She was ecstatic to have Blaise back but also couldn't believe it was real. She feared she'd wake up to discover it was too good to be true and that Blaise was actually gone—that her return had been a figment of Keira's imagination. It was painful to let Blaise out of her sight, to let her report back to work.

While Keira was incredibly grateful to the Russian scientist who spared Blaise's life, she was puzzled by his behavior. What was his reason for saving her?

On Blaise's second night back, Keira had asked her if she had more insight about that after having had some time to think. Blaise brushed a lock of hair from her tired face, agreeing that it was hard to comprehend. She ventured, "He wasn't a killer or probably even a criminal. I'm guessing he got forced into helping them because of his science background. His act of saving me might have been a way of defying his own oppressors.

"Looking back on it," she continued, "I think he was sneaking me goo packs and water. I'd assumed he was asked to do it, but maybe he was trying to increase my chances of survival. There are people who haven't lost their compassion despite all this suffering, all these power struggles."

Not knowing the motive behind an act made Keira feel vulnerable and less able to protect Blaise. It was hard to slay the monster when you didn't know what it looked like or where it lived.

In addition to the Russian mystery, Keira and Blaise didn't know what to make of the American voices Blaise said she heard before she arrived at the warehouse. Were they Chusei? Some Chusei were born in These United States, while others were foreign. But it couldn't be ruled out that the Russians had other American partners they were working with.

Although Keira had wanted to tell Blaise to stay home and never go back out in the world, instead she had sighed, trusting that her heart would slowly get used to the stress caused by fearing loss. Its resilient muscles would just have to learn to function in spite of the reality that the odds were against them to return to each other's side day in and day out.

SEVERAL DAYS after Blaise's return, Keira was at the office when she got a notification that the crime scene report for Liam O'Connor's abduction was available. Finally, she thought. There had been quite a backlog at the lab. She downloaded the report and began reviewing its contents carefully as Squirmy did the same.

"Look at this," Keira said to him, pointing to the DNA results on page five. "'While the individual could not be identified in the system from a strand of hair found on the crib, the genetic markings indicate majority Yupik Alaska Native ancestry.' Wow, that's practically an extinct people."

She continued, "I remember reading an article about that tribe once. They used to live in a remote part of Alaska. After the government forced everyone out of Alaska to set up a military outpost there about forty years ago, the Yupik people were relocated to a reservation. I think it was in Washington state. They suffered waves of deaths during disease outbreaks and ended up dispersing to other parts of the country. Years afterward, it was unclear how many survived and reproduced. Here's at least one."

Keira thought back on the memory she accessed from Tomoko, when Tomoko's girlfriend walked in the room while Liam slept. Based on the girlfriend's hair and complexion, Yupik definitely seemed possible.

Nothing else in the report struck either of them as noteworthy or provided a new clue to follow. This was the best lead they had.

Squirmy searched the database for the known whereabouts locally of anyone with registered Yupik ancestry. One result materialized:

Cora Brink, age twenty-seven, single, last registered job was as a lock-smith more than two years ago. Squirmy pulled up several photos.

Keira recognized her right away, from memory-scape to reality. "That's her for sure."

Squirmy smiled. "We're getting somewhere now, partner. It looks like her address is to an apartment building in District East 5. Let's start there and then check on her last employer if we don't hit the jackpot."

"Yep, absolutely. We can also try to find her, if necessary, by tracking Tomoko."

They strapped on their weapons under plainclothes and headed out onto the street, where the sun blazed and the dry air practically crinkled in their throats.

A few blocks from the metro station Keira's time piece buzzed with a message from Blaise: "Revol, code 13. New developments re CH/OC case. Might be blue danger."

Blaise and Keira used cryptic correspondence when they worried about messages being intercepted. "Revol" was "lover" spelled back-wards. Code 13 meant trust no one. Keira assumed that CH and OC meant Chusei and O'Connor. Blue conveyed that the threat could be internal—another cop or agent. Shit.

Keira wondered if the Chusei had bought off a cop or two or three. Who was clean? Who might be working them from within their own police ranks? She imagined the concentric circles of protection collapsing inward until all that was left was the bull's eye, pinned on her chest.

Keira shared the message with Squirmy, who now had good reason to be nervous.

CHAPTER 11
MOLE IN THE LIGHT

THEY KNOCKED on the door of Cora Brink's last known apartment. It was in an underground, nondescript building in a working-class section of the city. Underground apartments gave Keira the willies, but at least it was cool down there.

They heard the latch turn, and an elderly woman with frizzy gray hair answered the door. "Are you the census takers?" she asked, blinking.

Bingo. Perfect cover story, although it was not a census year.

Squirmy didn't skip a beat. "Yes, ma'am, we are. But I'm wondering if we have the wrong address since this one is registered to a woman named Cora Brink, who is twenty-seven years old. Unless, hmm, is she a relative of yours?"

Squirmy's ability to play a role on the fly reminded Keira of her ex-boyfriend Ian, who had an uncanny knack for inventing believable stories that got him out of trouble or into events when he wasn't on the guest list. Soon into their relationship, however, Keira wondered what kind of stories Ian was feeding her. He quickly became another ash heap in her long line of short-lived romances. Unlike Ian, however, Keira more or less trusted that Squirmy drew a line she could see.

The elderly woman smiled pleasantly and said, "No, but from what I remember that was the name of the woman who lived here before me." She invited them inside. Keira figured the woman was lonely, and even census takers are better company than no one.

They entered the dark, cool living room. She offered them iced tea and then looked pensive. "Now that I think of it again, Cora *was* the name of the woman who lived here with her father. He was very sick. The neighbors told me they had a hard time paying the rent and were evicted."

"That's a shame," Squirmy said. "Do you know where they moved to?"

"The neighbors said they had to go to the docks. So sad. The poor man probably didn't survive long after that."

The docks referred to a makeshift neighborhood near the defunct port of San Diego. It was a skid row, down-on-your-luck kind of place. A last resort. People there were essentially homeless but erected lean-tos to live in or turned broken-down cars and shipping containers into shelters. Dangerous street drugs with high rates of accidental overdose, plus violence and disease outbreaks, were common at the docks.

"How long ago was that?" Squirmy asked.

"Gosh, let's see. How long have I been here now?" She looked up at the ceiling. "I think three years."

Squirmy said, "We'd like to find Ms. Brink for purposes of completing the census. Do you know anything else about her or her father that could be of help?"

"Hmm, I don't know anything that would be helpful in locating her. The only other thing I recall—I probably shouldn't tell you this, but I guess it's okay since you're not cops." She giggled. Keira and Squirmy exchanged an amused look. "Sheila, who used to live next door but has passed, told me that Ms. Brink was as quiet and mysterious as a ninja, and that people would come to the door late at night and then immediately leave. Sheila suspected that Ms. Brink was into something like drug dealing, but that could all just be gossip."

Keira said, "Yeah, it can be fun to speculate about what goes in other people's lives, but it's hard to know what's real and what isn't from a distance." She figured, however, that the neighbor probably did have reason to suspect shady dealings of some sort.

"Stories can be more fun than the truth, I suppose," the elderly woman said. "But, boy, that landlord who kicked them out sure got his comeuppance. A couple of months after I moved in here, he was found dead hanging from the Coronado Bridge. I mean I didn't like him, but I would never wish that on anyone."

Keira and Squirmy looked at each other. Coincidence?

As Squirmy moved forward with the fake census, Keira began to wonder how dangerous Cora Brink was. How did she get involved with Victor and the Chusei? Her ethnicity lab results didn't show any Japanese heritage.

When Keira and Squirmy got up to leave, the elderly woman said, "It sure was nice to spend some time with you young people today. You come by anytime you want for iced tea and a chat."

What a sweet person, Keira thought. They thanked her on behalf of the country and made their way out the door and up the elevator shaft into the light.

Emerging into the sunlight again was harsh. Keira felt like an exposed mole unaccustomed to the aboveground conditions of daytime.

It seemed to Keira like the more she and Squirmy dug into leads, the more potential danger they found. They were in a game of connect the dots with frightening consequences for not doing it quickly enough. Adding to the uncomfortable mix was the thought that they couldn't trust their fellow officers to be who they purported to be.

All these thoughts made Keira increasingly uneasy as they made their way to Mario's Locks, the last known business that Cora Brink worked for.

When they got there, they discovered that Mario's Locks no longer existed. In its place was a mechanic shop. No one there knew anything about Mario or his defunct business. The crew said that when they signed the lease, the space had been empty for months.

Squirmy decided he'd head back to the station to look into the landlord's death and try to follow up on other loose ends related to Ms. Brink. Keira figured she'd head over to the Empress Hotel to see if she could spot anyone of interest leaving the building, like Cora, Tomoko, or Victor, and then tail the person. It was a long shot, but she didn't have the mental wherewithal to try anything more daring.

LATER THAT NIGHT as Blaise slept soundly, Keira woke up around 02:00 with a nagging feeling of dread in her stomach. She sat up in bed and looked around the room. Nothing was out of the ordinary, yet the sense that something was off persisted. She walked into the kitchen and looked around. All was clear.

Go back to bed, she told herself. You're freaking yourself out. She took a few deep breaths and then tucked under the sheets again.

Keira nestled against Blaise's back, kissing her shoulder softly so as not to wake her and wrapping her right arm around Blaise's waist.

As she listened to Blaise's rhythmic breathing, Keira tried to figure out what had just triggered her nervous alertness.

Blaise's message about a possible internal threat from law enforcement had definitely gotten to her. She felt like she couldn't relax or trust anyone, which in turn made it hard to do her job. Blaise later shared that the Bureau had found questionable use of police details by O'Connor, but the picture was still hazy until they could gather more information.

Keira had found herself questioning everything, which wound her thoughts and stomach into knots. Earlier that day she hadn't spotted any person of interest at the Empress Hotel, which didn't help with the rumination as there was not much to productively focus her attention on.

In bed, Keira eventually grew so exhausted from her troubled mind that she drifted back to sleep.

Then the bald man with the bright white teeth appeared to her as if in a dream. He did not smile this time and looked worried. "Wake up," he whispered. "You are in danger."

Startled, she opened her eyes to see a dark figure standing over her with his arms upraised—bearing a knife pointed down at her chest!

She leapt from bed and tackled the intruder at his waist. They struggled on the floor as Keira tried to wrest the knife from his hands. He was strong but awkward in his movements, allowing Keira to avoid a knife thrust intended for her neck. As they thrashed on the ground, she heard a drawer open and then out of her peripheral vision saw Blaise move.

Keira struggled to keep the man's hands down and was losing ground in the physical fight.

"Spring back, Keira. Now!" Blaise yelled. As Keira did, she heard Blaise's gun fire. The man's head ruptured from the force of the bullet to the side of his temple.

Panting, Keira leaned back on her haunches. Blood streamed across the tile floor a few feet from her.

Blaise turned on a light and then knelt beside Keira, turning her face to hers. "Are you okay, baby? Did he cut you?" She examined Keira's body for signs of a wound.

Keira shook her head.

"Thank the universe," Blaise said and pulled Keira in toward her chest. She squeezed Keira tight. "I've got you. You're okay. You're okay."

Keira tried to shake her state of shock as the adrenaline still coursed through her body. They both stood up and examined the crime scene in their bedroom.

Neither of them recognized the man on the floor. Blaise searched his clothing for a sign of his identity and found in his chest pocket a blue star. That meant he was law enforcement. The blue star was standard issue, an identifying badge to present during an arrest or to another cop when working in plainclothes.

"This case just keeps getting crazier and more complicated," Keira said. She felt nauseous as she gazed at the lifeless body, its blood oozing into the grout of the tiles.

Blaise stood with her arms crossed, looking pensive. "I wonder if we were both on his hit list, or if he came here for you specifically."

"I was wondering the same thing, but it's hard to kill two people with a knife." Keira paused. "How do we call this in? Do we just come clean about our relationship to our bosses?"

Since Bureau agents have identifying marks on their bullets, there would be no hiding the fact that the intruder was killed with a Bureau gun. Keira couldn't quickly think of a believable explanation that skirted the truth.

By dating, they weren't breaking law-enforcement rules per se, but inter-agency relationships were definitely frowned upon. Both of their bosses might question how they had dealt with sensitive information or think they'd endangered themselves or their colleagues. Keira didn't want to invite awkward speculation if she didn't have to.

In their situation, however, having a partner with Bureau training had most likely saved Keira. She doubted that she could have over-taken the assailant on her own. Her gun had been several feet away in the bedside table, practically useless to her there. But, she realized, if the man in the dream hadn't prompted her to wake up, she still would have been a goner and maybe Blaise, too.

Blaise said, "I don't see any other way to do this than to tell the truth. I'll call Devon. He'll be discreet and will know the best way to handle things." Devon played his cards carefully and thoughtfully, which had earned him trust with Blaise and the other agents who reported to him.

"All right. It is what it is. I'm going to call Squirmy's personal line just in case corrupt ears are listening to my codes over the monitor. I'll figure out with him how to deal with our boss later."

But instead of making the call, Keira just stood there looking down at the dead cop and the knife glistening under the electric light, suddenly feeling unable to move. It was like her feet were stuck in heavy mud and her legs couldn't figure out how to extract them.

"Hey," Blaise said quietly. She lifted Keira's chin with a gentle touch. "We will get to the bottom of who did this. I promise you that. No one is going to come between us. Not Russians, not Chusei, not corrupt cops, not law-enforcement bureaucracy. Okay? No one."

Keira nodded, fighting back an urge to cry. She felt ridiculous and then felt ridiculous for feeling ridiculous. After all, she had just fought hand to hand with an armed intruder who could have killed them both. She had a right to be upset. And this week had just been too damn much. She didn't know how much more she could bear.

Keira's body shook with the effort to contain the tears that couldn't be contained. Blaise embraced her and rubbed her back. She said quietly to Keira, "This has been an agonizing month for both of us, and you just woke up to someone trying to stab you. It's okay to be freaked out, angry, confused, or anything else that's going through your mind."

Blaise then moved her head back slightly and made eye contact with Keira. "But in order to stay safe and ready to face anything that might come at us, we both have to recognize what's going on with us. That's all. You've got to let me in on the thoughts running through your head that you sometimes keep to yourself."

Keira exhaled slowly and tried to overcome the state of being frozen in place, a rare one for her, and overly filtered, her default. Before she could overthink her response, she told Blaise how she'd been nervous earlier and had awakened, almost like with a premonition, and then how the bald man from her dreams had prompted her to wake up again before the intruder could stab her. She described the other visitations and messages she'd received from the bald man, knowing it all seemed crazy.

"It's so bizarre and probably sounds like nonsensical mumbo-jumbo, but I get the sense sometimes that this bald man is trying to communicate with me through these dreams."

Blaise seemed stunned, skeptical. She tilted her head, then looked down and cleared her throat. "Wow, that is trippy," she said before making eye contact again. "Do you think he could be a manifestation of your thoughts or instincts, echoing them back to you?"

Keira pondered the suggestion. "I suppose that could be."

Blaise smoothed Keira's hair behind her ears and rubbed away the salt from her cheeks. "It's possible that your mind touch works on multiple levels. I wonder if recently you've been able to tap into a different facet of it that's more intuitive."

"Perhaps, but I want you to stay open to the possibility that it could be something stranger than that." Keira did not know what to make of these dream messages and the way they were impacting her life. On a gut level, she believed the bald man was real in some way, not a creation of her mind. It all seemed so odd, and she could not make rational sense of it.

She looked longingly at Blaise, seeking the understanding that comes from a deep connection with another human being, even when something shared seems far-fetched, almost ridiculous.

Blaise's green eyes warmed and sparkled, returning with their gaze the commitment to be there through it all. "Absolutely, baby. I will stay open to all possibilities. I promise."

Keira sighed and then put her hand on Blaise's lower back under her shirt, feeling her warm skin, feeling her alive.

SQUIRMY WAS the first person to arrive on the scene. It was about 03:15. He was jumpy like a person amped on caffeine and surprised Keira by giving her a big hug.

"Gosh, can't you ever take a night off?" he laughed. "Let's get a look at this fucker." He put gloves on and followed Blaise and Keira into the bedroom. The dead cop was still splayed on his back, a blood pool surrounding him and the knife near his right hand.

Squirmy looked down at the knife with what appeared to be disbelief. It was sharp enough to carve leather with just a flick of the wrist. If the knife had made deep contact with any part of Keira, she would have bled out.

"Damn," he said, "this isn't exactly government-issued weaponry." He squatted down over the knife. Something caught his attention. "Look, Keira." He pointed to a spot just above the handle that showed the small insignia of a black bird. "It's a raven. This is a Chusei weapon."

So this cop was either on the Chusei payroll or owed the Chusei a favor. The weapon choice made sense because the Chusei liked to leave a brutal, messy message. That was their signature style, a way of warning others to fear the worst if they chose to tangle with them.

Keira was surprised that neither she nor Blaise had noticed the raven insignia before, but they'd both been spooked by the dead body in their bedroom. It felt personal, making them a little more like victims than investigators. It was good to have Squirmy there to turn the tables and get them back into problem-solving mode.

"Have you had the sense that anyone was casing you, Charlie?" Blaise asked.

He said he hadn't noticed anything out of the ordinary, and he'd been on high alert, reading clues into everything. He'd slept with the light on this past night in fact.

Keira suggested, "We should assume that you're also a target, Squirmy, or will become one. Maybe you are too, Blaise. You're sort of a dead woman walking. We have no idea whether the Russians or Chusei know you're alive."

Blaise's time piece buzzed. "Devon is here. I think he'll handle this well, but we'll see." She walked out of the room to greet him at the door.

Moments later Devon Woods' tall, lanky frame loped into the bedroom. "Hello." He nodded at everyone and looked down at the dead body. Devon had defined cheekbones and a strong chin, with kind eyes. The combination made him seem tough yet fair.

He said, "I'm concerned that there could be more corrupt cops in the mix listening in, relaying messages, and attempting to control the investigation." He paused, breathing out through his nose. "So, the Feds will take on the case of this intruder, but the O'Connor kidnapping investigation will continue as before."

Everyone agreed that was a good idea, not that their opinions actually mattered. It was Devon's call.

"Detective Kincaid and Detective Watts," Devon said, "I'll keep you looped in since your lives might depend on it. The Chusei don't like anyone knowing their dirty secrets."

Devon then explained how he would give Keira and Squirmy a dedicated communication channel outside of the city police force to use for discussing the investigation. That would reduce the risk of unauthorized surveillance. The Bureau would also put Keira and Blaise in safe housing. Devon offered Squirmy that option, but he politely turned it down.

After looking at the rumpled bed that two people had clearly been sleeping in, Devon said to Blaise, "It's up to you, Agent Richards, whether you want to be here when the crime scene team arrives. If you're looking for privacy, you'll have a better chance of securing it by not being around." He straightened the top bed sheet in one quick motion. "For both of your sakes, I'd like to present this as Agent Richards stayed here because she was concerned that Detective

Kincaid's life was in danger. She nodded off in that chair in the corner and awoke to the intruder standing over Detective Kincaid in bed."

"Thank you, sir," Blaise said. "I appreciate your discretion and will take you up on your offer."

"Very well. I will update you when I have a preliminary report. I expect the team in twenty minutes, which should give you two time to pack a few things. The safe houses have multiple beds and are in short supply, so I don't think other agents will find it unusual that you're staying there together. Detective Watts, maybe you could lend me a hand for a moment."

Keira and Blaise set to each packing a bag. Keira felt simultaneously exhausted and wired. She could barely concentrate on the task. She was surprised at how relaxed Devon had been about discovering their relationship. Maybe he suspected it already, or maybe he was looking the other way because Blaise and Keira had excellent reputations in their departments. It wouldn't be a good time to stir up unnecessary drama with such high-stakes cases to solve.

Keira and Blaise stepped out of the apartment to await a ride. It was still dark out, but the day had very much begun.

WHEN BLAISE and Keira arrived at the safe house, they checked it for any possible security breaches like hidden video cameras. They both felt paranoid. Blaise even ran a rapid test for toxic chemicals. From investigative experience, she knew an easy way to off two unsuspecting people was to pump odorless toxins into a room.

Deeming the safe house indeed safe after multiple checks, they flopped on one of the two beds. They both had permission to report to work at 13:00, so they'd might as well catch a bit of shut-eye in the meantime. Blaise spooned Keira and grasped her hand. "We're okay, baby. Try to let go and get some sleep."

Keira admired Blaise's calm but suggested they take turns being on watch. Although the bedroom door and apartment were password controlled, the two of them still didn't know who was truly trustworthy. Blaise didn't think she could stay awake. They settled on putting packing materials they found in the kitchen on the floor near the only door to the room.

Settling back into bed while facing each other, Keira closed her eyes but felt nervous. She wasn't sure that she could sleep. Blaise said, "Look at me, Keira."

Keira opened her eyes and met Blaise's disarming gaze. "We've got each other's back, but neither of us will be functional in figuring out what's still at stake if we don't get some rest."

Keira sighed. She needed to start to let go a little bit for her own sanity and Blaise's. Blaise nestled Keira's head against her breasts and kept her arms around her. Keira felt her own body calm down in waves, and before she knew it she was asleep.

She dreamed of her mother. The wind whipped her mother's long hair back as she stood on a boardwalk by the beach on a gray, blustery day. Keira recognized the scenery as Spring Lake, a shore town in New Jersey where they'd visited family members when Keira was six years old.

In the dream Keira's mother, now long passed, turned to her and said, "I am so glad you have found love, Keira. Treasure it and let it guide you. The world needs more love." She smiled in her knowing way, as the Atlantic Ocean churned behind her—whipped up into whitecaps that made their choppy charge toward the shore.

A buzzing noise interrupted the sound of the waves and wind, and grew more and more annoying. Keira opened her eyes and realized it was her alarm. Blaise started to stir.

Keira was surprised she'd had yet another vivid dream. Besides, her mother hadn't appeared to her in a dream in years.

While watching Blaise wake next to her, Keira thought about how incredibly lucky and happy she indeed was to have found love. She decided not to fixate on why her dreams had been intense lately and just be present in the moment.

Blaise sat up with a yawn and stretched her arms. Keira wrapped her arms around Blaise's torso and pulled her back down to the bed. "Not so fast," Keira said with a coy smile as she rolled Blaise on top of her and inhaled the lavender scent of her skin. "The world needs more love."

"Oh, I see," Blaise said, laughing as she leaned back and took her top off. "Let's see if we can fix that before work." She started to pull Keira's shirt off.

"That should be just enough time," Keira said, as Blaise's breasts grazed against her own. She felt her blood rush warm throughout her body, and let desire take over and fear drop away.

CHAPTER 12
BABY'S TEARS

TOMMY WOZNIAK, Keira and Squirmy's boss, called them into his office. He had been briefed by the Feds and was not happy they were handling the intruder case. He was also fuming about the internal corruption.

Keira figured that was mostly because Wozniak was more of a political face of law enforcement than a practicing cop. He would be responsible for answering to the press and public if word got out about cops trying to put a hit on other cops. So far, the news had not leaked.

"Look," he said, clasping his hands on the table, "I'm very sorry this happened to you, Detective Kincaid. I truly am. And we will do everything we can here to make sure that both you and Detective Watts are kept protected." He paused, as if considering carefully what he was about to say next. "I just would really appreciate for morale purposes if you two could keep this under wraps. If other members of the department start hearing about attempted hits by cops on cops, all hell's gonna break loose around here."

Of course that was what he'd ask, Keira thought cynically. What other choice did they have anyway? It wasn't exactly a request. She and Squirmy muttered that they'd keep it a secret.

Wozniak looked relieved after their quick acquiescence. "Great! Thank you. That's settled." He exhaled audibly. "Now, let's talk about what little we know so far. It sounds like Special Agent Woods will provide more details later today. But at this point we do have a positive ID on the perp.

"He worked for drug enforcement in the California 5 Division. His name was Samuel Petrini. His partner died while undercover investigating the Chusei last year, so I'm wondering if that had something to do with his own unauthorized involvement with the Chusei. That's obviously just pure speculation at this point. I don't have much to go on and will see what Special Agent Woods comes up with."

As Wozniak rubbed his chin and showed them photos of Petrini and his DEA partner before he died, Keira felt a little weight lift off her shoulders. Since Petrini had been in the fifth division, rather than the fourth, she felt less suspicious of her home base. Petrini's division served the greater Los Angeles area, where the Chusei had their greatest stronghold.

Nonetheless, she still planned to work with an abundance of caution. It remained unclear how extensive the corruption extended or how many cops were performing the Chusei's bidding. There could certainly be others closer to home or even within their department. Besides, she still didn't know how someone accessed Travis' place with a dead officer's fingerprints or whether she and Squirmy had been followed that day.

She was relieved that Wozniak did not seem to know anything about Blaise. It appeared that Devon had indeed kept their relationship under wraps.

"All right, guys, that's all I know at this point in time," Wozniak said. "By the way, I'm hoping to hear more progress on the Liam O'Connor kidnapping by the end of the week. It would really put a feather in our cap if we could name a suspect soon." He seemed to realize his timing was quite off for high pressure and caught himself. "But, hey, don't worry about all that right now. You should take it easy, Detective Kincaid, and take time off if you'd like."

Keira attempted to be diplomatic with what amounted to an underwhelming show of appreciation as they wrapped up the meeting.

After leaving Wozniak's office, she and Squirmy rolled their eyes at each other. "Well, what did we expect from Mr. Cop Photo Op?" Squirmy asked.

"Exactly what we just got."

They made their way to the Whiteboard to do some brainstorming together. They each logged in to a computer and then projected photos and other materials pertaining to the O'Connor case onto the surrounding wallscape, which had a dome shape. The Whiteboard allowed investigators to add handwritten notes and whatever else they found useful onto the wall. They could move the clues into categories, create work orders, and ask questions of Simon, a virtual assistant built specifically for law-enforcement personnel.

Some days Squirmy and Keira would sit in the Whiteboard room for hours, just looking at clues and thinking and asking questions. They were both analytical and visual, so when they didn't know where next to turn while working a case, it made the most sense to pause and consider what they knew so far and take a deeper look. Other cops felt the need to appear busy and get back out on the streets. But that was sometimes just a form of spinning wheels.

Squirmy projected photos of Liam's crib and the lasered window onto the dome, while Keira displayed Cora Brink's files in a separate section. They were both absorbed in thought when their time pieces buzzed.

Keira hit play on the audio message. A male suspect was at large in the Center Shopping District with a four-month-old baby girl he'd kidnapped from the child's home. He was on foot and considered unstable. Witnesses said he had a gun and was acting in an erratic, possibly inebriated manner. Use of deadly force was allowed only in the case of a clear shot without bystanders in the firing zone.

Keira and Squirmy immediately sprang into action. They strapped up and departed the station in the squad mod in under three minutes.

While Keira piloted the aircraft, Squirmy monitored the drone footage of the kidnapper on the move. "The man looks high and para-noid," he shared. "He's waving the gun at anyone who gets near him. The baby is crying. Clearly, this kidnapping was not well thought out. Maybe it was spontaneous. He saw the baby, knew the value, but he didn't think through this part of getting away."

It did sound like a crime of opportunity, Keira thought. She had a feeling that this wouldn't end well. She breathed slowly to try to lower her heart rate and stay calm.

They'd been given permission to land in a public square beyond where the suspect was currently located. He appeared headed in that direction with the baby. Police on the ground had cleared the spot of bystanders for a landing.

As Keira approached Sierra Square from the airspace, she saw people below clutching their children and hurrying away. The public was clearing out of the danger zone quickly, which boded well for a confrontation without bystanders.

Two police officers on the ground radioed clearance to land, and she descended straight down slowly and carefully. "Touching down in two point three seconds," the navigation system announced as the aircraft got close to the ground.

They landed softly, and Keira turned off the engine.

Squirmy nodded at her. "We got this, Kincaid." She nodded back.

As they stepped out of the gull-wing doors, two foot-patrol cops she'd never seen before approached.

"Detective Kincaid, drones have spotted the perpetrator headed this way with an ETA of two minutes and seven seconds," the younger one said to her. He was clearly frightened as revealed by his deer-in-the-headlights eyes. He had the anxious appearance of someone fresh on the job who had never confronted an armed person before.

Taking pity on him, Keira offered, "Let's have you and your partner proceed past us now and clear the way of people in the two blocks beyond just in case we don't stop him here."

He looked relieved before he sprinted away with the other patrol cop. Keira knew that she and Squirmy would stop the suspect in some fashion before he got to the next block, which had probably already been cleared. One of them would subdue the suspect, hopefully without needing to fire a weapon. She just didn't want to subject the newbie cop to the big bad world yet. He'd have plenty of exposure in the future, but today was his lucky day.

Time was ticking, though. They didn't have the luxury of even several minutes to prepare. Keira decided that catching the perpetrator off-guard was their best option, given their limitations.

"I'd like to try a surprise attack," she said to Squirmy. On their screens they watched the man walking wild-eyed through a now empty shopping block. "I'll hide behind that sculpture there," pointing to it in the near distance, "and wait for him to be a few feet from me. You hang back slightly out of his immediate view near the fountain in case I don't successfully take him down."

Squirmy shook his head. "I don't know about that plan, Keira. It's risky."

"I know, but we're running out of time for anything carefully planned. And his movements are too jerky for a safe shot in the leg. The baby is going berserk. I think a physical takedown is the best way. I'll attempt to pin him and then tranquilize him, but you'll have to close in quickly to grab the baby and keep her safe."

He exhaled loudly. "All right, Keira. Be careful. I've always got your back." He ran over to the fountain and crouched down out of sight.

She got in position behind the sculpture which, apropos to the situation, depicted a woman holding a smiling baby up to the sky.

The man drew close enough for her to hear the baby's shrieks. She looked again at her screen. If she could attack him on his right side and grab his gun, or knock the gun out of his hand, then the baby would stay out of harm's way on his left side.

He was about ten seconds away now. Via her time piece's audio recording from the drone tracking, Keira heard him say, "Stop your crying, little baby. It's all right," his words slurring together. The baby continued to scream.

She readied herself to pounce. But then he stopped walking and buckled at the knees. Shaking, he dropped the gun with a clatter on the cement. It did not go off.

Keira ran out from behind the sculpture just as the man began to fall toward his right side. She reached for the baby and pulled her safely away from his collapsing body. Holding the screaming child in her arms, Keira watched as the man began to writhe on the ground, spit droplets forming over his lips. He was overdosing.

Squirmy ran up just then and knelt beside the man, turning him on his side with the hopes that he might breathe on his own. Keira radioed for first-responder backup as the baby bellowed in her ear. Squirmy then rolled the man on his back and started CPR.

He looked in his fifties, his skin haggard from poor health. He had long legs and a paunch that looked out of place against the rest of his skinny body.

Keira knew that they had an extremely short time before he'd lose the fight against the toxins coursing through his body. He needed an immediate shot of tronsaphine to attempt to reverse the rapid acceleration toward certain death. From her screen monitor, it looked like the ambulance might not make it in time. Her gut felt hollow.

She held the baby up in front of her face and tried to make eye contact with her, but the baby looked away, hands balled up and screaming. The poor little thing, Keira thought, tucking her against her chest. She spoke soothingly to her and rubbed her tiny back.

The man began to convulse on the ground, the body's final battle. He had probably injected cheap black-market junk called Spun into his veins. Spun could be made inexpensively in rudimentary labs and was often cut with additives that were lethal themselves in high enough doses.

The man's body went limp. Squirmy put two fingers on the man's neck and shook his head at Keira.

Ambulance sirens grew increasingly louder, and soon paramedics swooped down on the scene. They checked his pulse and then put a sheet over the man and lifted his body into the back of the ambulance.

Another paramedic, probably a male in his early thirties, took the still crying baby from Keira. "It's amazing how loud and long they cry for, isn't it?" he commented. She smiled wanly. She'd been thinking the same thing.

The baby, dressed in a onesie with pink and white stripes, would probably not settle down until she was returned to her mother, who most likely was not her genetic mother, who in turn would most likely never meet her. These really were strange times, Keira thought, that we all muddled through in an attempt to keep our humanity alive in whatever way we could.

Squirmy appeared tense as he stood with his hands on his hips near where the man had died. Keira walked up slowly and gave him a chance to speak first, but he was silent. "Are you okay?"

He stared straight ahead. "My cousin died in a similar way. Took too much Spun. The ambulance didn't make it in time. I watched the light go out of his eyes just like I watched it go out of this guy's," he gestured at the spot on the ground where the man's body had convulsed mere minutes ago. "I can't believe we don't crack down more on these assholes who make this stuff knowing that it can kill their customers just as easily as it gets them high. Such a cheap price to put on life."

"I'm so sorry, Charlie. I didn't know that about your cousin." She searched for something comforting to say. "It's not much consolation I'm sure, but at least the baby survived this ordeal without getting hurt. She'll hopefully have a chance at a normal life."

"Yeah," was all he said. She squeezed his arm and then walked over to the gun on the ground.

Squatting over it she could see that there was fresh blood on the handle. She summoned Squirmy and pointed to it. "Let's hope he didn't kill anyone before he got here."

Keira radioed the cops at the crime scene where the abduction occurred and mentioned the blood. They told her that the deceased had hit the nanny across the head, knocking her out. Then he grabbed the baby. The nanny likely had a concussion but was okay otherwise. The man hadn't shot anyone, and no one else was injured.

At least there's that, Keira thought, as she ended the correspondence.

A crowd of looky-loos had gathered to take in the spectacle now that people knew the danger had passed. Media drones buzzed over the square, hovering at the mandatory distance of one hundred feet from the crime scene. Keira wished she could have a moment of peace to gather her thoughts before the circus began, but this was the way it went whenever the crime took place in a public space.

Keira then got a creepy feeling that someone was watching her. She turned her head toward the main part of the square. There she saw a petite woman with black hair begin to run rapidly up the steps. Within seconds the woman had disappeared into the crowd of curious bystanders.

Cora, Keira thought. That had to have been her. Light on her feet, knew how to disappear. But how did Cora know how to find Keira?

Keira's pulse quickened and her senses heightened as she realized once again that she was being hunted. Someone on the inside must have been relaying her whereabouts to the Chusei, or the Chusei were hacking the police's cyber system.

Though she was pissed and a little scared about another attempt on her life, she now saw an opportunity to build a trap.

Squirmy gave her a curious look like he could tell that something was up.

"I've got a plan," she said, and started walking toward the squad mod.

"It's about time," he quipped, and kept pace beside her on the way back to the aircraft.

~

AFTER A DEBRIEFING about the kidnapping at the station followed by another meeting that Keira attended without Squirmy, she asked him to join her on a walk. She wanted to make sure that no one could eavesdrop on their conversation at the office, which was also why she didn't express her thoughts aloud to him in the squad mod. She wasn't sure that her fan trick in the cockpit was foolproof.

As they strolled along the skywalk, a suspended walking bridge popular during sunset, she shared her suspicion that Cora had been in Sierra Square watching her and that someone on the force was probably relaying their whereabouts.

"We should set a trap," Keira said. "We could have Wozniak send us a fake order to report to a kidnapping at a particular location and see who else ends up showing up there."

She and Squirmy stopped in a quiet spot to admire the Pacific Ocean glistening in the distance beyond the rolling hills that were visible between clusters of skyscrapers. Keira explained, "It would be difficult to determine who had shared our whereabouts, but maybe

Cora or another Chusei goon will make an appearance. An arrest and threat of the death penalty for child kidnapping might get that person to talk, which could help us locate the source."

"I like that plan," Squirmy said. "I can meet with Wozniak and run it by him." Squirmy had a more amicable relationship with their boss than Keira did. Although she followed Wozniak's orders and was one of his top detectives, Wozniak seemed to pick up on the fact that Keira didn't particularly like him. He was vain and needed praise, which irked her. Besides, she had to keep some healthy distance to avoid questions that could reveal her power of mind touch.

Squirmy then shared with Keira what he'd just found out about the death of Cora Brink's former landlord about two and a half years ago. The man's body was discovered by a jogger taking an early run along the Coronado Bridge. Although investigators did not believe his death to be a suicide, there were no clues or DNA evidence to link anyone to a homicide. Whoever had done the crime knew how to cover their tracks. The video camera near the section of the bridge where the hanging occurred had been destroyed by a drone.

Squirmy had not been able to locate any information about Cora's father's death. He did learn that her father—who was White, not Yupik—had been a chemist granted leave due to radiation poisoning from the war. Squirmy said, "We all know that the government didn't do much to help those sickened from the fallout. There was very little money, supplies, or assistance to go around."

His comment triggered a terrible memory for Keira of her younger brother, Jacob, just fifteen years old then. During a raid in the early part of the war, their parents were killed by a missile strike on the commercial complex where they worked. Jacob had been at school a few blocks away, putting him close enough to the impact to become incredibly ill from the chemical exposure. He survived only to then struggle to breathe.

The hospitals had been overwhelmed, just as they were in the aftermath of all the various bombings and attacks during those dark days. Keira, a college student at the time, cared for Jacob for weeks, but his condition only deteriorated. She couldn't get access to a ventilator or medicine that might help him turn a corner, although she tried every day to find anything that might ease his suffering. All she had to work with was ibuprofen, a few herbs, and her love for him.

One night Jacob's gasps grew worse and worse, and fluid bubbled up through his mouth.

She held him as he died, stroking his curly hair and giving him assurances. "Go now to Mom and Dad," she had said. "You will be at peace, little brother. Do not be afraid for you have nothing to fear. It is blue skies and green fields ahead for you." That was something their mother used to say to them. "I'll see you on the other side." He had nodded and squeezed her hand. Moments later his friendly, curious eyes closed and his breath stopped; with it expired the last living member of her family.

Keira felt overpowered by the sudden memory. She tried to keep the remembrance of those horrible times as far away from her conscious mind as possible, but of course some days it was just impossible to continue to bury what could never be totally put to rest.

The memory of her brother's death now connected her to what she imagined was Cora's pain. If the landlord had indeed thrown Cora and her father out on the street, and her father had been gravely ill and subsequently died, it wasn't hard to see why Cora would take revenge. Killing her landlord was extreme, but Keira knew that people with nothing left to lose could sometimes snap.

"It could very well have been Cora Brink," Keira said. "Clearly, she's stealthy, and if something bad had happened to her father, then she would certainly have motive."

"This gives us some kind of theoretical window into her situation," Squirmy responded, "but it doesn't necessarily help us get any closer to her. She's a bit of a ghost in the wind at the moment, with no viable address or place of employment."

Keira considered returning to the Empress Hotel, but it seemed too risky now that she found herself directly in the Chusei crosshairs. Then she thought of baby Liam and what some mind touch with him might reveal. But for now, she was spent and just wanted to be with Blaise at "home" at the safe house.

CHAPTER 13
SWEET APPLES

KEIRA ARRIVED at the safe house before Blaise and felt antsy. She worried that she could have been tracked, but she had taken plenty of precautions while making her way to their temporary dwelling.

While she stood in what she thought was probably the plainest kitchen on the planet, she replayed the day's events in her mind and prepared herself mentally for tomorrow's work. She would have to get time alone with Liam to perform mind touch and would therefore need Squirmy to run interference. As she thought about how they might pull that off, her time piece buzzed. It was an alert that Blaise had requested access to the place.

Moments later Blaise walked in with an unusually big smile on her face and her red hair looking as vibrant as ever.

"I've got a treat for you," Blaise said and then kissed Keira playfully on the lips. "You'll never guess what it is!"

"A sex toy?" Keira joked.

"Ooh, you're bad in a good way," Blaise said while laughing. "Nope. What's red and crisp and delicious?"

"You, of course. You have to give me a harder riddle than that." Keira pulled Blaise toward her by the hips. She kissed her lightly at first and then deeply, running her hands down Blaise's back and up through her hair.

Blaise laughed and and teasingly bit her own bottom lip. "That's true, but this is even better. You're gonna love it!" She reached for the bag that she'd set on the counter. "Now close your eyes."

Keira did.

"Now open them." Blaise held two shiny, plump apples in her hands.

"No way! Are those real?"

"Absolutely, one hundred percent! Can you believe it? When was the last time you took a bite of real fruit, babe?"

"Wow, definitely not since the war."

Blaise set one apple down carefully on the table and approached Keira with the other. She held it up to Keira's nose. "Inhale that scent. It's incredible. I'd forgotten what an apple smelled like."

Keira took in the sweet and herbaceous aroma of the apple and pictured blossoms freshly touched by rain. Her mouth watered. "Amazing! Where did you get these?"

"From Devon. He occasionally gets real food, and I just think he felt sorry for us and wanted to cheer us up." Blaise's eyes twinkled with delight. "Here, you take the first bite."

"You should go first, hon."

Blaise giggled. "No, I want to see your reaction first."

Keira smiled and, incredulously, took a bite. What followed was like a crisp explosion of flavor—sweet and ripe—that felt luscious in her mouth. "Dang, I forgot how spectacular apples are!" As she chewed, Blaise beamed back at her.

Then she held the fruit up to Blaise's mouth, who took a bite and then looked like she was experiencing a sensory explosion. With her mouth full, Blaise's whole face radiated joy. Keira could see Blaise trying to formulate what the flavor was like and what it reminded her of.

There was something bittersweet to the experience, Keira realized, as it drove home how deprived they were of the good life of the past— real food, clean health, natural landscapes unmarred by war. But sharing this wholesome time capsule with each other was also to be treasured; in an era of so much negativity, it was important to revel in the positive when it appeared from time to time.

Blaise held the apple to Keira's lips again. As Keira put her mouth on it and prepared to take a bite, she thought of how as a kid she had always loved the texture of apples: firm and crisp, followed by a yielding and sweet interior. It dawned on her that she actually did perceive Blaise that way. A little resistant on the surface, which was good for self-preservation, but once Blaise granted access to her inside world, she gave so much sweetness and love.

As Blaise savored the next bite, Keira unbuttoned Blaise's shirt and unfastened her bra, lifting it up to release her full breasts. Keira rolled her tongue along Blaise's right nipple and then gently bit down until she could hear Blaise's breath quicken. Caressing the other breast by hand, Keira slid her free hand down Blaise's abdomen and inside the waist of her underwear until she could feel Blaise wet and warm against her fingers. Blaise's breath became shallow.

Blaise lifted Keira's mouth up to her own, kissing her in one big motion and then stopping as she inhaled sharply and made her mix of sighing, groaning sounds that Keira could never get enough of. Keira could feel the soft walls pulse against her fingers as Blaise made her way to a climax. In a burst of love noise and breath and throbbing, Blaise peaked.

She pulled Keira against her for a full-body embrace, tightly gripping Keira's back with one arm and gently cradling her head with the other arm that still held the apple. Blaise's breath carried the sweet aroma of apple as she kissed Keira's cheeks and mouth. "Wow, that felt fantastic!" Blaise smiled and then said softly, "Thank you, baby."

"No problem, love. I'll work for apples any day."

"Here, for your efforts then." Blaise giggled as she extended the apple to Keira for another bite.

They traded smaller and smaller bites until all that remained were the stem and seeds. "We should save the second apple for another day," Blaise suggested.

"True, but we can't wait too long because real food doesn't last forever, remember? That's crazy to think about with our non-perishable goo packs that could probably survive two apocalypses," Keira said. "But that's what's so neat about real food, now that I think about it. It's what makes it alive."

"Kind of like us," Blaise said.

"Yeah, exactly."

Standing there together at the safe house, Keira felt delightfully young on the one hand, but on the other hand she was aware of an older, more mature person within her stepping forward. She became cognizant of desire and responsibility melding in her mind. She wanted to stay playful with Blaise in their days ahead, but she foremost felt a desire to protect and care for her.

Keira tried to recall the old expression about admiration that had to do with apples. As soon as she thought of it, she said, "You are the apple of my eye, Blaise. I cherish you above everyone and everything else."

Blaise's eyes filled with tears. She placed Keira's hand on her heart and held it there.

THE NEXT DAY Keira and Squirmy paid Ms. Strauss and Liam a visit.

Ms. Strauss looked like she hadn't enjoyed a good night's sleep in a long time, but she was certainly in better spirits than when they'd met on the morning after Liam's kidnapping. A hologram image on her kitchen counter showed a sleeping Liam in his crib.

"How are you doing, Ms. Strauss?" Keira asked.

"I'm so grateful to have Liam back, but I'm still a nervous wreck. I can't sleep or calm my nerves. I'm worried that something will happen to him again, and I keep wondering if the same people who killed Stephen might want to attack me, too."

"I'm really sorry to hear that," Keira said. "If it's any comfort, based on our investigations, we don't believe that either you or Liam is in danger."

Although Ms. Strauss had already been caught up on the case, Keira repeated what they knew. Namely, Liam had been leverage that was no longer necessary, and Mr. O'Connor had paid a steep price for selling state secrets, ironically from the very buyers who most benefited from them. Ms. Strauss had been told the truth because of her own deep connections to the government. The average person, unfortunately, would have been given a version of events that cast no aspersions on the state.

Ms. Strauss nodded but exuded nervous energy. So this is what motherhood does to a person, Keira thought.

Squirmy explained how while they knew the Chusei were involved in the kidnapping, they needed more details as well as legally valid proof, which was the purpose of their visit today. He wondered if he could ask Ms. Strauss some additional questions while Keira looked at the baby room and Mr. O'Connor's study.

"I don't see why not. Liam is sleeping though, Detective Kincaid, so please be careful not to wake him."

"Of course. We really appreciate your cooperation."

Ms. Strauss gave Keira directions for how to get to O'Connor's study from the baby room, and then she sat with Squirmy in the living room with the hologram image of Liam in her peripheral vision.

As Keira walked toward the baby room, she sent Squirmy a message to turn Ms. Strauss physically away from the hologram for the next five minutes. She hoped he could get her to look at case files with her back to the kitchen or get her out of the room. He messaged her a 10-4.

Liam looked snug and sweet in his crib, as if the crazy world posed no threat to him at every turn. Such innocence in their tiny faces, Keira thought. Throughout the morning she'd been preparing for this mind touch by thinking about the memories she hoped to retrieve from Liam.

She was afraid if she picked him up that he'd wake and start to cry. She did have a baby dose of a sleeping agent, but she didn't want to have to use it. Besides, Ms. Strauss might wonder why he slept longer than usual. Instead, Keira tilted the left side of the crib down slightly, locking it into an angle that allowed her to get close to him, hopefully without waking him.

She pulled her hair back into a ponytail and moved her head slowly over his, listening to his tiny breathing noises. She pressed her forehead gently against Liam's, noticing the softness of his warm skin and the fresh scent of his little head. He started to lift his left arm and then dropped it, his tiny body slackening. She held his arms against his body to give him a swaddling feeling.

The first memory was of his mother's face, eyes sparkling and smiling at him as she laid him in the crib. The second one was of toys on a floor from a low angle. He must have been playing on the floor and reaching for them. As the third and fourth memories brought similar baby-type perspectives of daily life, she feared that she'd get nowhere with this mind touch.

But then the fifth memory opened in a different place. Since the viewpoint of the surrounding walls changed quickly and bounced around, Keira figured Liam was being carried and kept turning his head. The interior had the look of a decrepit warehouse, with exposed brick and wood beams. It was somewhat dark inside. In the distance voices murmured and echoed, but their sounds were indistinct. Liam started to fuss, and a woman's voice cooed to him, trying to soothe him.

Tall, bright objects were visible in a corner, but then Liam turned his head and they went out of view. But when he turned back, Keira could see them better this time. The objects were different heights—some with rounded tops and some with pointed tops. As Liam got closer, Keira realized they were surfboards.

The memory ended there and moved on to other benign baby moments. Keira pulled her head back and puzzled over the warehouse memory. Liam started to squirm. She caressed his arms and tucked them again against his sides, and he luckily drifted back into a calmer sleep. She returned the crib to its original angle.

Keira silently thanked Liam and wished him a nice doze, and then started walking toward O'Connor's study.

She pondered what she'd just seen. Ever since the war ended, people generally did not go in the ocean. The water was considered extremely dangerous due to toxins from chemical and nuclear weapons. Who, then, would be surfing these days? Or were those boards collector's items from a previous era just there for show?

Mystified, she made her way into O'Connor's study, which was fastidiously organized. Every little item in its place. She dug around but didn't find anything of importance, at least as far as she could tell.

It seems that he hid his tracks pretty well or perhaps kept up a firewall between work and home.

After exchanging parting pleasantries with Ms. Strauss, Keira asked Squirmy as they walked onto the roof if he knew of any people who still surfed or places where they did.

"Sure do. Haven't you heard of the Misfits?"

She shook her head.

"They are this renegade bunch of surfers who shack up together in abandoned warehouses by the waterfront of old San Diego. Rumor has it they stole plants in order to grow their own food supply and be off grid. The educated among them won't take government jobs and are essentially dropouts. Law enforcement tried to arrest them multiple times, but it seems that eventually the ends just didn't justify the means. They were hard to track and put up quite a fight. And then I think the idea was just like, good riddance. Let them go; they won't contribute to society anyway. But they sound pretty cool to me." He laughed.

Keira could tell that Squirmy was about to ask her what this had to do with anything and then caught himself. He knew it was better for both of their sakes that he not put her on the spot about how she came upon this seemingly random thread.

"Did Ms. Strauss provide any new clues?" Keira asked.

"Not really." Squirmy ran his hand through his wavy, brown hair. "The only thing that stood out to me was that O'Connor frequented a men's club called The Masters in the months before he was killed. She only found that out after he died because she traced his rides—now curious what he'd been up to. I'd like to see what that place is all about and why he was going there. It could be nothing, but we might as well explore any angle we've got."

"I say we start with the Misfits this afternoon, and then maybe you can check out The Masters tonight," Keira said.

"I believe that will be an incredibly pleasant way to pass the day, Kincaid." She chuckled as they hopped in the squad mod.

CHAPTER 14
BARRELING WAVES

KEIRA AND SQUIRMY perched themselves on the roof of an abandoned warehouse in a part of old San Diego formerly known as Ocean Beach. Over time Ocean Beach had transformed from a hippie hangout—nonetheless one with extremely expensive property values —to a warehouse district after sea levels rose, causing coastal destruction and inland retreat.

The thinking was that, compared to homes, it was cheaper to abandon shoddy manufacturing and storage facilities if rising water levels continued to pose a threat. The expensive residential areas moved higher inland into the hills, which made the insurance companies happier. In fact, all of residential San Diego essentially just pushed eastward, re-establishing itself at a safer distance from the encroaching seas.

Before the war, people continued to surf, swim, sail, and gather at the shore. They just didn't live there because of the potential for flooding. Then the war's damage made people fear the ocean for the toxins it contained. It was a hard loss for a city borne by the seas. No one ate seafood or played in the waves. Well, almost no one did.

Squirmy and Keira had discovered a clue to the Misfits' potential whereabouts from the police's cyber system. Heat-sensing scans from six months ago had identified a warehouse where it was thought that people were squatting. The location matched previous reports about the Misfits' headquarters. Squirmy was right that no one seemed to be actively investigating or tracking them.

As she and Squirmy positioned themselves on a neighboring roof, the drone they brought for surveillance kept shutting down seconds after being booted up. "What a useless piece of shit," Squirmy said.

"It's all right. We'll watch the old-school way, with binoculars and patience."

He shrugged and kneeled down.

Keira enjoyed being near the water again. The surf broke with power, as a swell brought in six-foot waves that crashed with a low rumble of turbulent white water. She found the consistent roar of the surf both soothing and inspiring. She hoped that in her lifetime the toxic waste might be cleared and the seas deemed safe again to immerse herself in.

"At least we're getting a beach day," she said.

"Absolutely, although I wish I'd brought an umbrella." The sun, when it emerged from behind the clouds, was strong and hot. They both were sweating and had drunk almost all the water they'd brought.

After sitting in silence for another twenty minutes, they got movement. Five people carrying surfboards emerged from the side of the warehouse. Through her binoculars, Keira could tell that two were women and three were men. They all wore full-body wetsuits that covered their feet and hands.

The five surfers trotted down to the beach. Once there they pulled up their hoods and zipped into them translucent face masks that appeared to have some type of breathing mechanism built into the mouth area. The surfers looked strange all suited up, almost otherworldly, like creatures accustomed to an entirely different environment. After strapping their board leashes around their ankles, they let out an excited yell and ran into the water.

The first one to catch a wave did a graceful bottom turn and then attacked the upper lip of the wave with an aggressive cutback. The second one caught so much speed riding up the wave that she launched herself up into the air and spun around, landing on the back side of the wave with a splash as her friends whooped.

Squirmy said, "Clearly, this isn't the first time they've played in the waves."

Keira laughed. "No, I'd say not. This is quite a show!"

As the second female surfer paddled hard to catch her first wave, Keira tried to get a good look at her face, but the mask she wore made for a slightly distorted view. All that Keira could really make out was a fierce, determined expression and what looked like a scar on her right cheek.

The mouth area of the mask was freakish—it gave the impression of a human skull transforming into a fish gill. Perhaps the filter ensured that they didn't swallow any water but could still breath. Keira wondered what their wetsuits were made of and how vulnerable their skin would be to the exposure.

The woman with the scar didn't catch the wave and shook her head in frustration before turning and paddling farther out. As she sat up on her board to rest and wait for another wave, she turned slightly to talk to a male surfer in the water near her. As she did, Keira could make out "Harper" stitched into the upper left arm of her wetsuit in blue thread. No one sold wetsuits to the public anymore, so it probably wasn't a brand name. Was that her name?

And then it hit Keira: Harper was the name of the person who sent the message to Spyder that said the ships hadn't left the harbor and asking if he had set sail yet.

Keira attempted to find a name on the others' wetsuits. After scanning with binoculars, she found the name "Dillon" stitched on a male's suit by the chest.

She shared these observations with Squirmy, who jotted down the names with his time piece.

Harper then caught a wave and rode it right, crouching low as the wave broke over her and she stayed in the hollow section. When she emerged from the brief barrel, she straightened her body and lifted her arms in victory, riding on until losing speed. Dang, Keira thought, this woman is a real firecracker.

Squirmy and Keira enjoyed the stellar surfing performance while it lasted. After about fifteen minutes of total time in the water, the five surfers paddled in to shore, catching smaller waves on the inside on their stomachs that carried them close to the water's edge. They all emerged smiling and forearm-bumping.

Then they trotted back toward the warehouse. They went around to the back of it this time and peeled off their wetsuits. They were completely naked underneath. All five of them had lithe, toned bodies. Keira thought they mostly looked in their twenties and thirties, with one guy possibly being a late teen.

Squirmy photographed each of them as Keira looked for identifying characteristics through her binoculars. A tattoo of surfers riding waves covered the side of one man's torso. Another male had an ancient Polynesian-style tattoo on his upper arm with swirling tribal patterns that emanated outward from a representation of a sea turtle.

They hosed each other off, rinsed their wetsuits quickly, and then dunked the suits in some type of open tank and let them soak there. Then they lathered their bodies and hair thoroughly with what looked like soap and did a second rinse. Afterward, each one helped another to irrigate their ears and nostrils and apply liquid eye drops. Finally, they each took two tablets that they passed around and placed under their tongues.

So that was surfing cleanup in toxic 2122, Keira thought.

The man with the Polynesian tattoo wrapped his arms around Harper from behind and kissed her right cheek. The youngest male walked by them toward the tank holding the wetsuits, which he slid a lid over to cover. As he did, Keira noticed a small raven tattoo on his left shoulder. The distinguishing mark of the Chusei. But none of the others had it.

She asked Squirmy to photograph that tattoo and try to get a close-up of the young man's face. He looked Hapa—part Asian and, in this case, part White. He had attractive facial features, with a small nose and pronounced cheekbones. There was something kind of gentle about him, even the way he moved. He wouldn't be one you'd peg as a Chusei tough guy.

After all the surfers went inside, Keira said to Squirmy, "The Chusei member didn't exactly fit the image, right?"

"Yeah, I agree, but it takes all kinds. Maybe a family member is Chusei and the kid didn't have much choice in the matter. The others seem unaffiliated, at least as far as not having the tattooed claim, but they might still do business with them."

"Right, certainly. Or maybe the Chusei have infiltrated the Misfits. Perhaps the Misfits have no idea there are enemies in their ranks, or maybe they're all working together. Then there's the connection of Harper with Spyder. We still don't know who took Spyder out or what he had been tasked to do before he was killed." Keira paused, considering options.

"Let's keep eyes on this place with a hidden camera," she suggested. "I want to see who comes and goes and when. I especially want to figure out a good time to ambush Harper. We need to find out what she knows and how these different players connect. Cornering the Chusei guy could be trickier and might backfire because the Chusei already have a hit out on me, and maybe on you and Blaise, but he is another possibility."

They had with them a special implantation tool that could embed a camera into a surface from relatively far away. Once installed, the video camera could be adjusted remotely to the angle desired. They decided to go with the side door where the surfers had exited to get to the beach. Keira hoped it was their main entrance.

Deferring to the better shot, Squirmy handed the tool to Keira. She set the sights on a beam a few feet above and to the side of the door. Holding the tool very carefully but relaxing so as not to jostle it and screw up the shot, she took two steady breaths and then fired. Bingo. Right where she wanted.

"Way to make it happen, captain," Squirmy said. He used the controller to pivot the video camera's angle to hopefully capture their faces while going in and out. "All right, we've got eyes."

"If nothing else, we'll find out when the surf's up again," she said.

"True. Maybe we can get our hands on some of those specialty wetsuits to get out in the water with and then see whether we end up growing a third arm in a few months—or losing several teeth."

Keira laughed and then turned toward the water for one last look at the crashing waves. She didn't really want to leave. But duty, as always, called.

As KEIRA and Squirmy were about to leave old San Diego in a pickup truck, their time pieces buzzed. It was a message from Devon with an encrypted access code to their safe communications channel.

Once logged in, they watched Devon explain through a video message that a possession of Keira's must have been tapped with a tracking device. The Feds figured this out from decoding a tracker found on Samuel Petrini. Petrini had followed the signal of it to her apartment the night he attacked her. It had also been pinged from a different device to trace her to the crime scene in Sierra Square. Now the tracer was reading as coming from the safe house.

Keira wondered what it could be attached to.

She and Blaise would not be able to stay at that safe house any longer, Devon said. Most likely someone had already cased the place trying to get to Keira, but the safe house was well protected by codes, a lack of windows, and federal security systems that would immediately register an attempted intrusion through the keying of a wrong code, for example. Plus, there were cameras monitoring the street, sidewalk, and entrances. The footage was being reviewed now in case it revealed any people or vehicles that may not have seemed suspicious at first glance.

Devon said he was sending two agents to the safe house to find out what the tracer was embedded on. They planned to use it to set a trap, which was what Keira had wanted to do earlier. But just as the thought of being part of the trap popped in her head, she heard Devon quash it. He insisted in his video recording that she not get involved and that the Feds handle this one on their own. He concluded by saying that Blaise had just been made aware of the situation. His agents would round up their belongings and move the two women to a different safe house tonight. Instructions would be sent to Blaise within hours.

Devon ended his message with pleasantries—may the bounties of the universe be upon you—and vowed that he and his agents would see this through to completion to the best of their abilities. "Blue through and through," he said, a motto of law enforcement.

Keira was relieved they'd figured this out but shocked. How had she been traced without realizing it? She felt played and one-upped. Was she losing her edge, her instincts?

Squirmy tried to put her mind at ease. "Someone on the force could have planted a tracker on your weapons or uniform, Keira. Even if it happened in broad daylight by a civilian, you and I both know how easy it is to embed these devices. We do it all the time. It doesn't personally make us skilled or clever or cutting edge. It's just the way the tech works."

"I guess." She sighed and shook her head. "I still feel like I've been careless, though, and that I've endangered your life and Blaise's. What if her abduction while tracking O'Connor was because of something I did?"

Squirmy looked at her with his head cocked, letting her know she was being too hard on herself, an opinion he often expressed. "I don't follow how that could be the case, Kincaid. That doesn't mean it's not possible, but you shouldn't beat yourself up over something you don't even know is true. This is the nature and danger of the job. We track criminals, and they track us."

He ran a hand over his unshaven face. Squirmy did look a little haggard and tired, Keira thought. "It's a messy race to the finish line," he continued. "All we can do is try to think of the next steps and be ahead of the competition. We gotta leave the past in the past and just see it as clues to the future."

She patted his back. "Thanks, Charlie. I always appreciate your way of putting things in perspective. And I know you're always there for me." She smiled at him. "Now get some sleep tonight, or get laid at the club if it's that type of establishment. Both have their benefits!"

He laughed. "Now you're talking!"

CHAPTER 15
TENDER LIPS

WHILE SQUIRMY MADE an undercover visit to The Masters, the gentlemen's club that O'Connor had frequented in the month before his murder, Keira met Blaise at the new safe house.

"I can't believe I put your life in danger again. I'm so sorry," Keira said when she walked in.

As it turned out, the tracer had been placed on one of Keira's shoes that she tended to wear about every other day. Thinking back on it, the days she had felt tracked coincided with the days wearing those shoes. She could not recall a time when she had been jostled or someone had gotten strangely close to her. As such, she had no lead on where, when, or by whom the tracer had been set.

Blaise stroked Keira's cheek and looked at her like she was being sweet but ridiculous. "You didn't do anything wrong, babe. We know the risks of being together, but we also know the rewards," Blaise added flirtatiously. "You have to drop this guilty conscience you carry around! I think it's time to share that other apple with you to get your pleasure centers firing."

Keira playfully rolled her eyes but still felt a bit glum.

Fortunately, when the agents had gathered and returned the women's belongings, they included the apple with the other bags. But the possibility that Blaise and Keira could have missed out on it served as a warning to them not to wait too long—only to find that time had run out and taken away the opportunity.

Keira gazed at Blaise's small nose and cream-colored skin, against which her green eyes and red hair shone with a natural resplendence. Keira had so much she wanted to say to Blaise but didn't know how to just jump in and say it. She had felt since she was a child that she was too reserved, that she wanted to open up more but wasn't sure how to go about it. Her default behavior, as a result, had been cautious observation.

Although Keira believed their love for each other was as plain to see as a color and as clear in feeling as a body immersed in water, she wanted to get better at expressing it verbally.

She decided on the spot that she'd might as well declare her love in the way she wanted to, even if she stumbled, because the day very easily might come when her chances ran out.

Keira cleared her throat and steeled her nerves. "When you disappeared, I realized how much I had depended on you to feel something, Blaise. It's like you represent to me the last fragments of beauty and hope in this depressing, dysfunctional world. I feel angry some days because the universe always seems to be threatening to take you away from me, like maybe I'm not supposed to be happy or something. I don't know. Anyway, I never for one moment took you for granted, but I regret that I never really told you what you meant to me so fundamentally. I didn't express my love enough."

Blaise's eyes shimmered as she held Keira's gaze without awkwardness or self-consciousness. "I've always felt so much love from you, Keira, and admiration. It's beautiful to hear you say it, but I want you to know that I was always aware of the strength of your dedication to me. It didn't matter whether you said it enough or clearly enough because I felt it."

Although Keira was vulnerable in the moment, she wasn't uncomfortable. It dawned on her that vulnerability wasn't something she always had to shield herself from.

As Blaise hugged her, Keira sensed her own heart rate settle. She was calming down again. Blaise always helped her to find her center whenever she lost it.

Before giving the decision more time to process, time she couldn't bank on, Keira made up her mind. "I want to marry you, Blaise."

She paused to let the statement set in, both for Blaise and herself. Same-sex couples didn't qualify for marriage certificates, but Keira craved the symbolism.

"I know we can't marry in the legal sense," she explained, "but we can in the spiritual one. I read how people used to exchange rings that they wore on their left hands to signal their commitment to each other. It's because the ring, like love, is endless with no start or finish."

Blaise began to cry while still smiling. Keira wiped the tears away and pressed her lips to Blaise's. Then she pulled back and asked in a soft voice, "Will you marry me, Blaise?"

Blaise let out a little squeal and lifted Keira off the ground. "Yes, a million times yes!" She laughed and then worked her hands into Keira's hair, pulling her face forward for another kiss. "I can't wait to call you my wife."

They held each other and rocked side to side slightly, as if keeping time to their own wedding tune.

"Tomorrow I'll start looking into where we can find rings and champagne that's not crazy expensive," Keira said. "I suppose flowers are out, but we can dream."

"This is a dream already. Anything we gather later is just extra. The amazing part is here right now."

They locked eyes and smiled at each other for so long that Keira felt like her cheeks were stretching to new limits. Then she reached for Blaise's hand and led her fiancée toward the bedroom so that the ache and the joy they felt for each other could find proper release.

KEIRA WOKE AROUND 05:30, with Blaise sound asleep by her side. She stroked Blaise's exposed shoulders and back, and then pulled the sheets up to cover her. Blaise nestled deeper under the covers with a murmur. Her long eyelashes closed on each other like the feathers of a little bird taking respite from a long flight.

Asking Blaise to marry her was the best decision she had ever made, Keira thought with a satisfied smile.

Her mind's attention then shifted to the bald man from her dreams who had insisted that she alone held the keys to her own destiny. Perhaps she was beginning to realize that and trying to make life actually happen, rather than just reacting to life happening to her. For so long she had felt as though she didn't have agency. She had lost her family. Her career was chosen for her. She fell in line, doing what she was told to do.

It wasn't that Keira lacked a rebellious side or a skeptical part of her personality. It was that the resistant, questioning parts of herself often got thwarted by the need to survive.

She thought about how her adult life had mostly been an exercise in pushing down what wanted to rise up. Perhaps falling in love and almost losing that person made her realize that the time had come to really fight, to put her foot down, to make things happen.

The dream man's statements about having the power to shape your future through your own thoughts still eluded her somewhat. She didn't know exactly what he meant, but she had noticed lately that when she maintained a clearer, more positive headspace, better possibilities and even outcomes seemed to materialize. The best outcome of all was hearing Blaise say yes to her marriage proposal with unmistakable excitement.

Blaise's red hair streamed across the pillow, like fiery comet dust left in the wake of celestial glory. She was gorgeous, absolutely stunning. Keira had begun to wonder if the Russian scientist just couldn't bring himself to kill such an exquisite creature.

Gazing at Blaise sleeping inches from her own body, Keira for the first time truly yearned for a baby with her. She imagined what a child created from Blaise's DNA would look and act like. What an incredible life form that child would grow into. Of course, the male part of the equation proved problematic. Who could fill that role, and how would it even happen? Was Blaise fertile enough to become pregnant? Probably not based on her physical exam results. The practical lost its grip against the stronger force of desire. Looking at Blaise, Keira just wanted a baby with her.

Okay, now I'm really losing my head in love, she told herself, but she allowed the fantasy to captivate her. Why not dream a little? It certainly didn't hurt anything. It did open up the vulnerable part of her that she'd learned to keep suppressed over the years, but she wanted to change that. She hoped in time that she could let Blaise and others in deeper to her interior world, without making them pass through so many walls and filters.

Unfortunately, it was 05:45 now. She had to get prepped for work. Keira kissed Blaise's forehead and whispered near her ear, "It's time to get up, love."

Blaise stirred a little and then opened her eyes with a series of blinks. Once she got her bearings and seemed to almost arrive into the moment from a faraway place, she smiled at Keira and then stroked her face. "I was just dreaming about you, baby," Blaise said.

They kissed and held each other, Blaise's body bed-warm and skin soft to the touch. "Don't you wish that we could call in a love day instead of a sick day?" Blaise asked. "Like I need to take a day to just make love and feel love, and not be part of the workforce?"

"Hmm, maybe you should run that by Devon," Keira chuckled, "because I think it's an excellent idea that could really build morale at the Bureau."

"He'd be a fan." She ran her fingers through Keira's hair and along the curve of her cheek. "All right, I guess I'll get up and just try to get by knowing that I'll return to you tonight and every night after that."

Keira clasped both of Blaise's hands and brought them to her lips. "Tonight and forever."

CHAPTER 16
SPOON-FED MEDICINE

SQUIRMY MET Keira on the street on their way to work. They still tried to avoid talking in the office about important details from the case until they could figure out who was a threat and who wasn't.

Keira hadn't heard whether the trap had been set yet by the Feds. She anxiously awaited that news but to no avail so far.

Squirmy's visit to The Masters hadn't produced any definitive clues. He said the club catered to a high-end clientele. Although everyone had to check time pieces at the door, he recognized some top-ranking government officials by sight without needing to do an image search. On the surface, the club provided prestige, elite networking, booze, and access to beautiful women (from flirtation to everything else) for outrageous sums of money.

"It's very possible that underhanded deals are being fleshed out there, but I just didn't have enough context to find my way in that environment or to really work the club," Squirmy said as they passed the Monument to the Child, a multimedia public exhibit. Keira found it odd how the abstract metal sculpture of a young boy would get covered up by a three-dimensional neon light display of a boy and then revert back to the sculpture. Watching the switch made her feel like she was going to have a seizure. While grateful for public art and supportive of its intention, some of the politically motivated pieces felt like public torture.

"That monument is ridiculous, don't you think?" Squirmy observed, shaking his head. "Anyway, my hunch tells me that if O'Connor was frequenting the club in the months before the shit hit the fan, then it's likely he was meeting someone related to this case, whether Chusei, a hacker, another government official, whatever. He may have even been serving as ears for the Chusei and reporting back. But it was no dice, Kincaid."

"That's all right," she said, suddenly picturing Blaise's face staring into hers that morning. What was it about the love you could see in someone's eyes for you that felt better than anything else in the world? She still buzzed over Blaise but tried to focus. She continued, "It's good to know about it for background. Maybe a connection with the club will lead to something later, maybe not. But the most important question is: Did you have any extracurricular fun?"

He chuckled. "Just some strong martinis. But those alone were definitely worth the trip. And the exotic dancers weren't too hard on the eyes, I'll tell you that much."

"All this pleasure in service to the state. Who said work isn't sometimes fun?"

Suddenly, the soft ding-ding-dong of a public-service announcement rang throughout the busy streets. Everyone stopped to listen and put their right hands over their hearts, per government edict. Keira and Squirmy followed suit.

President Richard Miller appeared in a 3D hologram across city billboards, his receding hairline and fake teeth broadcast for all to see. "Greetings, citizens of These United States," he began with a friendly yet solemn tone. What a wanker he is, Keira thought. "May the bounty of the universe be upon you," he continued, "in God's great nation."

"And with you," everyone mumbled in unison because it was expected of them.

"I come to you today with exciting news."

Squirmy gave Keira a furtive look of we'll see about that. He disliked Miller's fake, power-hungry approach to governance too. Neither of them had voted for him. In fact, many skeptical citizens suspected that their votes simply didn't count anymore when the election outcome wasn't the desired one by those in power. Polls had shown Miller trailing by double digits heading into the last election day, and nothing had happened to cast his opponent in a negative light in the run-up to the vote. It was highly suspicious that Miller came out on top.

With Congress weakened by the barrage of executive orders that the White House justified due to extenuating circumstances for protecting national security—and the Supreme Court taking many liberties with interpreting the Constitution, which had been amended more times in the past decade than in any previous decade in the nation's history—the executive branch steered eerily toward dictatorship.

"I want to thank each and every one of you for your sacrifices to this country. Without your help, we wouldn't be able to make the strides we have. Fertility is up. Food production is up. The economy is roaring. I have reason to believe that in two years, we will return to the consumption of real food." President Miller smiled with his mouth but not his eyes, giving him the grim appearance of creepy liar. He swept his thinning hair back with one hand and tried to use the pregnant pause to maximum effect.

"Wait for it," Squirmy muttered to Keira. "The political pitch is coming."

"But that will only happen if you elect me once again as your president. Unfortunately, we have reason to believe that there is widespread fraud among the voting registrars. While our staff here is working tirelessly to address these issues, we are starting to believe that a fair election may not be possible by Dec. 31. While no decision has yet been made and we are doing everything in our power to meet the federal election deadline, I need you to know that these extraordinary times might call for extraordinary measures."

Keira's heart sank. Of course he'd go for one last power grab as Congress and the country turned against him.

"You're a fucking liar, you shitbag!"

Keira turned around to see a skinny man, who appeared to be in his mid-twenties, giving the hologram president the double bird.

"Power without compassion for the people will never prevail!" he hollered.

Two heavily armed street cops in military fatigues swept in on the man from the front and behind. One clubbed him in the gut while the other put a hood over his head, cinched it, and pulled the man's hands back to cuff him. The two of them then dragged him away, his head flailing and feet scrambling as he tried to resist.

The first cop who had done the clubbing pulled a syringe from his weapons vest and injected it into the protestor's arm. The two cops were so efficient in their tactics that it was chilling to watch, even for Keira, who was obviously accustomed to making arrests. She had never used a hood on a suspect, however, finding it too similar to the behavior of criminals who resort to torture. It was clear that these street cops had mastered their maneuvers through ample practice.

Within seconds the fight in the arrested man's body went out. The cops quickly dragged him to an armored patrol vehicle, where another policeman monitored the situation from behind a machine gun.

People in the crowd appeared shocked, but they kept their hands over their hearts and avoided eye contact with the police. Keira was relieved that she and Squirmy were dressed in plainclothes, one of the benefits of blending in as detectives.

The president's words droned on. Keira couldn't separate sound from meaning as she thought about the protestor and what would happen to him.

So many political dissenters just "disappeared" these days. Because a semblance of democracy still infused other types of legal proceedings, Keira surmised that Miller and his cronies were able to get away with eliminating activists and off-the-cuff protestors. There weren't enough protests to cause enough people to question what was happening to the arrestees, especially since the lower courts seemed to otherwise mete out justice as usual. Not that it was always fair by any means, but it wasn't all that different from how things were before the war in that the poor mostly got screwed, while the rich hired lawyers who got them better outcomes.

It didn't help that the press would be fed lies about grassroots political dissenters dying of drug overdoses, accidents, and disease.

Keira wondered how many of the dissenters were instead test speci-mens at the Labs. Or perhaps they were just outright killed.

Reporters then spoon-fed the false information they'd received from the government back to the public. Although some journalists attempted to crack open the truth by any means necessary, many were far too afraid to publicly question the veracity of official statements.

At what point does a person decide that it's worth it to put a target on their head? That was a question Keira often asked herself. Now that she'd fallen in love with Blaise and been reunited with her, she didn't think she could ever sacrifice her personal happiness for the sake of a political cause. Nonetheless, she knew she'd keep trying to find indi-rect ways to resist the increasingly authoritarian state, in part by doing good acts as an investigator. Sometimes that meant letting someone go when the hard-and-fast rules called for an arrest.

She and Squirmy followed their gut instincts on the job; when they could give a good person the benefit of the doubt without laying the heavy hand of government on them, they did. A number of times they'd corroborated their stories that the suspect had left the scene before they'd arrived, or had escaped after spraying them with teargas, or any other plausible excuse that fit the situation and allowed them to let someone go without a charge. Minor acts of resistance. They were better than taking your medicine straight, she thought.

The president faded from public view. The crowd quickly dispersed, with mothers holding their children's hands and shushing them. Given that the First Amendment hadn't protected the protester's right to free speech, it was best to assume it might not protect one's own.

Keira and Squirmy exchanged glances that said it all and then joined the quiet, terrified masses on their way to work and school.

BLAISE HAD FOUND a new development in the Russia probe that she shared with Keira that evening. Over the past six months, the Chusei had wired large amounts of money to what appeared to be Russian handlers. The Russian government tended to run its dirty business through dirty hands. That way if things went awry, they could blame the criminal underground and pretend that they had nothing to do with it.

Since the timing of the wires coincided with the ramping up of warehouse and mining production in Russia, Blaise and her team believed that the Chusei's transactions were funding the Russian production of food and weapons.

The Chusei carried a reputation as reliable bankers for the criminally inclined. As such, it could just be that the Chusei were loaning money to the Russians at profitable interest rates for themselves. But it couldn't be ruled out that a greater partnership existed between the Russians and the Chusei.

The recent digging into of leads also had led to a mysterious detail that puzzled Blaise. An American spy embedded in Moscow had intercepted correspondence between a member of a Russian crime syndicate and a Russian government official. One translated message within the longer chain was: "We now think the American redhead was Sparrow's daughter. We might have hell to pay for killing her. His people will even the score if they find out."

"Then make sure they don't," the government official had replied.

While it was possible that the Russians had recently killed another American female redhead (or, like in Blaise's case, thought they had), Blaise could not ignore the likely possibility that the message directly referred to her. Red hair was statistically uncommon—found in probably less than a half of a percent of the country's population. And even fewer people got embroiled in Russian-American espionage.

Sparrow's daughter? Blaise's father had died during the war. A roadside bomb explosion killed both of her parents while they strolled the streets of San Francisco on a trip to visit Blaise's ailing aunt.

An only child, Blaise supposedly had two living cousins, but she had not been able to find either of them in recent years and doubted they were actually alive. War records were shoddy at best, with too many millions of Americans having died in a short period of time— plus the systems and backup systems that housed the records often got destroyed by missiles and cyberattacks.

Blaise's father, Paul, had been a corporate executive who frequently traveled overseas for work and was gone a lot. Blaise had previously described him as having a calm, kind demeanor. She doubted he was the "Sparrow" of whom they spoke, yet something nagged at her about it. She said she had considered the possibility of mistaken identity. Clearly, she could resemble someone enough to be confused for his offspring, but her gut just couldn't sit with that. She wasn't sure why.

Keira and Blaise stood in the safe house kitchen, puzzling over the possibilities. Keira said, "I know that this is very strange to think about, but now that you're an agent, is there anything about your father's behavior looking back on it that resembles that of a criminal or spy?"

Blaise looked away, appearing upset.

"I'm sorry. That was insensitive. I don't want you to feel like I'm interrogating you."

Blaise exhaled audibly. She leaned back against the counter in the tiny kitchen and crossed her arms against her chest. "You're on the right track. I need to think like that. It's just hard because it's my dad. There's a part of me that doesn't want to know if he was involved in anything shady. I mean, I don't believe he had been, but look how easy it is to live a double life. We see it all the time."

Keira nodded. "Right. But keep in mind that the double life typically takes a toll. Unless people are total sociopaths, they have a hard time carrying out acts of deception over and over again. They're angry or they drink too much. They can be silent and brooding. But in the case of a spy, it might be a gentler form of detachment, like just not disclosing much about comings and goings in order to keep the family safe."

Blaise grew quiet, her eyes seemingly staring into the void like she was contemplating something that had not fully formed yet. After a long pause, she said, "I feel like I can't bring myself to look at him like an agent would because I don't want to see his true nature if it's reprehensible—and then be seen by you in that light. I mean, what if he was or is a double agent, a traitor who let me believe he was dead while he ran off to be a badass in Russia? Would you then trust me?" She flexed her hands.

"I would never stop trusting you over anything your family did.

Your father made his choices, whatever they were. He led his life. You had nothing to do with that. It's not fair to make the innocent guilty by association." Keira ran her fingers through her hair, trying to think of what else to say. She settled on a belief she often held: "We just find the truth and carry on because of it or in spite of it. That's the only way to live anymore. Besides, with threats coming in from all directions, we can't afford to ignore any intel that comes our way, as hard as it might be to swallow."

Blaise nodded and relaxed her face, appearing slightly less troubled by the hypothetical. "Okay, although it makes me sick to my stomach to do this, I'll start looking into him and all the ugly possibilities." She sighed. "Tonight can we just let it go and take a bath? I need some distance from this."

"Of course." Keira could see the wheels turning in Blaise, that Blaise was thinking and repelling the thinking at the same time.

Keira drew the bath and then massaged Blaise's shoulders and back. While soaking in the warm water together they didn't talk. Keira liked hearing the sounds of the water sloshing against the tub and of their breath moving in and out. She realized it was nice to take a break from analyzing and conversing, and she let the day fall further away.

THE NEXT MORNING, Keira awoke alone in bed. She walked out to the living room to find Blaise hunched over her portable computer, staring intently at the screen.

"Good morning, love," Keira said.

Blaise appeared startled at first but then stood up with a smile and approached Keira. "Thank you for being so sweet to me last night. I really love you for that—and everything else."

Keira hugged her. "How are you feeling this morning? You're up and at 'em early."

"Better. I'm definitely feeling better. But to be honest, a memory kept bothering me last night. I didn't sleep well." She paused.

"You can tell me anything, but you don't have to."

Blaise sighed. "I'd like to get this off my chest."

130

Keira nodded her support.

"When I was probably ten years old, there was a night when I tossed and turned and couldn't fall back asleep," Blaise said. "I got up to head to the bathroom. When I walked past my father's home office, I was surprised to find him standing there with what looked like recording equipment, speaking a language I didn't recognize. His back was to me, but he seemed to sense my presence and turned around. It was his look that strikes me now. He had the appearance of someone getting caught doing something he wasn't supposed to be doing.

"He ended the recording immediately and then seemed to quickly compose himself, almost like an actor falling back into character. He smiled and asked what I was doing up at that hour. When I told him I couldn't sleep, he offered to rub my back and warm up milk for me. We walked down to the kitchen together, and he acted totally normal from that point forward. And then I just went back to bed and didn't think much of it."

She paused and ran her hand through her hair. "I think he was speaking Russian, which I didn't recognize at the time. I had assumed that he was up late doing business, but why would he look like his identity had been compromised if that were the case?"

Keira asked, "Do you remember what the recording equipment looked like?"

"Sort of, but it's a hazy image in my mind."

"I remember one time seeing photos of spy messaging equipment from the turn of the century in a book on detective work. I'll see if I can track those images down again. But that's really interesting about your father's reaction. I think your gut is telling you that he was being deceptive in some way because, as you say, he might have looked annoyed or startled if he was doing regular business. The fact that he looked compromised and then had to catch himself and realize it's just his ten-year-old daughter, so be cool, implies something else altogether."

Blaise stared at the floor and clenched her jaw. "It's so frustrating and unsettling to think that the past is also uncertain now, just like the future. I mean I always assumed that my parents and my childhood were what they appeared to be. Realizing they might have been built on falsehoods makes me feel like nothing is real."

Keira sighed in sympathy. "It doesn't mean that you have to throw it all away or that your parents' love wasn't real. I'm sure it was. Your father perhaps had a job like ours. He might have been a good guy, Blaise, who couldn't tell you what he was doing for his own protection and that of the country."

Blaise nodded. "That's certainly possible. But it's also possible—"

Their time pieces buzzed simultaneously. It was an alert from Devon. They looked at each other and then opened the encrypted message that read: "The trap failed last night but gave us good intel. Still on it." A video link followed.

Keira felt her heart rate pick up. She expected results from the trap, not just intel. Blaise shook her head in disappointment and then voice-commanded her time piece to play the video in hologram mode.

They watched together as two male Bureau agents sat at a table in the corner of an otherwise empty room. The agents must have decided to move the tracking device to a new location because that room wasn't at the old safe house.

The agents kept their attention on their time pieces. One nodded to the other. They stood up but squatted low, guns at the ready—and flanked each side of the door.

A green light then flashed on the door. As soon as she saw it, Keira knew it was cast by a heat-sensing device. The perpetrator would see that two males stood crouched, ready to fire. The trap was blown.

The agents also knew what the green light meant. They rushed to open the door, but smoke wafted in and they began to cough and recoil. The perpetrator was apparently well prepared. By the time the agents could open the door, the hallway was empty. The suspect gone.

Blaise clicked to play the video from the hallway view, starting from the beginning of the scene. A petite person—a woman, Keira assumed—walked quickly down the hallway dressed in all black with a white skull mask over her face.

When she got close to the door, she squatted down and with her right hand pointed a heat-sensing gun up at an angle, safely out of the line of fire of the door. Almost immediately, she grabbed a smoke bomb from her pants pocket with her left hand and released it. She darted away like a shadow, barely making an impression that she'd ever been there.

That must be Cora, Keira figured. Light on her feet, doesn't leave a trace, tough, quick, and ready for the worst.

Keira asked Blaise, "Why wasn't an agent standing guard on the street to pick off the fleeing suspect?"

"Right? Let me ask." She voice-messaged the question to Devon.

Devon responded, "The agent positioned on the street followed another suspect around the corner, seeing him first. He missed the female one. That's how she got in and out no problem. These guys were clearly prepared. They created a decoy. Normally, we would have had a fourth agent on duty, but he called in sick and we couldn't get a backup in time."

Keira was frustrated. They were all getting closer to results but still had nothing to show for their efforts. She asked Devon what the valuable intel was.

Devon explained that night drones pursued the van leaving the scene. Several miles down the road, both suspects removed their masks. He sent a still captured by one of the cameras of their faces.

When it came through, Keira knew without hesitation that she was looking at Cora and the young guy with the raven tattoo from the Misfits' surf warehouse. They both had serious expressions on their faces, like they too were stressed out from the night's disappointment. Keira imagined there'd be hell to pay to the Chusei for failing to make a hit. Not that she felt sorry for them.

Devon then said that the van eventually parked at the Empress Hotel. The Feds planted a tracking device on its undercarriage, but it hadn't moved yet.

"At least there's a second chance to find them," Keira said. It wasn't much consolation, however, given that multiple assassins were still out there trying to take her out.

CHAPTER 17
RUNNER'S HIGH

KEIRA AND SQUIRMY had video footage of their own to review. Although the video camera they had planted outside the Misfits' door hadn't produced any smoking guns, it had still proven valuable.

Footage showed Cora and the young Chusei guy coming and going at various hours of the day and night, indicating that they most likely lived there. A handful of other people appeared to visit at random times but not reside at the warehouse.

Harper, however, followed a very predictable pattern. She departed every morning in workout clothes around 07:15 and returned around 08:15 sweaty. They figured she was running. Since Harper's departures could be better timed, confronting her first still seemed like Keira and Squirmy's best bet.

They would need special permission from their boss, and then a judge, to detain and interrogate her offsite, temporarily taking away her rights to an attorney. Detectives could conduct this form of questioning, called BAM Interrogations (for By Any Means), in extenuating circumstances only. Given the Chusei's multiple attempts on Keira's life, the fact that Cora and the other Chusei suspect appeared to live at the Misfits' warehouse, and the connection between Spyder and Harper, Squirmy thought they had as good of a chance as any to secure permission.

Keira usually eschewed BAM Interrogations because she felt queasy about taking away people's legal rights, but she worried that time was running out. She thought their best bet for getting ahead of this investigation, rather than letting it close in on them, was to corner Harper and get her to talk. Squirmy agreed.

He filled out the request form and sent it to Wozniak.

As they waited, Keira walked toward her desk, thinking back on the footage of the busted trap. She found it chilling that Cora carried the same equipment that law enforcement used, like heat-sensing guns and smoke bombs.

In theory, it should have been extremely difficult for private citizens to get their hands on those tools and weapons. Ever since the Second Amendment was overturned at the end of the war, citizens lacked legal access to guns and other forms of self-protection. While anything could be procured on the black market for a certain price, the selection was typically low quality. It was clear, then, that the Chusei had friends in high places. They had penetrated the blue shield and now had the means to play hard ball on the same playing field.

Keira felt ill at ease. She figured that taking back control by homing in on Harper would help her to, if not exactly even the score, at least tip the balance toward her.

The trapped must set a trap of her own, she thought.

She sat down to fill out more reports related to the kidnapping and overdose incident at Sierra Square. For a department that could play fast and loose with the rules on the one hand, there sure were a lot of bureaucratic hoops to jump through on the other.

Squirmy stopped by about an hour later. "Wozniak said the BAM is all but guaranteed and to proceed with planning it while we wait for the official stamp. He wants us to make the scoop tomorrow morning. I say we call this one Operation Keira Freedom."

She laughed. "Freedom sure sounds good to me, buddy. I could use a night of uninterrupted sleep in a home that's not a safe house."

They headed to the Deception Room to look through simple disguise options that would be easy to incorporate into tomorrow's plan. For work of this nature, wearing the uniform of a factory worker or mechanic was preferable to the more deeply undercover setup facilitated by the Impersonator. Besides, triptoline could be dangerous and counteractive when the intent was to surprise and intimidate.

The mechanical wardrobe spun outfits around one at a time for a series of two seconds. They watched military fatigues go round, followed by sequined dance costumes. "I'm a really good dancer, you know," Squirmy joked.

"I bet. I'm just not sure Harper will want to tango. And she probably won't let you take the lead."

"Don't underestimate my footwork, Kincaid."

"I've seen it sober and it's really, um, notable."

A delivery-driver uniform came around. "Pause," Keira ordered the AI system. She said to Squirmy, "There's a government storage facility on Newport Avenue, which is near the Misfits' place. I think we'd blend in with this outfit."

Although drones and robots handled most deliveries in the country, the government had actual humans perform its deliveries for fear of a cyber hack that could overtake AI and lead to the compromise of government trade and intel.

"Good call, Kincaid. It's time to deliver some justice."

She laughed. "You're on fire today!"

"I'm always on fire. You just don't always appreciate my quick wit."

"Ah, I see. You're obviously hard to keep up with."

"Especially on the dance floor."

She rolled her eyes and suggested they look at vehicles next. In the meantime, they commanded the AI system to take their physical dimensions and create tailored versions of the delivery outfits in their trademark drab brown cloth.

They had many other decisions to make in a short period of time, but Keira was glad to have the time pressure to keep her focused.

At 07:05 the next morning, Keira and Squirmy sat several blocks from the Misfits' warehouse in a vehicle made to look like a government delivery van.

They had sent a bumblebee, an incredibly tiny drone that was hard to detect, to hover near the Misfits' headquarters. The plan was to use the bumblebee to follow Harper once she stepped out.

The van felt stuffy and claustrophobic, Keira thought, but she realized those sensations had to do more with her mental state than the conditions in the vehicle. She pulled her brown delivery cap down lower on her forehead and tightened her ponytail. She did what she most hated to do: she waited.

"I thought I was the squirmy one."

Keira smiled. "I'm a bit antsy today, too. That's for sure." She thought about Blaise and their last kiss before Keira left that morning. Blaise had clung to her and made Keira promise to be careful, which was different from Blaise's usually steely exterior before work assignments.

Since Blaise's abduction, they'd both become more afraid of loss and more appreciative of life. As such, Keira found herself in a new frontier of emotional awakening that was simultaneously terrifying and electrifying. She did not know what it was that she was supposed to do next.

"Here we go, Keira." Squirmy pointed to the van's monitor, where the bumblebee's video was being broadcast. Harper had emerged from the door of the warehouse wearing shorts and a sports bra.

They watched as she made her way to Sunset Cliffs Boulevard, where she turned south and began jogging, the bumblebee following her movements from what they calculated was an undetectable distance.

Keira observed the way Harper moved her body. She was nimble on her feet yet strong in her movements, appearing to glide effortlessly through air and crush it at the same time. She had given the same impression in the water. Keira felt slightly in awe of Harper's physicality and knew she wouldn't be easy to subdue.

"Let's let her get about a half mile down the road before we intercept her," Keira suggested as she looked at a map on her time piece. "If she stays on this current path, then she'll arrive at the corner of Sunset Cliffs and Orchard Avenue, which has empty buildings except for squatters. We don't want witnesses."

Like in many parts of the city, buildings damaged from wartime attacks remained abandoned. Given the postwar population decline, there was a glut of residential and commercial space. The uninhabited buildings were such an eyesore that a citizens' brigade advocated for their removal, saying their existence acted as a depressing reminder of what mankind had lost. So far those requests had gone unfulfilled, and the buildings indeed reminded everyone of what had been taken away and never replaced: people, community, solidarity, belonging.

Squirmy nodded his agreement to the plan and gave voice commands to the van, which began to drive east of Harper's location. The idea was to head her off from the south rather than overtaking her from behind.

Keira took slow, steady breaths as the van proceeded quietly along the route. She picked up her distance-stunner weapon and visualized aiming and firing it. She'd probably have only one chance to get the subduing arrow in Harper's body before the agile Harper fled around the corner and out of firing range.

The van stopped near the intersection. Keira nodded to Squirmy and forearm bumped him. "We've got this, Watts." She needed to tell him that in order to convince herself.

"We do indeed, Kincaid."

Keira hopped out of the back of the van and ran over to a decrepit building on the corner. Using her climbing equipment, she ascended about twenty feet before stopping and hanging with her feet against the building. She stayed out of Harper's oncoming view, instead monitoring Harper's movements from the bumblebee feed on her time piece. Keira counted how long it took Harper to run a block. For three blocks in a row, she completed each one in four seconds. Consistency helps with aim, she thought.

When Harper was one block away, Keira shifted her feet so that she hung out over the building's corner. While counting to four, she steadied her body with a deep breath and squared her shoulders. Harper appeared on the street below. Keira set her aim on Harper's left thigh—and fired.

Harper buckled over. Keira could see through the weapon sight that she had hit her target right where she wanted. She watched

Harper writhe on the ground and attempt to extract the tranquilizer dart, which embeds under the skin and quickly subdues the nervous system. She sure was a fighter.

Once Keira's feet touched the ground, she ran over to Harper, who groaned and cursed loudly. Squirmy emerged from the van at the same time, as planned. Just as Harper turned her heard toward Keira with the fierce expression of a lion letting a hunter know it's not over, she lost consciousness. Squirmy grabbed her under the arms and hoisted her up, while Keira picked Harper up by the legs.

When they got her in the van, Squirmy quickly closed the door and ordered the van to drive north and then east to the predetermined interrogation site. Given Harper's strength and tenacity, they took extra precautions to tie her hands and legs. The look she flashed before passing out was the most intense warning Keira had ever seen in a suspect's face.

"She's tough as nails, Squirmy. We're going to have to be very careful. I also think we should avoid mind games with her and be direct. My gut tells me that's the only way to win her attention, if not her cooperation, which could be unlikely."

Keira placed a blanket under Harper's head to keep it from bouncing around on the van's hard floor. As she did, she looked more closely at Harper's face. A small, jagged scar whiptailed like lightning on Harper's right cheek. She had full lips, high cheekbones, and long eyelashes—the classic hallmarks of feminine attractiveness —but she also gave the impression that she could care less about any of it. Keira found her formidable and knew they were playing with fire.

Her time piece buzzed with a message from Blaise asking for a status update. Blaise also shared an image, that looked decades old, of a handsome man wearing the International Intelligence stripes. The name under his photo was Hank Sparrow. Blaise wrote, "Pater unfamilias. Photo is def him. Name?!?"

So that was Blaise's father! He did have her nose. Other than that, Keira didn't detect much of a resemblance. His expression in the photo was inscrutable. He was a spy after all with the I.I. stripes to prove it and looked like one, she thought.

She messaged Blaise, "The lion sleeps. Will wake with a roar. Wow! Do you have proof that he died during the war?"

While awaiting a response, Keira monitored Harper's vitals. Her pulse was normal. If they waited for her to wake on her own, they were looking at about an hour. The other option was to revive her with a reversal drug. Keira didn't want to do that because it jacked up the heart rate, which agitated the person. She figured they shouldn't push it with this spirited one who had six-pack abs and ripped legs. Imagining her fiercer than usual was slightly terrifying.

Blaise's return message sent a vibration over Keira's wrist. Keira read, "Not sure anything is foolproof anymore. Be very careful. Moon & back." The last part referred to the old expression "I'll love you to the moon and back."

Keira smiled and dictated, "Moon & back," and sent it to the sky.

CHAPTER 18
THE LION WAKES

ONCE HARPER HAD DONE her own proverbial trip to the moon and back, she woke with a gasp and immediately tried to rise. She was strapped on her back to a narrow hospital bed. She glared at Squirmy and then at Keira.

But strangely, her glare softened as she looked at Keira. It was replaced by an expression that Keira interpreted as recognition and acceptance—almost calm. Harper stopped struggling against her restraints.

This was not what Keira was expecting at all. She suddenly felt thrown. A furtive glance from Squirmy communicated the same confusion.

It's not like they had time to huddle and come up with a new plan in front of Harper, Keira thought, so they were just going to have to ride this out, whatever it was.

She carefully removed Harper's gag, ensuring that her hand didn't get within biting range. With her mouth unencumbered, Harper smiled. Then she said to Keira with a tone of awe, "You are the one with the gift. We've been waiting for you."

For a moment Keira wondered if they'd accidentally administered the wrong drug through the tranquilizer dart. Did they get Harper looped on something? There was always the chance of a bad batch of chemicals or drug mislabeling.

Seemingly reading Keira's confusion, Harper continued, "I know this sounds bizarre. It's weird to me, too, but give me time to explain. Could I have some water first, though? I'm so thirsty."

Squirmy and Keira exchanged a look of mutual bewilderment. Each seemed to hope the other would have an idea of what was going on and what to do. Squirmy spoke first to Harper. "Of course. One moment."

As he rummaged in his backpack for his metal water bottle, Harper's eyes locked on Keira's. Keira had the odd impression that Harper could see through her and knew everything about her, including what she was thinking right now and what flavor goo pack she'd had for breakfast.

"Chemical blueberry," Harper said with a laugh.

Keira thought she might pass out. What in the world was going on?

A flash of light crossed Harper's hazel eyes. Her gaze then neutralized and became soothing. "Sorry, I shouldn't have spooked you like that."

Since her arms were still restrained, Squirmy slowly poured water into her open mouth. She drank thirstily for several seconds, paused, and drank some more. Appearing satiated, she thanked Squirmy, who now held an empty bottle, and then turned her attention again to Keira, who was still reeling from what had just transpired.

Harper said, "I only occasionally can access someone's thoughts like that. I promise that I don't know everything you're thinking right now. Obviously, just sheer observation and intuition tell me this is spooking you and that you have a fear-breeds-respect view towards me." She laughed. "Most people do."

"I can imagine," Keira said, smiling wanly and crossing her arms against her chest.

"The Manifestors have been trying to reach you, Keira. They refer to you as the Incomplete One."

The revelation struck Keira as both plausible and ridiculous.

Squirmy laughed. "Sounds like an insult to me, Kincaid." To

Harper he said, "There's nothing incomplete about this one, I can assure you. So who are these Manifestors you talk about?"

Harper stared at Squirmy, waiting an uncomfortable amount of time to respond, as if trying overly hard to gather her composure. She leaned her neck to one side and stretched her bound arms as much as possible given the restraints, her muscles undulating ropelike as she moved. It was like watching one of the companion cyborgs of old. Robotic. Playing at being human, yet also awe-inspiring and phenomenal in their construction.

Finally, Harper stated matter-of-factly, "It's true there's nothing incomplete about her in the sense you're thinking of. In the sense they're thinking of—of destiny—her mission remains very much unfinished and her potential untapped. She has been chosen to do great things. You will both see. It will become apparent in time."

Keira felt weightless and a little dizzy. She wished that she could brush this off as quackery. She recognized, however, a foreign truth that resonated with her; she just needed to learn the right language to understand it. She also knew in her gut that the bald man of her dreams was part of this.

Almost on cue, Harper nodded and said, "You're right. The Light One has been trying to reach you and protect you from what we call the shadows. You are beginning to open up receptivity as you become more vulnerable. He was never able to reach you until you fell in love and almost lost her."

Squirmy turned to Keira with a look of what the hell is she talking about?

"I know you believe that Cora has been trying to kill you," Harper continued, "but she is actually trying to save you. Although she has done bad things in the past out of obligation to the Chusei, she double-crosses them now. See, we needed someone on the inside to do our bidding on the outside." She looked right and left, as if scanning the room for danger, and then back to center. "Would it be possible to untie my hands, or at least tie them more comfortably?"

Keira wondered if they should be careful and keep her restrained, but her gut told her she could trust Harper. She nodded her consent to Squirmy, who unfastened the wrist restraints.

Light flashed over Harper's eyes again. "Shall we start at the beginning? There really is no other place. It's a long one. I suggest you sit down for it."

Clearly, they needed to accept the reality that they had lost the lead as the interrogators of this investigation. They took a seat as she suggested.

∼

HARPER BEGAN her revelation with a short benediction. She closed her eyes and placed her hands palms up on her thighs. "Into the light we go. Where it takes us we soon shall know. The shadows we diminish in order to start what we must finish."

She opened her eyes and nodded to Keira and Squirmy one at a time. "Peace to you and to the universe." Then Harper put her hands in prayer position near her forehead and bowed slightly toward them.

Squirmy mouthed at Keira, "What is this bohemian woo woo stuff?" Keira met his eyes with I get it, but let's be patient.

"Manifestation is an ancient practice that was mostly long forgotten by the time the war rolled around," Harper began. "Those who practiced it believed that they could use their thoughts and energies to bring into their lives what they longed for, as long as those desires were driven by good will. The concept was psychological and spiritual in nature. Some people considered it kooky." Harper laughed, surprising Keira with a moment of levity after quite the serious preamble.

"But then something very interesting began to happen. We do not know the cause. It may have been energy shifts in the universe from all the wartime upheaval, or exposure to chemicals or programming. But whatever it was, some people began to find that they could more easily manifest outcomes they desired in their lives. That skill was awakened strongly in a select few and began to increase in magnitude for others. In addition, these Manifestors, as we call them, developed the ability to recognize the gift in others who also possess it and then reach those people in untraditional ways.

"That is how they found you, Keira, once you started to find yourself. It is often through dreams that they communicate with each other."

This made sense on the one hand and certainly aligned with Keira's impression that the bald man had been communicating with her while she was slept, but it also shattered everything she held true about the limits of human ability. She supposed, however, that if she and her mother could perform mind touch, then why couldn't other people possess different forms of access?

Since mind touch was an ability to tap into a channel of communication and energy that others could not, it did not seem unreasonable to think that there were other ways to access those seemingly hidden channels. She had always wondered whether other people had strange gifts like mind touch, but other than her mother she'd never met anyone who did—at least as far as she was aware.

Keira's mother, who had been a research psychologist, never found definitive answers as to why they possessed the ability. As a researcher she had sought as much information as she could find, but it was a classic case of insufficient data—of science not having all the answers and of bearing witness to what could not be explained. There were only rumors, uncorroborated, of electromagnetic experiments that had inadvertently led to mind-touch ability.

But Keira's mother had wondered if she herself as a young child had been involved in some type of electromagnetic experimentation. Her mom had memories that began to surface that promised to offer a window of clarity into that theory, but they vanished as quickly as they appeared, much like the accessed memories of others. As a psychologist, she also questioned whether she was creating those mental images due to the power of suggestion.

Keira, then, learned more from her mother about how to practice mind touch, including self-monitoring the temptation to take advantage of it, rather than where it came from and where it might lead beyond the obvious. She remembered her mom once saying, "Just because we can get answers that way doesn't mean we should. You will actually learn more about people by interacting with them the regular way. By talking, asking questions, showing genuine interest, and caring for their well-being."

Keira pulled her attention back into the room and began to wonder whether Harper was a Manifestor or if Cora was. Spookily, but now not so unexpectedly, Harper shared, "You might be wondering if I possess the gift. I do not, but I have what we call Enhanced Intuition. I can read people more deeply than what is considered typical."

Harper paused and held Keira's gaze for an uncomfortable amount of time before speaking again. "We are interested in creating a new normal for future generations because, let's be honest, this civilization in its current state is an unworthy shell of human experience. There's no heart or guts to it. It's like a ghost lingering in a lost realm, unsure of what to do or where to go next. The Manifestors and those of us who align with them are trying, while recognizing our own limitations, to use these surreal gifts for the betterment of humanity."

Squirmy said, "No offense, but this sounds like some idealistic mind-fuck nonsense. If you're so enlightened, why are you working with known members of the Chusei?"

Harper chuckled. "I get such a kick out of people's skepticism! I get it. I know it sounds wacky. That's a fair question. As I explained earlier, Cora is double-crossing the Chusei. We need people's gifts and have to sometimes forgive their pasts."

Harper seemed to weigh what to say next. Her prolonged pauses and speech patterns were certainly unusual, Keira thought.

"When Cora killed her landlord to take from him what she believed he took from her father, she put a price on her head literally and figuratively," Harper explained. "In the literal sense, she owed the Chusei the unpaid debts of the landlord, who had defaulted on his drug payments to them. When the Chusei saw how nimble and stealthy she was, they decided to put her to work for them as repayment. This got her deeper and deeper into a lifestyle she didn't want and couldn't control. You don't exactly tell the Chusei that enough is enough. It doesn't work that way. There's no real path away from them."

She sighed. "The figurative price on her head, of course, is that you can't play creator in choosing when someone lives or dies. You will pay for that in some way, whether it's a debilitating sense of guilt, terrible loss, or some other form of karma that rights the score. She is attempting to make up for what she's done, knowing full well that her time is most likely limited."

Harper stared straight into Keira's eyes. "Some say life is unfair; others say fair. I believe that we can only determine the relative fairness based on our actions. It is only until we fully engage with life that we can get a sense of its meaning. And it is only then that we can integrate ourselves into its fabric according to its terms and our own." She put her hands into an accordion and stretched outward from her shoulders.

"But most people, unfortunately, prefer to hide in the shadows. To live partial lives. They believe it's safer that way—that they're protecting themselves. All they're actually doing is failing to live. That to us is one of modern mankind's strangest paradoxes. We underlive in order to merely live, when in fact *fully* living is the only way to feel alive."

Squirmy whistled through his teeth. "That's quite a philosophy you've got there. You should have your own self-empowerment show. But back to the facts: What happened to Spyder and Travis?"

Harper glared at Squirmy and then abruptly erupted into laughter, startling Keira again, who by now felt like a jumpy fawn. Harper said to him, "I like you, even though I don't. I think you know exactly what I mean by that." She paused. "To answer your questions: Travis is alive. We saved him from the hit that was sure to come after your interrogation. Spyder is dead as you know. He was killed by the government, which you obviously don't know."

The three of them sat with that information for a moment. Keira felt immensely relieved to hear that Travis was alive. She had been struggling with remorse for inadvertently putting him in harm's way.

Before Keira or Squirmy could ask follow-up questions about Spyder's death, Harper put up a hand and shook her head. "I know you both have many more questions, but it is not my place to answer them all at this moment. The Light One, however, would like to meet you face to face right now, Keira. Come here, please." She beckoned Keira to her side.

Keira hesitated and looked at Squirmy. He was slouched forward in his chair, seeming exasperated. She exhaled and locked eyes with Harper again, who nodded—her eyes like an open portal.

Keira approached the hospital bed on the left side, deciding she'd might as well go all in. What other choice did she really have? Besides, if she could, she'd like to have the opportunity to communicate with the strange bald man whose messages had captivated and puzzled her.

Harper lightly squeezed Keira's hand and held her gaze with assurance. "It's okay, Keira. Have faith in the universe. Don't let the fear of what you don't know keep you from the beauty of discovery." She smiled. "In a moment, you'll press your forehead against mine. The Light One will meet you."

Harper then surprised Keira by pulling her into a tight embrace. Who would have thought this ferocious force of a woman could also be tender? Despite the strange and uncomfortable experience of meeting Harper, Keira simultaneously had the impression that she was exactly in the right place at the right time and with the right people.

Harper lightly pressed her hands against Keira's cheeks and nodded, as if in agreement with Keira's thoughts of right fit. Then Harper settled her head back on the bed and closed her eyes. Keira took three deep breaths, which steadied her heart rate, and leaned over and against Harper's forehead.

When their skin touched, Keira felt an immediate surge of warmth in her forehead. That warmth then began to circulate down her neck and into her core and limbs. It felt like she was a soft cloud stirred and then lifted by a breeze. The sensation brought to mind sunshine and a hug and a mother's nurturing gaze all at once. Keira recognized the force behind these sensory impressions.

It was love. There was no other word for it. She gave into it and let the love spread throughout her being.

CHAPTER 19
PATH OF LIGHT

WITH HER FOREHEAD pressed against Harper's, Keira floated along what appeared to be a pathway of light. The warm sensations continued to circulate through her body. She sensed that she was being guided, rather than forging her own way. It felt good to yield to the flow rather than trying to create or control it.

The path of light gave way to an exhilarating blue sky. Keira soared over the treetops of a forest, inhaling a scent of pine and awakened soil.

Moments later the light returned, whitening her visual field. When it receded, she found herself flying mere feet above the top of the ocean, as dolphins leapt out of the water in a series of graceful arcs. A baby dolphin breached the surface and came within inches of Keira's face, emitting a squeal that sounded almost like laughter.

Then the light enveloped her again. She heard bird songs and the thunderous cascade of plummeting water, and emerged to find herself floating above a giant waterfall. Droplets caught the sun's attention and turned to rainbow hues as she drifted by. The roar quieted, and the all-encompassing light returned.

Keira felt as though she rode a slide downward, upward, and then outward in a free fall that kicked up her adrenaline.

The rush of speed began to slow and slow and slow until her

motion stopped completely. She hung suspended in the light space, awash in white light and buzzing from the exultant experiences, the warmth still flowing through her body.

The white light slowly receded again, giving way to rich colors in her visual field that morphed into recognizable forms. She blinked several times to adjust her sight.

There in front of Keira, about ten feet away, was the bald man.

He sat on a giant lotus leaf, his body wrapped in draping white cloth. He smiled for what seemed like minutes. The top of his head and face glowed with so much light that it was difficult to make out his specific facial features, although Keira would recognize those gleaming teeth from her dreams anywhere.

Below them was a pond covered with lotuses in bloom. The heady fragrance of flowers filled Keira's senses and seemed to drown everything else out. She felt weightless and suspended in time.

Nonetheless, she was slightly nervous. The fantastic visions and sensations gave way to the questions that rarely leave us: Why am I here? What am I doing with my life? What is the point of any of this?

The Light One opened his palms upward as if to say, I understand. He made eye contact with her, holding her gaze softly yet with conviction. She did not yet feel the desire to speak and waited for him to begin.

After a few more moments, his voice interrupted the expectant silence. "Keira, thank you for choosing to join me." He spoke slowly with a deep, calm voice. "It has not been easy trying to reach you!" The Light One laughed heartily, causing his belly to shake. The unexpected levity reminded Keira of Harper. There was something quirky about both of them. But the bald man's entire being emanated kindness, putting her nerves at ease for the most part.

"I know you are wondering why you are here and why I've been trying to tap you. Naturally, you want answers." He exhaled slowly and smiled. "Please know that while I can reveal part of your role to you now, part of it you will have to discover for yourself. And, truthfully, some of it still remains to be figured out. I certainly do not have all the answers. No one does. And therein lies the beauty of unfolding destiny. We can only write so much of the story; some of it writes itself."

She nodded and thought about what he'd just said. Although Keira obviously liked having answers, from her job as a detective she was accustomed to the often frustrating pursuit of figuring out how the pieces fit together as well as what the emerging picture revealed. She cleared her throat. It sounded strange to actually hear her voice in this dreamscape or whatever it was.

"I understand what you're saying," she said, "although I really don't understand any of this on a deeper level. I do know now that I owe you my life for waking me up during the break-in. I wouldn't be here, or Blaise, if you hadn't woken me." She paused and then added, "And thank you as well for getting me to believe in the idea of having agency in my life."

He smiled. "Much of that work was your own intuition, Keira. On the night of the attempted murder, I gave you a little nudge just in case. We Manifestors all look out for each other! There are no debts of gratitude that you or anyone else has to repay. We take more of a philosophical approach to life and only associate with those who choose to voluntarily associate with us. As such, please know that you do not have to fulfill our requests. That choice is entirely up to you, Keira. In fact, you are here with me right now by your own volition. If you hadn't wanted to meet me, your mind would not have opened up the proper channel to allow it."

He pulled a small purple crystal from his robe and cupped it in his right hand. "Catch!" He tossed the crystal through the air to Keira. With what seemed to be through no effort of her own, she caught the crystal in her own two hands. Light roamed up its surface and around its edges, in a never-ending circulating pattern. The crystal was warm to the touch.

"As I'm sure you're realizing," he continued, "this scene around us is not real in the sense that we are not occupying this physical space." He gestured to the pond below and the space between them. "Neither of us is actually floating on air in a physical world. In fact, that crystal is not an object that you'll be able to hold in what we call the real world. It does not have mass or take up space." He adjusted his white cloth around his shoulder.

"It's almost as though we are thought projections as we talk here. It's like seeing a hologram on your time piece, but unfortunately this is not some alternate physical reality that we can inhabit instead. It sure would be nice, though, right?" He laughed. "I love nature, so I conjured up these natural landscapes for us to enjoy together during this meeting. Your perceptions were open enough to take them in."

Keira took a moment to process what he was saying and to realize that although she felt as though she was floating in mid-air, her feet stood firmly on the ground by Harper's temporary bedside. Squirmy was standing near her right now, probably wondering what in the world was happening as her forehead was pressed against Harper's.

It was trippy to contemplate that she was experiencing a flight of fancy—a mind voyage to reach someone. It reminded her of mind touch in that she accessed another person's inner world, but this was a whole other level. It was like sharing utopia with someone. It was creation.

Mind touch didn't foster direct bonding with another person; accessing their memories provided a one-sided perspective. She felt like an investigator when she did mind touch. This experience, however, made her feel part of a vast whole. She exalted in the headiness of it, while also being slightly afraid of what it all meant and where it would all lead.

"Unfortunately," he said, "we cannot be spared from the human experience. For those of us who are Manifestors, we actually access our power by allowing ourselves to be vulnerable—by feeling sadness, joy, and the whole kaleidoscope of human emotion."

He paused and inhaled slowly. "What we cannot be is numb. Numbness cuts off our channels of communication. That's why I could only begin to access you when you feared you had lost Blaise after her abduction. As your heart opened more and more, I could start to reach you." He smiled and gave her time to absorb his meaning.

He continued, "As you all too clearly know, the world sits on the brink. While we collectively struggle to pull ourselves up from such devastating losses, corruption threatens to plunge us backward. Not only has our government pushed the limit of what is considered fair and equal treatment to human beings, but powerful crime syndicates like the Chusei and Russian operatives present dangers just as spine-chilling. At times, as you know, the government gets involved with these organizations to further mutual interests. We need help in figuring out those connections, exposing them, and severing them." He sat up straighter and then leaned forward toward her.

The bald man continued, "We are trying to fight back against the dark inclinations, against the corruption. Sometimes that entails working inside the system and sometimes outside of it. The more people we can enlist to our side, the better the chances that we'll succeed. 'Life, liberty, and the pursuit of happiness' have begun to fade, but they mustn't. Without those beliefs, These United States loses its identity—and its promise to future generations to safeguard the best opportunities we can for them, given our limitations."

He waited, his invitation indirect but obvious. Keira clasped her hands together in her lap. She knew she had gifts to contribute as well as doubts about those gifts. She knew that life was not worth living in numb despair and resignation, grinding on from one day to the next with no real purpose. She'd might as well up the stakes. Perhaps this was the right time, or maybe there was no such thing as the right time. She wanted to give it a chance and said, "I'm prepared to fight the good fight in whatever way I can, given my own limitations."

He smiled, his teeth gleaming. "That makes me happy. I had an intuition that you would!"

She laughed. "I bet you did."

"It's safest to give you instructions on an as-needed basis because what you know can be used against you. People also have a way of subconsciously broadcasting what it is they're trying to hide. So, we'll work in breadcrumbs." He drifted on his lotus leaf closer to Keira until he was only an arm's length away.

His smile radiated pure joy as his eyes changed color from blue to purple to green and then orange. The colors of his pupils kept swirling into a new hue over and over again every second. She couldn't look away.

"You are a guardian of love and truth, Keira. It's not just what you do; it's the value behind it. I suggest you seal those vows with Blaise as soon as possible. I'll send you two a bottle of champagne." He smiled. "I have a weakness for wine, plus access to an old wine cellar! Then I will give you an assignment."

She smiled back at him. "I look forward to that champagne and, more importantly, to getting married. Thank you for wanting to celebrate us."

"My pleasure! My parting words of advice for now: don't fear Cora. She really is going to help you. Also, don't hesitate to ask Squirmy to have your back in more ways than you have already. He's very capable and valuable to you—and to us."

Her mind seemed enveloped in a warm fog. "I know I should ask you a million questions right now, but I can't actually think of one. It's the strangest feeling."

As he smiled serenely, white light emanated from his mouth. "When we are in the moment, we can finally stop questioning. Enjoy the pause while it lasts, my dear Keira, and try to return to this feeling of presence whenever you can."

"Okay. Thank you. I will."

"Very well. Be with the light, and may the light be with you."

In the next moment Keira found herself inches from Harper's face with her hands gripping the metal frame of the makeshift bed.

She turned to see Squirmy wide-eyed, clearly bewildered yet fascinated. He said, "I had no idea I was guarding a national treasure, Kincaid."

CHAPTER 20
BANDS OF GOLD

AT THE OFFICE the next day, a drone delivered a package to Keira's desk. When she opened it, a handwritten card sat atop a bottle of champagne.

Making sure no one was watching, she closed the box and opened the card to read, "Dear Keira, there's no time like the present to declare your love. As promised, the bubbly is enclosed. And in case you don't have any, I've provided two wedding rings that a dear friend once asked me to safeguard when she knew her time was limited. She made me promise to pass the rings on to two individuals who would treasure them as a symbol of their love—a circle, not a line, because love is infinite and boundless. Many blessings to you and Blaise in your days ahead together as one. In kindness, Michael (Only Harper calls me the Light One!)"

Keira was impressed and excited that Michael knew about the old-fashioned ring tradition. Very few people did anymore.

She was also relieved that she didn't have to call Michael the Light One, as that did sound rather pretentious.

Keira reopened the box and moved the packing paper around. At the bottom of the package was a small, purple jewelry box shaped in a heart. Lifting the ceramic top, she found two etched golden bands shimmering inside. They had a subtle swirling pattern engraved into their surfaces. She choked up as she watched the shiny gold catch the light and thought about how beautiful it would be to put one on Blaise's finger.

Squirmy walked in, surprising her. She quickly set the precious contents back in the box. "Supplies from your otherworldly comrades, Keira?" He chuckled. "It's probably best you don't answer that."

"Agreed." She blushed. Although Squirmy hadn't quite wrapped his head around what he'd witnessed yesterday in the room with Harper and later learned from Keira about mind touch, he was being a good sport.

Keira, for that matter, also struggled to come to terms with what her interactions with the Manifestors had meant. Her brain craved a rational explanation that she knew she'd never get. Her gut told her to trust Michael and Harper. She believed that more layers of truth would be unearthed over time that would allow her to dig deeper into what was going on. While she was apprehensive about abiding by Michael's wait-and-see approach because no one craved uncertainty, she accepted his terms.

Squirmy had told her that while her forehead was pressed against Harper's, a resplendent white light had emanated between and around their touching heads. He said it was bright, beautiful, and mesmerizing. He couldn't look away and completely lost track of how much time had passed while it happened.

She didn't believe that light appeared during mind touch based on seeing her mother perform it, so she wondered if it had to do with journeying, in a sense, to Michael. Maybe it was his light that Squirmy saw. There were obviously way more mysteries and questions than answers at this point. Regardless, it was fascinating to get the perspective of someone on the outside looking in.

Keira felt it was important to tell Squirmy about her mind-touch abilities, as there was no way to make sense of what he'd witnessed and heard from Harper without acknowledging them. She was also following Michael's advice to rely on Squirmy more, which started with being forthcoming. As she'd suspected, Squirmy had figured prior to yesterday that she could either perform mind touch or possessed some other surreal gift. She could tell he was intrigued by all of it but was relieved that he didn't bombard her with questions. She was one who liked to open up incrementally after her initial walls-up phase.

Squirmy and Keira found themselves in a bit of a predicament with Wozniak because they couldn't tell him what had happened with Harper. Plus, they needed to protect the Misfits now, even Cora, which made both of them uncomfortable. How could they trust that the person who appeared determined to kill Keira was actually on her side?

Yesterday when they returned to the office, they told Wozniak the raid had been a bust. They said the Misfits had fled the warehouse before they arrived and their whereabouts were unknown. Wozniak had clenched his fist, sworn several times, and asked what they'd been doing all morning then. They said they'd combed the warehouse looking for leads and had followed one clue to another location that also turned out to be a dead end.

He had glared at Squirmy and Keira and then seemed to catch himself. Sighing, he acknowledged, "Even the best lose some battles. Even the best! All right, let's regroup. But I need something promising from you two very soon."

They had given their assurances and quickly turned toward the door before he could ask more questions.

Thinking about that awkward encounter with Wozniak now, Keira said to Squirmy, "We need to come up with something to deliver Wozniak in the next day or two to get him off our asses. Between our disappointing update, the Feds' takeover of the intruder case, and the fading limelight, he's one step away from a full-blown tirade. So, if my trippy friends don't send some magic here shortly, we'll have to find another way to reveal the Chusei's role to him."

Squirmy agreed, but neither of them had any brilliant ideas. They decided to check back with each other later. Squirmy ambled out of the room and headed to the Whiteboard.

Keira sat at her desk thinking about how a person couldn't always get to the truth while trying to face it head on. It was like sailing a boat straight into the wind and ending up motionless or, as sailors called it, in irons. Instead, a boat has to be sailed at angles to the wind, making a zig-zagging approach through tacks and jibes in order to catch the gusts and head, however indirectly, to where the captain wants to go.

Her investigative sails were luffing as she tried to aim right for the answer that would crack the case wide open. She needed to be patient and believe that she would find a new angle. Sometimes she had to give her mind a break, as ideas often filled her sails when she least expected them.

In the meantime, she had mere hours to put together what she decided would be her and Blaise's wedding that evening. She felt in her gut that she should take Michael's advice and marry Blaise while she could. Nothing and no one could be taken for granted, and opportunity was best seized rather than overanalyzed. Today was November 11, 2122, or 11-11-22. Since $11 + 11 = 22$, Keira liked the significance of the date and wanted to seal their bond—and make their individual parts add up to a greater sum.

KEIRA TOLD Blaise that she had a fun surprise for her but left it at that. Based on the work duties she'd been tasked with, Blaise had permission to use a Fed motorbike for the remainder of the day, which was perfect for Keira's seaside wedding plan.

They drove west on the motorbike, with Keira holding tightly to Blaise's slender waist. As they got closer to the ocean, Keira could feel the moisture in the air as she inhaled the salt scents. The sun would be setting soon.

The last few blocks before the beach were comprised of gritty warehouses, mostly abandoned. Seagulls soared overhead, screeching in their cacophonous way that was somehow still pleasant. Keira wondered if the odd pleasantness had to do with the fact that whenever she heard seagulls, she knew the ocean was near.

They parked and walked, holding hands, onto the beach. They headed south for a couple of minutes through the soft sand to the edge of a breakwater, then climbed the rocks to the top of it. At the end of the breakwater, waves thumped against the rocks, sending up spray that cascaded back down with a gentle woosh. The spray wasn't high enough to touch their skin, which could be dangerous, but the surging and retreating water was close enough to connect them to the rhythms of the sea.

Keira removed her satchel and set it on the rocks. Then she pulled Blaise close to her and kissed her lips and cheeks. As Blaise smiled, the breeze pushed her red hair back, while the descending sun imbued her eyes with a golden radiance.

"This is our day, Blaise. If you still feel it's right in your heart, then I want to marry you here tonight, right now."

"I had a feeling that's what this getaway was all about!" Blaise beamed. "There's nothing I could want more, Keira." They drew closer together until their faces were inches apart. "I'll love you forever," Blaise said softly.

"And I will always love you, Blaise. I promise to care for our love, and for you, to the best of my ability."

The wind billowed Blaise's hair around her shoulders and tossed it gently against her cheeks. "I thought about what I might say when this moment came, Keira. I want you to know that I vow to support your needs, to lead with respect, and to nourish our relationship with constant infusions of love. Always with love, always with you."

"Then it's settled!" Keira declared. She pulled the purple, heart-shaped box from her bag and held it up to Blaise. "Take a look inside."

Blaise gingerly removed the top of the box. When she saw the rings, she drew in her breath. The unearthed bands glimmered in the lingering low light of the golden hour.

Blaise held the rings while Keira set the jewelry box back carefully in the bag. Then Keira guided one ring onto Blaise's left ring finger and then watched as Blaise did the same for her.

"With this kiss, I thee wed," Keira officiated with a big smile. As she went to press her lips against rosy-cheeked Blaise's lips, she noticed how Blaise had become even more beautiful in the elements and the joyous moment.

"I thee wed, Keira." Blaise's eyes sparkled with happy tears and the top of her nose crinkled.

As Keira looked at her blushing beloved and ran her fingertips over

Blaise's newly adorned hand, she thought of how lucky they were to have each other.

Blaise also gazed admiringly at Keira and then at their newly bejeweled hands. "Where did you get these gorgeous rings, love?"

Keira told her about Michael's note and the wedding bands. "He also gave us one more gift!" Keira laughed as she grabbed the carefully packed bottle of champagne and presented it to Blaise. "Let's open it together." She set Blaise's hand on the cork and set her own on top of Blaise's. "One, two, three!" They uncorked it together with a loud pop.

Then they stood there grinning as the effervescent champagne bubbled up and over like the love they poured into each other.

KEIRA LAY in bed at the safe house the next morning, stroking Blaise's hair and remembering their wedding toast at sunset as the waves lapped the rocks. Blaise still dozed. Keira admired Blaise's sparkling wedding band on her left hand that gently clutched the pillow. We did it, she thought. We are now married. The thought filled her with warmth and pride.

Her time piece buzzed. With a groan she turned to the bedside table to check it. It was Devon's assistant. Cora was on the move in the van they'd set a tracker on while it was parked at the Empress Hotel. This was the first time it had left the hotel garage. A still from the drone footage showed Cora in the driver's seat headed northeast on the interstate toward Riverside.

Cora clearly wasn't headed for her, which was a relief, but Keira worried about what would happen if the Feds did successfully track and detain her. She had accepted a type of indirect responsibility for protecting Cora, at least until she knew more and could confirm the Manifestors' assertions that Cora was trying to help her.

She ran her fingers through Blaise's silky hair one more time and kissed her forehead. My wife, she thought, and liked the sound of it in her mind.

As Keira made her way into the kitchen for a glass of water, her time piece buzzed again.

She looked down to see Michael's face, which was a surprise. She never gave him her time-piece number, so how did he get it? She figured he had ways of gathering intel through networks in the real world in addition to his other exceptional and inexplicable abilities. Still, she felt a little uncomfortable.

Keira tapped his voice message. "Good morning, Keira, and congratulations on the wedding nuptials! Tying the knot is such sweet fun. I'm sorry I couldn't give you more time to savor being a bride; duty calls at inopportune times. I have a special delivery for you today at 09:30. Please go alone and wait in the lobby of the defunct Mermaid Inn. I know you won't be happy with the way the meeting starts, but please try to keep an open mind. Things aren't always what they appear to be. That's all I can say for now. May the blessings of the universe be upon you!"

She found his warning odd. She wouldn't be happy with the way the meeting starts. What did that mean? Who or what would meet her for the delivery? Keira grew tense but knew there was no point in overanalyzing a vague message. And how did Michael know they'd had the wedding? Her head hurt from all the unanswerable questions, and it was only seven o'clock. She took a deep inhale and steadied herself. No time to honeymoon today apparently!

CHAPTER 21
MERMAIDS MEET

AFTER STOPPING briefly at the police station, Keira made her way toward the Mermaid Inn.

She had told Squirmy about Michael's message in case something went wrong. He had suggested tailing her, but she said no because Michael had requested that she go alone. Squirmy didn't like the sound of it, but he agreed to let her handle the situation solo and asked that she check in with an update as soon as possible.

The self-driving car she'd chosen at the station drove at the speed limit along the surface streets near what had been at one time a military base. The Mermaid Inn for years had served as a seedy hotel on the outskirts of the base that catered to the sexual needs of stationed sailors. Rooms were rented by the hour; few questions were asked.

The base got blown to bits during the war. The government didn't bother cleaning up the mess after the decision was made to move all military bases to new secure locations, often underground, that only officials with security clearance knew the coordinates for. Somehow the inn still stood, spared by bombs but bearing the deep scars of neglect.

Keira parked a block away and cautiously made her way on foot to the inn with its broken windows and discolored stucco. The stained glass mermaid, done in shimmering pieces of turquoise, green, silver, and gold glass, remained. Keira smiled as she thought about the dreamy mermaid, perched above the second floor, still beckoning sailors—and those who'd keep them company—home. Wish me luck, she said silently to her.

She walked up the rickety stairs, watching for wood rot. The front door, which no longer had a knob, was slightly ajar. She slowly pushed it all the way open and stood back in case it was a trap. After several seconds of peering around and listening for footsteps, she cautiously stepped inside. The floor and furnishings were covered in so much dust and debris that the lobby was practically unrecognizable. What kind of delivery was she going to get here? She started to feel on edge.

Her time piece buzzed. It was a security update from Devon's assistant. Cora's location was unknown. A 3D mannequin of her was found in the van apprehended by the Feds. She was considered on the loose and could be armed and dangerous.

Keira felt a sharp jab in her right arm and looked up to see a small figure in dark clothes one story above her.

Cora? In her peripheral vision, Keira caught the outline of a needle sticking out of her upper arm before everything went black.

KEIRA CAME TO IN A CHAIR, her vision fuzzy at first and then clearing with multiple blinks. Her hands and legs were bound. A gag in her mouth made it hard to breathe. The small, windowless room was dimly lit. Another chair, empty, faced her. Shelving racks on both sides contained dusty boxes and partially used cleaning materials. If she was indeed still at the Mermaid Inn and hadn't been transported to a different location, she figured this was a supply closet.

She tried to get her bearings and review what she knew. All she could remember was receiving the update on her time piece about Cora's ruse, then feeling a jabbing pain in her arm, seeing the dark figure, and realizing it was probably Cora.

Tranquilizing and binding someone to a chair didn't exactly translate into "I'm here to help." She questioned whether she'd walked straight into a trap like a full-blown idiot. But she remembered

Michael's message when he'd said, "I know you won't be happy with the way the meeting starts, but please try to keep an open mind. Things aren't always what they appear to be."

She definitely wasn't happy with the way this one had started. Although she began to wonder whether she'd been duped by the Manifestors, she decided to keep an open mind and be ready for anything, including confirmation that she'd been a fool to trust a man in the clouds.

As if on cue to reveal what was going on, Cora opened the door. She wore loose black clothes and stepped lightly. As she sat down, she pushed the hood off her head and looked at Keira with neither disdain nor sympathy. She had coarse black hair down to her shoulders and attractive brown eyes that appeared to be calculating her next move. She was beautiful but, like Harper, seemingly unaware of her looks. It appeared as though Cora had other things on her mind.

Cora crossed her right foot to her left knee and placed her hands in her lap. There was something very purposeful, but also painfully shy, about her.

She rubbed her forehead and spoke quietly. "I was just wondering how many people I've killed, or left to be killed by someone else. I've lost count. Even some of their faces are now unclear. Most were dirtbags. Some were not. But all their deaths took a toll on me. Love counteracts the spirit's decay, as do good deeds. Yet there is always that shadow crossing the heart, eclipsing the light."

She looked down at her feet and then up at Keira, who read resignation in Cora's expression.

"Michael and Harper hold high hopes for you, Keira. I have no supernatural power, no heightened ability to manifest outcomes, but I do read people well. I believe wholeheartedly in them and what they're trying to do. By extension, I support the mission of protecting you and providing you with the intel you need."

Keira began to feel more assured that Michael was indeed in her corner. Nonetheless, she didn't plan to let her guard all the way down. Still gagged and unable to speak, she nodded at Cora.

Cora pulled a brown wig from her bag and put it snugly on Keira's head. After adjusting the wig slightly, seeming to want to get it just so,

Cora took a photo of Keira. "I need something to show for my efforts. We want Victor to believe that I have you captive." She paused. "But this gets complicated because I'm also going to need for him to believe that I killed you." Cora grabbed an aluminum can from the shelf and stepped behind Keira. Keira couldn't see what she was doing but smelled paint. This was getting weird.

Cora stepped in front of Keira. Using an old paintbrush, she then quickly painted what looked like a jagged circle on Keira's shirt in the center of her chest. "With the low light and low photo quality, this will look enough like blood," Cora said. "Sorry, but I'm going to have to splay you in the paint on the floor. Your hair will be okay under the wig, but you'll want to throw these clothes away. Here we go. Try not to move."

Before Keira could utter a sound, Cora tipped the chair back slowly until Keira was all the way pressed against the floor. Cora gently pressed Keira's face to the side and adjusted her shoulders and knees. "There. Good as dead." She took another photo, checked it, and appeared satisfied. Then she lifted Keira back into an upright position in the chair. "I'm going to take that gag out now and untie your feet. No offense, but I'd rather keep your arms bound in case you aren't as trustworthy as Michael says you are."

Fair enough, Keira thought, as Cora pushed the wig off her head and removed the gag. Keira inhaled thirstily, craving the unobstructed flow of air. She had started to feel lightheaded; the paint smell wasn't helping. When Cora untied her feet, Keira rolled her ankles around and lifted her legs to the front and side to try to get the blood flowing. A simple "thank you" was all she could manage. She felt nervous around Cora and unsure of what to say.

"This ruse will only buy so much time," Cora said, sitting back down across from Keira and leaning forward onto her knees. "Victor will find out you're alive and will come after me and you. I have ways of protecting myself, but they are limited, especially against the Chusei, whose resources are vast and unrelenting. You, I suppose, will have to take Victor down before he can get to you."

Keira puzzled over where this was going.

Cora continued, "I did the actual kidnapping of the O'Connor boy as the indentured servant I am to the Chusei, but I'm sure you figured out that Victor was the one who ordered it. However, I don't believe you're aware of the much bigger fish that he and the Chusei are working for. Brace yourself for this one: Victor has been doing dirty dealings with the Russians to shield President Miller, who's really behind it all. In return, Victor and the Chusei get weapons, government backing, and power."

Keira was dumbfounded. "You're telling me that Victor is the go-between for the president—our president—on shady deals with Russia? Why is our government selling Green-Y to the Russians if it could potentially help Russia increase its arms supply?"

Cora exhaled. "That part I have no idea about. I got lucky, if you could call it that, in finding the link to Miller. I suspect that very few members of the Chusei—and certainly only the higher-ups—know about Victor being a front man for Miller. I just happened to overhear and see some things not intended for me."

She paused, seeming to carefully weigh her next words. "Look, if you can get Victor, you might get enough clues to expose Miller for the scoundrel he is, but that's a long shot. Miller has the means to cover his tracks and knows how to hire fall guys like Victor, who in turn hire fall guys like O'Connor. They're like a line of dominos. When one goes down, he knocks the next one down, who then knocks the next one down. Maybe they'll all tumble, but I doubt it because there are many forces working hard to make sure that one fall doesn't topple the whole twisted kingdom."

Cora stood up and moved her chair against the wall, appearing antsy. "We both need to get going to take advantage of the borrowed time. Here's what I can tell you. A law enforcement mole who was sending your whereabouts to the Chusei, in addition to the tracker that was put on your shoe, was killed last week in the line of duty. I don't think you knew him. His name was David Smothers."

Keira didn't recognize the name.

"However, a computer program the Chusei recently embedded in your department's tracking system is also relaying information about you. Brandon, the young Chusei you've seen me with, is working on deactivating that program. He should have that finished by the end of today. In the meantime, don't log in or out of the Blue Finder for search requests or walk in or out of the police building today, as that also tracks you. Plus, keep in mind that Victor thinks you're dead. Assume all's fine by tomorrow morning as far as that hack is concerned. I'll get word to you if it isn't."

Keira sat there, feeling bewildered and wanting things to slow down but knowing they couldn't and wouldn't.

Cora cut off Keira's hand restraints with a sharp hunting knife. Then she handed Keira a large envelope stuffed full with papers. "That's a dossier of sorts on Victor. I'll leave it up to you to figure out the next steps with him, but here's one helpful tidbit before I go: Every single day at 07:30 he walks out of his house to feed his koi fish in the pond in the backyard. He likes to do this alone and doesn't have a security guard at his side, although one stands near the sliding doors keeping watch."

Cora stopped talking and looked at Keira, seeming to size her up or reconsider her in some way. Cora sighed and tapped Keira on the side of the knee. "You've got this. Good luck. Unfortunately, it's time for both of us to get back to our respective rat races."

Before Keira had a chance to respond or ask a question, Cora was out the door. Man, she's quick, Keira thought.

She stood up and turned around to see the imprint of the chair and her body on the red paint below her. Seeing her own death, however fake it seemed from this perspective—a trickery of props and staging, still gave her the chills. She touched her wedding band and twisted it slightly, reminding herself that she was alive and in love and married.

Holy fuck, she thought. How did I get involved with such deep corruption that ran all the way to the White House? Her mind reeled with the morning's revelations. She questioned her reality. How could this be true? Why was she involved?

She called Squirmy on his personal line.

"What's happening, Keira?"

"Dang, what isn't?"

"Are you all right?"

She sighed loudly. "Yep, but this is a bigger shit show than we'd ever imagined, if what I've been told is the truth. Can you meet me at the old Navy Yard on the northeast corner? Don't tell Wozniak where you're going. Please bring me a full uniform from the station—and caffeine."

"Roger that, Kincaid. I'll be there in fifteen."

She ended the call and told herself to put one foot in front of the other. It would all come together, or it wouldn't. But she knew that nothing good at this point would come from standing still.

CHAPTER 22
KOI FISH

TWO DAYS LATER, Keira and Squirmy crouched down at the edge of Victor's yard.

From their surveillance mission the previous day, they knew where the security guard waited and that Victor, who had stood dressed in a black silk bathrobe, took about ten minutes to feed and watch his koi fish. It was clearly a meditative moment for him to spend by himself in the morning and a time when his security guard appeared bored and distracted.

They didn't have a warrant for Victor's arrest because all their intel was received from uncorroborated sources. The dossier Cora provided hinted at connections to the kidnapping and the Russians without proving any of them. They still had little of concrete value to base their investigation on.

Keira and Squirmy wore full face masks and glasses that shielded their eyes from recognition software. They wouldn't have the time or means to drag Victor offsite, especially since they hadn't even told Wozniak of their operation, so everything was going to have to go according to plan or, if the plan took a turn toward chaos, be aborted as carefully as possible.

From the dossier, Keira and Squirmy had discovered to their dismay that Victor was an active, generous donor to various law-enforcement groups. He was also the president of a nonprofit organization that provided quality health care to low-income families. While it's possible that Victor had a heart of gold underneath his cold-blooded criminal façade, Keira and Squirmy saw his philanthropic activities as buffers.

They didn't even bother telling Wozniak that they were investigating Victor Watanabe, after they learned of his last name from Cora's files, because a quick search would have Wozniak wondering if they were crazy. Any gaffe in trying to link Victor to the O'Connor kidnapping would be an internal and public-relations nightmare.

And, interestingly, although Victor Watanabe was a known associate of the Chusei, nothing in official law-enforcement logs revealed him to be the kingpin he was. Thomas Saito and Kenichi Yamamoto were the identified heads of the Chusei, from whom all commands came down. Victor seemed by design to fly under the radar and simultaneously maintain a stellar public appearance. It was starting to make more sense how he could work with Miller rather seamlessly. You can't really pin crimes on a person who can't be pinned down.

There was a slight chill to the morning's air and a dryness to it that made Keira's nostrils itch. It was 07:25. Squirmy sat on his haunches next to Keira behind a low retaining wall. They had hiked a couple of miles across barren preservation land to try to approach Victor's property unnoticed. Keira was surprised that he didn't have higher walls, but some people believed that high fences just made would-be burglars more intrigued.

Although they'd identified the kind of security system he had and where its cameras were set up based on registration records filed with the police, which many insurance companies required for theft claims, they both knew he likely had a second system installed by a black-market vendor. That was common practice for criminals. Keira was concerned about how much time they had before a second system could detect and perhaps attack them. As for the first system, they'd identified one blind spot in the camera angles, which was why they crouched where they did.

They knew that once they moved from their position to subdue the guard that they could be spotted. From their surveillance they expected that one other security guard on the property might swarm them. Other than that, it was anyone's guess.

Squirmy hadn't wanted to proceed, but he gave in to Keira's resolve.

Although she'd worried about how to move forward with the investigation given the strange new revelations and the deep repercussions for national security that might be at stake if Cora's assertions were true, Keira had also reminded herself that she needed to take the next step and see where it led. Besides, the clock was ticking. Soon Victor would know that Keira was alive and that Cora had deceived him. They had a window of opportunity created by deception.

Yesterday she had pictured performing mind touch on Victor and having an aha moment from mining his memories. She began to believe more and more that mind touch was the next step she had to take.

At first Squirmy had looked at her with skepticism. "You want us to risk our lives because you have a hunch that his memories will serve up something useful? We might become memories ourselves, Kincaid."

"That's true," she had acknowledged. "It's not an amazing idea, and it definitely puts us both in danger. I don't know why exactly I see it and believe it, or why I'm not coming up with other ideas. Do you have anything better?"

Squirmy had suggested tailing Victor and waiting for a more opportune moment, but as they fleshed it out, it seemed unlikely they'd ever find Victor unattended by a huge, tough bodyguard or in a place where it wouldn't create a scene to approach him.

So here they were, fumbling along in the detective's dark, as Squirmy called it. But as he'd said yesterday, "Whatever, Kincaid. We may be on to something big here, something worth taking a risk for. If you believe it, I'm in. What the hell else am I going to do anyway— scratch my balls and make excuses to Wozniak?"

The bodyguard and Victor emerged from an arched walkway about thirty feet from Keira and Squirmy. The bodyguard stopped and stood with his back to them as Victor continued toward the koi pond, dressed once again in a black silk robe. He was lean and walked with calm purpose.

Keira gave Squirmy the nod to start.

Squirmy pulled a night-night from his vest, pulled the top off, and tossed it gently toward the guard. It hit the dirt slope and rolled down to the edge of the patio and stopped. Keira slowly counted to fifteen. She expected the guard to get woozy from the gas but not lose consciousness yet. Keira and Squirmy stayed low and quietly stepped over the retaining wall. Then they moved quickly while crouched down, attempting to make as little noise as possible.

The guard's legs began to buckle. Squirmy grabbed him from behind as the guard went completely lights out. Squirmy supported the man's bulking frame with his own body as Keira grabbed the guard's gun from his belt. Squirmy set him down without a sound or struggle. So far so good.

They nodded at each other and began to move steadily toward Victor while staying low to the ground. All was going well.

They were about twenty feet from Victor when Keira heard a cracking noise to her side. Squirmy must have stepped on something. Damn!

Victor turned around.

Seeing them approach, he dropped the bag of fish food and reached into his right waist pocket. Keira sprinted toward him. Just as he pulled a pistol from his pocket, she tackled him. The gun fell onto the raked sand surrounding the pond with a soft thud.

Victor groaned loudly on his back. Squirmy put a gag into his mouth and kept him still with a head lock. Keira pressed Victor's chest down with her right arm as he thrashed around.

He glared at her unafraid. She knew he couldn't see her eyes through her security glasses, but she figured Victor knew who she was. There would be no time for formal introductions. She ziptied his hands and then pressed her forehead against his. His body went slack.

Immediately she saw herself walking to work. It was creepy to see her own image in someone's memory. Suddenly the view of her was zoomed in, with her profile in full view as she tucked a strand of hair behind her ear. Clearly, he had either been watching her through drone footage or binoculars. In the memory she lined up at a Jolt shop for a dose of caffeine and checked her time piece. Just as she started to realize from the outfit she was wearing that the memory was probably from last week, the scene shifted.

She now saw in Victor's mind's eye a pretty young girl who smiled as she poured tea for what looked like stuffed animals seated around a table. The little girl looked up at Victor and said excitedly, "Daddy, we're starting the tea party!" Her long brown hair hung past her shoulders, and her teeth looked like those of a five-year-old: cute despite their odd angles and gaps. In the dossier, there was no record of Victor having a child. That memory faded from view.

In the next one, Stephen O'Connor sat several feet away on a couch. He nervously held a drink in his right hand and twitched his nose. Keira saw a folder open; from the perspective it was clear that Victor was holding it and examining its contents. A picture of a familiar man appeared in Victor's hand. The man sat in front of a row of computers, an intense expression of focus apparent on his face. It was Spyder, Keira realized. The next picture showed Spyder standing on the metro zoning out.

O'Connor said, "He will be dealt with. We know he's been the intel engine driving Go Slow. Our mutual friend is losing patience with them but doesn't know the solution we have in mind."

"Very well," Victor said. "Leave no trace. The hacker probably has breadcrumbs tied to everything he does."

"I'll create reports to make a convincing case that he's a threat to national security. Agents will take care of him," O'Connor replied.

In the next memory, a woman struggled against the restraints that bound her in a chair. Two Chusei guards stood next to her. The woman's hair covered her face as she fought against all odds to break free.

When Victor got closer, the woman tossed her head back and looked up. As her hair dropped away revealing her face, Keira recognized her. It was Catherine Strauss, Stephen O'Connor's wife.

"Ms. Strauss, I am sorry it had to come to this, but I promise you that we will find a good home for your son. He will always be well taken care of, I assure you."

Tears began to fill her eyes. She whimpered, pleading for her own life and the freedom to continue raising her precious child.

Victor continued, "I'm going to blindfold you, Ms. Strauss, and give you a couple of minutes to pray and prepare yourself for the life beyond this one. May the blessings of the universe be upon you. May you have the courage to embark on the next part of your sacred journey."

Victor moved his arms in an X pattern in front of his chest. He must be an Endower, Keira realized. The Endowers believed in reincarnation, karma, and a spirit world where souls waited for their next role in a wheel of existence without beginning or end. One of their signature prayers was an X across the chest that symbolized the end of the current life but the infinity of lives that both preceded this one and awaited the person moving forward.

A guard handed Victor a blindfold. He tied it around the trembling head of Ms. Strauss. The other guard, after Victor's instructions, lit cedar incense that the Endowers believed helped the spirit world locate and receive a new soul.

"We have to go! NOW!" Keira felt hands on her back, pulling her to her feet. At the same time, she heard a whirl and a bullet exploding. Squirmy shouted, "We gotta run! The drones are on us."

Keira looked up and saw three drones in formation above them. She put her hand on her gun and began to run toward the preservation land. Bullets sprayed sand up around them. Squirmy and Keira knew to run in a random zig-zag pattern that threw off the drones' aim. But the strategy wouldn't last for long.

They cleared the retaining wall and then hunkered down behind it. Keira immediately took aim at one drone and fired. She hit it. It began to fall, peppering the air with bullets for a couple of seconds before it went dead. As she aimed at the second drone, a bullet struck Squirmy in the arm.

"Fuck!" he yelled and sank down to the ground.

She steadied her aim, knowing they had very little time before the drones closed in and finished them off. She had to hope that Squirmy could hang on in the meantime.

Keira pulled the trigger and hit the second drone. As the third one began to swoop toward them and prepare to take them both out from point-blank range, she grabbed a decoy from her weapons vest and whirled it 90 degrees away from her. The drone immediately switched course and followed the decoy.

Her pulse pounding in her ears, she looked up to see Victor running into the house, his hands ziptied in front of him, yelling to a body guard. Keira grabbed a tourniquet from her vest and quickly wrapped it around Squirmy's arm. "You got this. Stay with me," she said to him as he clenched his teeth in pain and appeared to be fading.

A huge security guard came running out of the house and turned toward them wielding a machine gun. She pushed Squirmy down lower and quickly shot at the man's knees and then his chest. She hit his right knee as he started to press the trigger. That threw his aim off just enough to send the bullets flying about twenty feet away from them. He fell, and she shot several more rounds at him.

Without waiting to see if the guard was alive or dead, she helped Squirmy to his feet and they began to scurry away. When they were at least fifty yards from Victor's house and shielded by the slope of a hill, Keira called in an emergency chopper landing. She didn't think they'd make it out alive in a vehicle. More drones could await them or perhaps live body guards. Once they were up in government airspace and protected by its missile systems, it would be very hard for any Chusei weapons to strike them.

She heard a low whir and looked up to see a drone rapidly approaching. She fired and missed when it veered. It closed in on them and fired. Keira hit the ground and brought Squirmy down with her. He groaned loudly upon impact. She immediately pointed her gun upward again and squeezed the trigger. The drone dropped in a free fall toward the parched earth. She scanned the sky for more drones but didn't see any.

A buzz on her time piece alerted her to the chopper's planned landing coordinates. They needed to get about a quarter mile east of their current location.

She helped Squirmy to his feet. He was fading fast. She pulled her pill packet from her weapons vest and quickly sorted through the pills until she found the orange ones. Adrenaline. She put two in Squirmy's mouth and told him to chew. His face had become almost completely drained of color. Blood covered his right arm, but the tourniquet had stemmed the bleeding.

"We need to move, Charlie. You can do this. The adrenaline will power you through until the chopper arrives." He winced as she helped him to his feet, and they began to walk as quickly as he could muster while she supported some of his weight.

There was a soft thump behind her. Keira turned her head to see a guard closing in on them, a sword raised above his shoulders. She set Squirmy down awkwardly with a thud and prepared to fight.

The man swung the sword toward her thighs, but she dropped to the ground and scrambled away.

She reached for her gun and realized it wasn't in her holster. He swung the sword at her head. Keira ducked, barely missing the decapitating blow. Then she pounced forward at the man, hitting him at the knees and causing him to fall backward. As she wondered whether he still held the sword, knowing it could slice through her neck or other soft parts at any moment, she heard a shot fired.

The guard's body went limp. Keira looked up to see that a bullet had struck him through the temple.

She looked over at Squirmy, who held a gun in his left hand. A righty, Squirmy had somehow managed to shoot the guard with his non-dominant hand.

"Dang, Squirmy. If I knew you could shoot so well with an adrenaline boost, I'd put one in your goo pack each morning."

He smiled and then began to pass out.

She ran over to him and strained to pick him up. He was mostly dead weight at this point. She put his arm over her shoulders and hoisted him up by the hips. She felt the strength course through her body from her own natural adrenaline as she carried him toward the landing location. The intensity of the task drowned out all other thoughts and sensations.

Out of breath but still feeling powered by her body's physical response to threat, Keira felt tremendous relief when she saw the chopper overhead and watched as it descended on the predetermined site.

Just as she loaded Squirmy and herself into the chopper and closed the door, she heard bullets pelting the exterior. Luckily, the helicopter was practically bulletproof. The pilotless chopper began to ascend, rising to the tune of bullet fire against metal. Squirmy was barely conscious.

The helicopter followed her command to fly to the closest government hospital. She stroked Squirmy's hair and told him, "You're going to make it. I give you my word."

CHAPTER 23
CHECKING THE VITALS

WHILE SQUIRMY WAS BEING CARED for at the government hospital, Keira stepped out of his hospital room to contact Wozniak.

She had to come clean to a certain extent to Wozniak because Squirmy required government medical care, which of course was going to raise questions about why and how the incident occurred.

Wozniak was furious to hear about their unauthorized investigation.

"His blood is on your hands, Kincaid! What the hell were you thinking?" On her time piece she watched Wozniak's face turn red with rage. "And Victor Watanabe? Are you on drugs? He's one of our biggest donors. What a goddamn disgrace!" He banged both hands on his desk.

"We had full face masks on. I don't believe he got a positive ID on us," Keira stated matter-of-factly. The first part was true. The second part probably wasn't, but she couldn't afford to have Wozniak overreact and kick off a worse chain of events than was already in motion.

Wozniak went through a panoply of cusses and frustrated facial expressions. Keira thought, this is going swimmingly.

He closed his eyes and stopped talking. Opening them he said, "I need to let my blood pressure drop. I think you're going to give me a stroke." After a few seconds, he calmed down enough to speak directly to her again. "You're not going to breathe a word of this fiasco, Kincaid, to anyone until we we can confirm whether or not Mr. Watanabe knows you're behind it. Stay at the hospital and keep me in the loop on how Squirmy is doing. And for God's sake, don't even try to get any other crackpot detective work going. I don't know what is up with you lately, but you're skating on thin ice."

She nodded. "Yes, sir" was all she could muster and all she felt the moment deserved. He hung up.

At least he didn't pull her off the case, she thought. Maybe he couldn't think straight enough at the moment to make that call, or maybe he did find it convincing that Victor Watanabe was instrumental in the O'Connor kidnapping. It wasn't unheard of for police to collect money with one hand and provide a pass on the other. There weren't too many donors who didn't want favors repaid in kind. She had left out the alleged Miller connection for now because she knew it would make her sound like an out-of-touch conspiracy theorist.

A female nurse was leaving Squirmy's room as Keira approached it. The nurse said she was in a hurry to attend to another patient, but she told Keira that he was stable and expected to fully recover.

Keira stepped into the room to find him fast asleep and breathing loudly in a low snore. She walked to his bedside, squeezed his hand, and watched his chest rise and fall. It felt comforting to see signs of life in him.

She was still trying to wrap her head around the day's events and couldn't find enough clarity yet as to whether she had been foolish and, if so, had subjected her partner to harm unnecessarily, or whether Squirmy's injury was just an unfortunate consequence of good detective work that organically can go bad.

"I'm sorry, Charlie, to have put you in the line of fire," she said in a quiet voice. She squeezed his hand again and watched him breathe.

She felt her physical strength giving way and tears forming in her eyes. She fought back a desire to just crumble on the floor and let the overwhelm wash over her. Toughen up and focus, she told herself. There is no time to process this in full right now. You have to just keep going. She silently thanked the universe that Squirmy would be okay and asked for courage to move forward with the case.

Then she stepped out into the hallway and found an empty call booth where she contacted Blaise through her time piece.

"What happened, love? Are you okay?"

Keira gave Blaise a quick version of what had transpired and where she was. "I don't have time to rehash much of what's gone down, but I was wondering if I could ask you for a favor."

"Of course." Keira could tell that Blaise was worried and wanted her to pump the brakes. She hadn't been supportive of Keira's plan for directly approaching Victor anyway. But both of them knew that some investigations required bold steps that could backfire.

Keira explained what she'd seen related to Ms. Strauss' abduction and probable killing. She asked Blaise to check on Liam and to see if there were any signs at Strauss' home of a struggle.

Keira watched as a male nurse entered Squirmy's room. She hoped to catch him to ask more about Squirmy's condition and release plan.

Blaise said she'd jump on it. "I love you. Be safe."

Safe was relative, Keira thought, but she assured Blaise that she would be.

Keira walked back toward Squirmy's room wondering what move to make next while avoiding Wozniak's wrath and Victor's radar.

When she opened the door, she found the male nurse pressing a pillow down on Squirmy's face as Squirmy's body struggled against the suffocation attempt.

The man looked up at Keira.

"You bastard!" She pulled her baton from her waist belt and swung it at his knees as he lunged at her with his bare, powerful hands. She heard the baton strike his knee cap. He yelled in pain and doubled over. As he tried to rise, she used a backhand motion to clock him with the baton against his chin. He fell back and stayed down, the fight knocked out of him. She rolled him over and cuffed his hands behind his back.

Then she hopped up to check on Squirmy. She pulled the pillow off his face. His eyes were open as he groaned. "Nod if you're okay, Squirmy." He nodded. She pressed her hand against his neck and felt his pulse racing. "I'm going to get real medical personnel in here to check on you." He nodded again, his expression stuck between shock and relief.

The man on the floor moaned in pain. Keira dragged him a few feet to a heavy shelving unit and ziptied his hands to its base. If he pulled it down it would just crash on him. It was the best option available in the room. She pulled his shirt to the side to see his left shoulder. Sure enough, he had the Chusei raven tattoo.

Then Keira opened the door and flagged down the first doctor she saw. After telling him what had happened, the doctor requested security through the hospital's alert system and then approached Squirmy's bedside to check on him.

A beefy security guard arrived within a minute, the surprise apparent on his face that the woman in front of him had subdued the much bigger man on the floor. "Does he work here?" Keira asked.

"I've never seen him before, Officer," the guard said. He reached down to scan the man's ID badge. The search produced no results. "This must be a counterfeit badge. I have no idea how he got in here and where he got these scrubs."

Keira was impatient. "How about you start to look into that? In the meantime, please send a guard to watch this room. Where there's one assailant, there can always be two."

The man's eyes widened. "Yes, Officer," he replied and left.

Meanwhile the clearly flustered doctor attended to Squirmy, checking his vitals and adjusting the IV.

Keira then called Wozniak and asked him to send at least two officers: one to run prints and process the arrest and one to protect Squirmy. She didn't exactly trust the sophistication of the security force in this hospital, which was ridiculous given it treated police officers and other government workers.

Wozniak didn't hesitate or badger Keira. At least he could be reliable in urgent situations.

The assailant started to thrash around on the floor. He cursed loudly at Keira, which caused the startled doctor to drop his instrument tray. She wanted the doctor to be calm enough to tend to Squirmy, so as the nervous doctor bent over to pick up the instruments, Keira removed from her weapons vest a syringe containing sedative and jabbed it into the assailant's arm.

Moments later instead of losing consciousness quietly as expected, the man began to convulse. What a day this was, she thought. "Doc, it looks like he's having an allergic reaction to the sedative," she said. "Can you stabilize him? I am so sorry about all this." She wanted the perpetrator alive for questioning.

The poor doctor began attending to the would-be assassin and paged for a nurse to bring a reversal drug.

As Keira watched them stabilize the arrested man, Blaise sent her an encrypted message asking her to meet in person when she was able. Blaise conveyed it was urgent and about Ms. Strauss.

Keira replied that she'd run into a stumbling block at the hospital but would meet as soon as she was able.

Shortly after sending that message, reinforcements from Keira's department, twins Mitch and Mikey, arrived.

Mitch ran the man's prints and then showed the results to Keira on his screen. Tony de la Cruz, age 34. He had a mile-long rap sheet for petty crimes and armed robberies. He'd served three short jail sentences.

"When he's healthy enough to transport," Keira told Mitch, "please interrogate him in the station and try to find out who hired him and how he was able to get past security with his fake badge." In a low voice so that the doctor and nurse wouldn't hear, Keira said to cut him a deal on his next jail sentence if they had to. She wanted desperately to find a tangible link to a Chusei higher-up like Victor so that she could finally make an arrest that mattered to the investigation.

Squirmy was asleep. She squeezed his hand and told Mitch and Mikey to keep her apprised of any developments. They nodded and returned to their duties. She hoped they wouldn't mention to Wozniak that she'd left. Although she was concerned about leaving Squirmy's side, she felt like she needed to get back into the world to get her finger on the pulse of the case.

∾

SHE MET Blaise a few blocks from the hospital in an unmarked Fed vehicle. When Keira closed the passenger door, Blaise reached for her and pulled her into a tight embrace. Blaise kissed the top of Keira's head. "Your work on this case keeps making me so nervous."

"I know. I get it. It feels like I'm never ahead of this one. It's not exactly calming to play a game of high-stakes catchup, but I'm being careful, babe. I really am." She sighed thinking how the days since getting married certainly weren't giving them time or energy to celebrate.

Blaise sat back and almost studied Keira. Keira got the impression that Blaise was concerned about her in a different way, as though Keira was not all there mentally.

"What's that look about?" Keira asked in irritation.

Blaise seemed hesitant. "I went to check on Ms. Strauss, love. She was alive and doing chores while Liam napped in his cradle. Other than seeming rather dull in her demeanor—maybe she's depressed or exhausted—nothing appeared out of the ordinary with her."

Keira was taken aback. Could mind touch retrieve fragments of imagination? Was it possible that she could access people's dreams, nightmares, or fantasies—not just their memories? It didn't seem like that had happened to her before.

She mulled over the news about Ms. Strauss. It didn't sit well with her. It just didn't. "I'd like to see her for myself," Keira said.

Blaise appeared about to say something but stopped, perhaps picking up on Keira's resoluteness. "Okay. Sure. Let's go."

Blaise plugged in the coordinates, and the car started its journey. Keira stared out the window at the tall skyscrapers passing by like an impressionist's painting of glass reflecting crowds and clouds. The low and the high, mixing and transcending.

When they got close to Ms. Strauss' home, Keira asked Blaise to park a block away. Then Keira programmed and sent over a bumblebee drone, as she couldn't justify another official visit to Ms. Strauss' home. Wozniak would lose it and think she'd lost her mind. Maybe she had with all this craziness about the Manifestors and Miller.

Perhaps this was all some sort of crackpot conspiracy theory cooked up by wacky individuals that she had believed in her stress-addled brain. Maybe she was getting psychologically rundown and paranoid, allowing people to mess with her. But that didn't ring true to her. In her gut she felt she was aligned with a real, not imagined, purpose. However, she needed proof.

The bumblebee located Ms. Strauss from outside the building and began to transmit the live video recording to Keira and Blaise. The drone was then able to get in the home through an open window. They could now see Ms. Strauss' every movement from close range as they watched the footage together on the dash screen.

Keira started thinking that she really had been led astray by a false memory as she watched Ms. Strauss rhythmically mop the floor. But Ms. Strauss' mopping pace was so incredibly consistent that it started to seem strange. Keira wanted to keep watching to figure out why the woman's physical movements appeared off to her.

Ms. Strauss then walked into Liam's room, where he cried in his cradle. She picked him up and set him effortlessly on the changing table. While he wiggled around, she changed his diaper like it was the easiest thing in the world.

Keira had an impression of something not being quite right, but she couldn't put her finger on what it was. Had Ms. Strauss been drugged? The woman looked exactly how Keira remembered her, but there was a robotic aspect to her movements. She was efficient but lifeless.

They watched for another five minutes. Keira could sense Blaise getting antsy, but Keira needed to see more. This was just too weird and required an explanation.

After preparing what looked like baby formula in the kitchen, Ms. Strauss entered O'Connor's office. She reclined on the floor and turned on her side with her back to the wall. It seemed like an extremely odd thing to do. Then she reached behind her and inserted what appeared to be an electronics cord into the back of her head.

Her eyes opened wide and never blinked.

"Holy shit," Blaise said.

"Exactly," Keira muttered. "Exactly."

CHAPTER 24
A HEAVY HAND

IN ALL HER years working for the force and in all her research, Keira had never heard of criminals covering up a homicide with a replicant. To create a true-to-life replica of a person and then set it to carry on that person's life duties, including caring for a child, was both profoundly disturbing and game changing.

Was Ms. Strauss one of the first ones, or had this been going on for some time unbeknownst to law enforcement? Who was manufacturing and programming these replicants, and how instrumental were the Chusei in the process? The Chusei obviously had the means to acquire one, as evidenced by Ms. Strauss' replicant, but their involvement beyond that would need to be investigated.

People lived increasingly in isolation, making the ruse more viable than would seem reasonable at first thought, Keira figured. It did not appear that Ms. Strauss had many friends. Beyond Liam, she had only one living relative. Who would be around her long enough to suspect that something was wrong—that she was not the person, or a person, that she appeared to be? Keira got chills thinking about it.

Keira remembered a conversation she'd had with her mom about how the country had experienced waves of social isolation followed by waves of social cohesion. There was a coronavirus pandemic about a century ago, for example, that resulted in people working and attending school from home, wearing masks whenever they left their houses, and keeping their distance from others in public. It led to a collapse in social norms and social graces. Partisan politics became more divisive. Murder and road rage increased. Inflation soared as too many people chased too few goods, from cars to baby formula.

Americans increasingly saw their fellow man, especially if he held different political views than they did, as an enemy. Some people thought the government had gone too far in restricting individual freedoms in order to fight the virus' spread, while others thought it didn't do enough. The two things everyone had in common were agitation and unhappiness.

Keira's mom had explained to her how researchers believed that it took years from viral endemicity for people to start treating each other better on a societal level and coming back together as a country. Part of that stemmed from a decline in popularity of social-media platforms and a reintegration of people back to physical workplaces. People decided they wanted to spend less time on their phones and more time in nature and in the company of others.

But decades later, tech replaced many human-filled jobs, kicking off a new era of displacement, anger, and isolation. Income inequalities widened, while deaths of despair soared. That led to the Human-Centered Revolution, ushering in a turbulent transition followed by years of universal income and other measures intended to keep all people afloat. The period had its ups and downs but ultimately paved the way for a conservative backlash with an attempted return to what some considered traditional values. Critics called that brief movement the Stepford Wives Reversion. From there, of course, more societal upheaval and solidarity ensued.

Rises and falls. Change and repetition. Push and pull. Disease, war, distrust, triumph, unity. It was all there in the rearview mirror for anyone who cared to look. Keira wished she lived in a time of relative social cohesion, but she knew the current isolation, if history could serve as precedent, would not last forever.

She was in her office at the station combing through files. Knowing that Victor would be looking for her, she tried to limit her movements outside the office and take extra precautions. It was nerve-racking expecting a drone or person to attack at any moment. She felt on edge.

The assailant who tried to take out Squirmy at the hospital would not talk. Keira looked at his file and saw that Tony de la Cruz was of mixed Mexican, Italian, and Japanese descent—the latter explained the Chusei link—and was married. The Chusei had probably promised to take care of his wife if something happened to him while on assignment. Keira figured they'd also undoubtedly made it clear that they'd kill her if he ever talked. Messing up the job was bad enough. Now he had to do damage control by not spilling intel. He'd be a silent dead end for her.

She looked up Tony de la Cruz's wife, Celia, and also retrieved the records for his brothers in the hopes of gaining something even remotely useful from their files.

Squirmy was still recovering at the hospital. Keira had conversed with him briefly over their time pieces. He was groggy but on the mend. She felt reasonably assured of his safety with Mikey standing by and increasingly grateful for his rapid recovery, plus his escape from two potentially fatal encounters in one day. Squirmy seemed to be defying the odds, as did Keira for that matter.

Earlier in the day Wozniak's mind had been completely blown by the drone footage of Ms. Strauss. He was at a loss for words on how to proceed, but he had given Keira the green light to do whatever she thought was necessary while asking her to at least try to be discreet. He didn't ask how she'd come by the footage, which was a relief. She sensed that he felt over his head in unexplored depths. She could certainly relate.

As Keira examined the files for de la Cruz's brother Marco, she noticed that he worked for the Empress Hotel under their "curated experiences" division, which referred to the experience dens. It was common for multiple siblings to work for the Chusei because the crime tribe demanded loyalty and relied on leverage. Having multiple family members employed typically covered both bases. The oldest de la Cruz brother lived in Maryland, so there was no reason to contact him yet. Keira figured it was too dangerous to pay Celia a visit. She decided that checking out the experience dens tomorrow was her best option. Keira downloaded Marco's 3D image and physical description.

Then she turned her attention back to the existing case files hoping to find new insights on old material.

After coming up empty with her searches, she became frustrated and started pacing. As she rubbed a knot in her shoulder and thought about how best to close in on Victor again, Blaise called.

Blaise had been reviewing recorded transcripts of the Fed's intercepted correspondence from Russian persons of interest, she explained. "I was hoping to find clues I might have missed the first time." Keira found it amusing that they were doing the same thing—a process they both knew all too well.

Blaise continued, "One thing that leapt out at me today was a reference to 'the rise of the machines.' I searched for that term and found it three times in the transcripts. Each time the context is pretty vague, but there's like a gravitas around each mention. Earlier I thought it might refer to illegally reviving industry, but now I wonder if it has a much more specific meaning related to what we saw yesterday."

Keira's heart raced. If the Russians were involved in creating or using replicants, what was their end game? Furthermore, what did Miller know about the replicants? "This is getting sci fi crazy," she said.

THE NEXT MORNING around 08:30 Keira showed up at the experience dens and waited in line in the alley adjoining the Empress Hotel. In front of her, a skinny man wearing a tight black hood from his threadbare sweatshirt shifted his weight between his feet over and over again. His hands twitched.

She wore a medical mask to protect against contagion. The experience dens at this hour of the morning tended to attract the down and out and the real junkies, as opposed to the partiers or the curious.

She counted ten people in front of her. The line moved fairly quickly, with a muscular security guard letting one person in at a time for vetting. Although the background checks weren't as deep for the dens as for the penthouse services, it was never a good idea for cops to show up as themselves. Besides, Keira had a Chusei hit on her head. Courtesy of the Impersonator, she assumed the fake identity of Nicole Ferguson, a megastore employee.

As she made her way to the front of the line, the security guard glared at her. She said the code word "soar."

He inspected her belongings. "Go," he muttered, his chin pointing to the entrance.

The door opened automatically. An illuminated arrow showed her where to walk in the dark entrails of the experience dens. She followed the arrow down a ramp about two floors below ground before arriving at the reception desk, a small table where a grouchy woman with thick glasses sat vaping.

"Fingerprints."

Keira pressed her impersonated fingertips against the sensor.

"Nicole, please select your experience while I run your background."

Keira swiped through selections on the screen: nature immersion, cosmic awe, cuddle cure, torrid affair, coke dreams, lowered inhibitions, sunrise scenes, ocean explorer, serotonin soak, rock star fantasy . . .

"Is Marco here today?" Keira asked. "I heard he can hook it up."

The woman exhaled her vapor, which smelled like bubblegum, and stared at Keira through the ridiculously thick lenses of her glasses. It was hard to read the intention behind the stare, but Keira's best guess was curiosity overshadowed by irritation. Or maybe she just couldn't see Keira's face well.

"That may have been the case, but he doesn't work here anymore. Today you'll see Shania. Please make a selection."

That's odd, Keira thought. The employment records uploaded to government servers are accurate almost up to the minute because failure to report changes could bring hefty fines and the possibility of getting a business permit revoked. Even crime tribes like the Chusei kept clean employment records.

She chose rock star fantasy since it was the option in front of her. She didn't want the receptionist scrutinizing her for longer than necessary.

Maybe Marco was getting a shakedown for his brother's failure. She didn't particularly want to move ahead with the purchase, especially since she knew she'd feel lingering dissatisfaction afterward that would be hard to shake. A maddening craving for more pleasure always followed a trip to the dens.

But she couldn't leave now without arousing suspicion, so she continued with the transaction. The receptionist pointed the way to the waiting room.

Once there, a few other people sat far from each other looking slightly agitated. One skinny man sweated visibly around the temples and avoided eye contact.

What a creepy feeling in here, Keira thought, despite the soothing music and scent of peppermint. Neither was enough to wash away the human desperation. Keira felt nauseous as she tried to breathe through her mask.

A couple minutes after taking her seat, she heard commotion in the hallway and a yelping noise. Moments later a bodyguard could be seen dragging a man down the corridor. The man yelled out, but with his head stuck in the guard's tight headlock, the noise wasn't very loud.

Keira wondered what he had done.

A female employee then walked down the hallway crying and holding her nose. Blood gushed through her fingers and onto the floor. Poor thing. The man must have punched her. Keira figured the guy would be lucky to make it out of the dens alive. At the very least, the Chusei would give him a beating he wouldn't soon forget.

Keira felt really uncomfortable but tried to stay calm and not give anyone reason to notice her. Several minutes later the woman with the thick glasses appeared in the waiting room and walked up to her. She whispered, "Shania had to leave. I could get you another appointment in an hour or refund you your money."

Keira was relieved at her chance. "I can't wait that long, so I'll take the refund. Thank you."

"Very well. Until next time."

I don't think so, Keira thought. She headed upward toward the exit at ground level as quickly as she could. When she opened the door, she did a double take.

Nailed against the wooden wall was a bloody hand. Underneath was the message: "Hands off our staff, or be dealt a heavy hand."

Keira gagged and fought back the urge to puke. She walked quickly down the alley. Could they have cut the man's hand off this fast and already displayed it?

That didn't seem likely, which meant it was probably some other offender's hand. Damn, how many people had been maimed at the dens for getting out of line? A disgusted feeling churned in her stomach and slithered into her joints and muscles. She couldn't wait to hightail it out of there.

CHAPTER 25
FANNING THE FLAMES

KEIRA WAS FAST ASLEEP LATER that night when Michael summoned her.

"Keira, wake up!" she heard. She thought she was dreaming and turned on her side with her eyes closed. "Keira, catch!" She recognized Michael's voice and looked up to see the purple crystal floating in the air toward her. She caught it and watched the light race along its surface, reflecting the sun and sky. Was she awake or asleep? This was all getting so confusing.

Michael smiled with his sparkly white teeth, his head radiating light.

"What time is it?" she asked.

"02:04."

"Couldn't this little tête-à-tête have waited for a more normal hour?"

He laughed. "What is a normal hour? They all seem perfectly normal to me."

Ugh, his cheeriness was irritating. She wanted to go back to sleep. Her eyelids felt heavy.

"It is so tempting to doze away," Michael said, "and I do know how you yearn for rest. Soon you'll get it, I promise, but for now duty calls you away in the wee hours of the morning, my dear. You are needed at the Misfits' warehouse stat!"

She groaned. "Really? Why?"

"You'll find your answer there! Bring Blaise. And, Keira, go now!"

Michael faded from view. Keira opened her eyes in the dark of the bedroom. A part of her wanted to pretend that the exchange with Michael had been a dream or figment of her imagination, but she knew in her core it was real in whatever way that meant and that she should follow his instructions.

Reluctantly, yet with an opening mind toward her newest mission, she summoned a very sleepy Blaise awake. After dressing quickly and arming themselves, they left the safe house together and headed into the darkness of the earliest hours of the day.

THE RIGHT SIDE of the warehouse was engulfed in flames. A window exploded when Keira and Blaise were half a block away, causing Keira to instinctively cover her face and duck.

"We should call this in!" Blaise shouted over the din.

"There's no time! We need to see if anyone is in there. The left side is still clear! We have a chance."

They sprinted toward the burning building. Keira could feel the heat increasing as she got closer and closer to the disaster in front of her. The flames billowed from blown-out windows, consuming the oxygen that spurred the fire to become brighter and more destructive. Keira could hear building debris falling. The right side's roof might soon give way, she thought.

Keira ran to the entrance where she and Squirmy had planted the surveillance video camera. Blaise kept right behind her. "Keira, this is crazy! We could both die. How do we even know if anyone is in there?"

"Harper and Cora might be inside. I need to do this. Maybe you should stay, love."

Blaise shook her head, looking resigned to the crazy task and to the Manifestors' pull on Keira, which was still quite the mystery to both of them, and motioned for Keira to move ahead. Keira opened the unlocked door to find a warehouse plunged in darkness on one side and engulfed in flame on the other.

She picked up motion in her peripheral vision. To her left just where the light gave into the darkness, she saw Cora standing on the second-story walkway, her gun pointed at a male figure with his hands up. After having tracked Cora and having been tracked by her, Keira would recognize Cora's frame anywhere, even in this poor lighting.

Keira drew her own gun and motioned to Blaise to stay behind her.

The male said, "Cora, it's not too late to change your mind! This happens to all of us who carry out dirty deeds for too long. We stop trusting and go adrift. I understand."

Keira recognized his voice. It was Victor!

Why would Cora hold him at gunpoint in a burning building instead of running for her life?

Keira heard a snap to her right. She turned, gun pointed. Harper stood five feet away, motioning to Keira to lower the gun and walk toward her. Keira glanced back toward Cora unsure what to do.

Harper whispered, "That is her fate, Keira. This is yours." She waved her hand rapidly at Keira and Blaise to join her.

What other choice did they have? The building seemed likely to crash down around them at any moment, and it wasn't necessarily wise to step between a loaded gun and a target.

As they followed Harper through a dark passageway, Keira gripped her gun firmly with both hands, pointing it away from her and down.

A gun fired in the distance. Keira nearly jumped. Did Cora shoot Victor? Or did Victor shoot Cora? Keira met Blaise's gaze, whose eyes told her to proceed with caution. Blaise wasn't one to trust anyone at face value either.

Harper led them through a door and down a slowly descending ramp. It grew cooler and damper as they made their way deeper underground.

Above them the sounds from the fire-loosened debris falling to the floor grew muffled, although the disaster was still close enough to make Keira feel jumpy. Harper turned on a solar lantern and told them to hurry.

Keira assumed that Harper was leading them to safety on foot through a below-ground exit, but when she heard the roar of a jeep engine, she began to wonder what the actual exit strategy was. A few seconds later in the dim lantern light, Keira could see two men standing beside the jeep holding machine guns.

"Where are we going?" Keira asked Harper.

Harper turned her head but kept walking with purpose. "To safety, Keira. You need to trust the Light One. This is part of his plan."

Fuck this, Keira thought. She wanted to grab Blaise and find their own way out. But she looked around and saw no exits. If she resisted Harper's instructions and failed to find a way out, she and Blaise could die in the flames. Still, whatever plan Michael had in mind was not sitting well with her. She longed for more control and certainty, yet here she was below a burning warehouse about to board a jeep flanked by men toting machine guns.

Blaise, seeming to read her thoughts, said, "We have no viable alternative. Let's just see where they take us and figure it out from there. We have our guns and our wits and each other. We'll be okay."

Keira exhaled and nodded. "You're right. I just wish I could trust what this was all about and where it was leading."

Blaise squeezed Keira's shoulder. "Don't we all?"

Harper finished loading items into the jeep and called to them. "We need to go. Now!"

Keira and Blaise exchanged an expression of here goes.

As they climbed into the back of the jeep, there was a thunderous crashing sound above them. Keira wondered how much longer the ceiling would hold.

The jeep took off. Keira put her right hand on Blaise's knee and watched as the vehicle carried them through a long, dark tunnel lit only by their headlights.

Keira asked Harper again where they were going.

"All I can say right now is to safety. Hang on. It's going to be a long drive."

Long indeed. They drove along a network of underground tunnels for several hours, stopping occasionally to open the steel door of a closed tunnel in order to continue their journey.

Harper explained that the tunnel network had been financed and built decades ago by a paranoid entrepreneur named Silvester Donatello who wanted to ensure that he, his loved ones, and his products could be transported to safety should an explosion or government takeover or some other calamity impact normal life from above. Ironically, Silvester died of a drug overdose mere months before the war hit —when the tunnels really would have come in handy for him.

In his last years, Silvester became increasingly alienated and paranoid, Harper explained. As such, he kept the tunnels' existence a secret from everyone except his one trusted friend and confidant, the Light One. Silvester gave Michael the blueprints and codes for the doors should he ever need them.

Michael utilized the tunnels during the war, Harper said. The underground network offered a way to keep people safe and to store goods like non-perishable food and medicine. What was now the Misfits' warehouse had been Michael's central operations of sorts, an unassuming spot where he could come and go without too much fear of being monitored by the government, which he assumed would mismanage the tunnels or use them for the wrong reasons.

Silvester had originally used the warehouse for goods storage. The warehouse sat above the first tunnel, making it the perfect spot to escape a threat without being seen. The tunnel doors all closed immediately after being traversed, which made it unlikely that anyone would find the network. If they did somehow find one part, they couldn't access the rest of it without the codes.

Keira wanted to know more about Michael's activities during the war and how the Misfits got involved, but after a sleepless night she didn't have the energy to be actively inquisitive. She tried to stay awake, but her eyelids felt heavy.

The jeep suddenly started climbing upslope and then leveled out before arriving at another tunnel door. The man in the passenger seat jumped out. He opened what looked like a peephole on the tunnel door and looked through it for several seconds. He then nodded at the driver and signaled an all clear. He thrust open the door, allowing blinding sunlight to flood into the tunnel.

Keira blinked repeatedly and looked away. It was hard for the eyes to adjust to so much light after being immersed in so much darkness.

Harper handed Keira and Blaise pairs of sunglasses. Keira gratefully put hers on over her watering eyes and felt immediate relief.

The jeep drove through the open door, which swiftly closed behind it. They were out in the open now, on a sandy wash in the desert.

Creosote bushes dotted the flat landscape, which extended to distant mountains glowing in the early morning sun. As the jeep made its way over the terrain, fishtailing at times in the deeper sandy areas, Keira looked back at the tunnel exit. The door appeared to have been painted the color of desert sand, with tumble weeds and other vegetation stuck to it. It was so well camouflaged that she wondered if she could find her way back to it if need be.

Finding this all so disorienting and strange, Keira again asked Harper, "Where are we going?"

Harper pretended to zip her own mouth closed.

It had been worth the chance to ask, Keira figured, as she settled back into silence.

The sun's warmth felt nice after the cool darkness of the tunnels. The jeep rumbled on, passing badlands and highly stratified rock formations pushed together by pressure and time. All was still.

Keira found her surroundings hauntingly beautiful. The pervasive quiet, coupled with the immense unoccupied space, gave her the sensation that the world had truly ended this time but that the earth had offered them an inspiring place to start over.

Her time piece rumbled. Notifications she'd missed while underground now flashed on her screen. One was a video sent to her and Squirmy from a user named Phoenix. After running it through scam software to ensure it wasn't an attempted hack, she hit play.

To her surprise, in the hologram she saw Cora and Victor in what appeared to be the warehouse earlier this morning. But Victor wasn't being held at gunpoint.

In the video, Victor gestured impatiently at the flames around them and said, "Let's get to it, Cora. This building won't hold much longer. Where is Charlie, the detective?"

Cora pulled her gun and pointed it at Victor's head. "Step back a pace, and put your hands up."

Victor looked surprised but quickly collected his composure. He did as asked. "What is this about?"

"This is about putting things right. Finally. I never wanted to do your bidding. You told me I needed to work off my landlord's debts to the Chusei. The debts have been repaid many times over, yet you have never let me go."

"I understand your frustration, Cora. I will let you go now. I promise. Just lower the gun and lead me to Detective Watts. This will be your final mission. You have my word."

"It's too late. The clock has been set in motion and is about to strike."

"Cora, it's not too late to change your mind! This happens to all of us who carry out dirty deeds for too long. We stop trusting and go adrift. I understand."

Keira realized that was the part of the conversation she had overheard in the warehouse before Harper summoned her. She kept watching the tense scene play out on her time piece, hoping that Cora would prevail in the end.

While continuing to hold Victor at gunpoint, Cora said, "We both know I wouldn't be safe. The Chusei would hunt me down to atone for wronging you. You know that Detective Kincaid is alive and that I staged her death. You must think I'm naive to believe I'd survive that betrayal. Besides, this O'Connor kidnapping appears to be some sort of deal with the Russians, and I want no part of that. I renounce the Chusei credo once and for all. I will set things right."

"Cora, wait!" he pleaded. "I will protect you. I can say that you died here. No one will know. The stakes have gotten higher, the deals shadier. I understand why you want out. I didn't like kidnapping a baby either. Please."

A look of uncertainty crossed Victor's face. He suddenly reached toward his lower back for his own gun. As he started to bring it around, Cora shot him in the forehead.

Victor fell backward and toppled from the balcony one story down to the bottom floor. Cora looked down at his crumpled body and then toward the flames encroaching toward her. The fire was no more than twenty feet away. It was unclear if she had any route to escape. The video ended there.

"Is Cora alive?" Keira asked Harper.

Harper didn't speak but held Keira's gaze for an unnerving amount of time. Keira felt a sense of dread as she waited. She had grown fond of Cora after initially fearing and hating her.

"Cora volunteered to stay behind and make sure that no trace existed of our plans, items, or exit strategy," Harper explained. "I doubt that she survived the fire given how quickly it progressed. If she did make it out alive, we asked that she not contact us for some time in order to protect her identity and whereabouts as well as ours."

Harper sighed and continued, "Maybe it's better not to know and just to hope. Cora is like the mythical phoenix rising from its ashes in order to be reborn—in this realm or another." Harper wiped away tears.

Phoenix was the name of the video user. Keira thought that if anyone had a chance of pulling off a perfect exit and staging a come-back, it was Cora. As the jeep rumbled on, Keira said a silent prayer to the universe asking for Cora's safekeeping.

"Wait, did the Misfits start the fire on purpose?" Keira asked, the possibility dawning on her.

Harper sat silently for several moments. "Hold your questions. The answers will come in due time."

Keira was growing increasingly irritated by the stonewalling. After cussing several times in her head, she resigned herself to waiting. Harper would not crack; she knew that much. The fire had imperiled their lives, but she and Blaise were alive. Maybe the fire was necessary. Maybe it was just an accident. She was starting to lose a sense of what was going on and where she fit in with any of it.

She turned her thoughts to the video. She believed it would provide sufficient evidence to implicate Victor and the Chusei in Liam's kidnapping as well as the intended abduction of a police detective, Squirmy. If they were Cora's final moments on earth, they certainly had tremendous benefits for solving Liam's case, at least somewhat, which Wozniak would be happy about, and for opening the door into further investigation into the Chusei's Russian ties, which could lead to possible links to President Miller if they indeed existed. As such, Cora had left Keira in a favorable position for tying up loose ends and pursuing new leads.

A gut feeling struck Keira that Cora had a future role to play in her life. Rise up, Phoenix, she thought. I'll be waiting for you.

She glanced over at Blaise, who smiled tenderly at her. Keira leaned in and inhaled the sweet scent of Blaise's skin. They embraced for a moment, their bodies jostled by the jeep's movements. It always seemed like something tried to tear them apart, even an unsteady off-road ride, but the strength of their bond somehow kept finding a way to keep them together.

Keira sat back against the seat, thinking about how amazing the sun felt on the crown of her head and how freeing it was to be immersed in the elements. The city could seem stifling sometimes, but here there was so much space to wander through.

With all these pleasant thoughts and impressions trickling through her mind, plus the stress of the last several days weighing on her body, Keira fell asleep as the jeep continued its trek through the expansive desert.

CHAPTER 26
SHADE OF THE BADLANDS

WHEN KEIRA AWOKE to Blaise gently shaking her, the jeep was parked under a wooden shade structure covered with palm fronds. She was groggy and thirsty. "Where are we?" she asked.

"Michael's compound. That's all I know. Let's get some water—I'm parched—and see Michael, who apparently is here. Harper told me where to go. We couldn't wake you, so she and the guys with the machine guns unloaded and walked away."

Keira got out of the jeep and stretched her limbs. She had slept hard and felt rested but disoriented. Even with sunglasses on, her eyes took a moment to adjust to the brightness once she walked out from under the shade structure.

In front of them was a gorgeous fountain, with two hummingbirds flitting about in the streams of cascading water. Beyond the fountain was a small building covered with pastel tiles that shimmered in the sun. Mesquite and palo verde trees around the grounds provided patches of shade and greenery. Off in the far distance, a mountain range marked the horizon, giving the landscape a reassuring sense of containment.

Keira and Blaise smiled at each other. "What a gorgeous place," Blaise remarked. "Harper told me we'd find water and something to eat in that building."

Once inside they found a table holding a large water container, dishware, and what looked like real food. Keira wondered if the food was fake and just there for decorative purposes, but as they got closer, she thought that the nuts, bread, salad, and more certainly looked real. "Am I hallucinating this, Blaise, or is this an actual feast before us?"

"I was just asking myself the same question. I guess we'll have to find out."

Keira poured them glasses of water. Inside the water container, slices of lemons and limes bobbed among ice cubes. Keira was so thirsty that she rapidly drank two glasses in a row.

"This water is incredible," she said. They both marveled over the citrus flavors on their tongues from the infused water before placing food on their plates.

Keira tentatively took a bite of salad in case it was fake. The crunch of the lettuce and its watery, fibrous goodness covered in a tart yet sweet dressing awakened her taste buds in full force.

After sampling the assorted nuts, deviled eggs, and slices of mango, the two women forced themselves to stop. They didn't want to get sick and had no idea how their digestive systems might react to the meal of the decade. They sipped another glass of water, savoring it as they looked out the windows at the desert scenery. Keira felt in a trance and questioned whether her experiences were real or imagined. Was this some sort of simulation?

Just then the floor opened up about ten feet in front of them as a glass elevator entered the room. The doors retracted, and out stepped Michael.

He grinned and rushed over to them with his arms open for hugs. "Ladies, how happy I am to see you! Welcome to Brighter Days. This is a very special place that has been many years in the making. Would you like a tour?"

Before they could answer, he beckoned them to follow him into the glass elevator. Once inside, he asked them to close their eyes for the big reveal.

Keira reached for Blaise's hand as the elevator quickly descended with a whoosh. When it settled to a stop, Michael said, "Now open your eyes!"

They found themselves in a desert modern room with wall-to-wall windows perched over an expanse of badlands. As she stepped forward, Keira felt as though she hovered in space, practically within touching distance of the chiseled formations. She marveled over the badlands' deep vertical grooves, subtle hues of red and purple, and the channels cut between them. It was like seeing a topographical model brought to life. The room itself spoke to the chic days of Frank Sinatra with its retro minimalism and clean lines. Keira had never seen a design style like it before.

Michael beamed. "This has been my vision come true as an architect. It took a long time and tested my patience, but the final result has been more than worth the effort." Keira didn't know that Michael was an architect, but it seemed a fitting occupation for someone who could dream up other realities and endeavor to make them take form. He told them how what he had originally planned to be his retirement home expanded in scale into a self-sustainable compound.

Members of the Manifestors and Misfits had teamed up, he explained, as well as recruited others to build greenhouses to grow food, create computer surveillance systems to effectively shield the compound, and design a banking system for transferring and procuring funds via a legally formed shell corporation. Those were just a few of the systems in place for what had become in recent months a fully functioning autonomous center, although Michael conceded that there were still some kinks to work out. "I am hoping that the two of you will be instrumental in addressing some of them."

Before he could elaborate, the sound of approaching footsteps interrupted them. Keira turned around. It was Tomoko! By some miracle of timing, Blaise got a call on her time piece and stepped away to answer it.

As Keira and Tomoko smiled at each other and exchanged polite pleasantries, Keira noticed what looked like an emerging baby bump. Tomoko shot her a coy look. "Don't worry, it's not yours." Michael burst out laughing, while Keira's face grew hot.

Tomoko handed Michael a paper that she said was a greenhouse order form. Then she turned on her heels with a somewhat sad expression on her face and left as quickly as she'd come.

Michael told Keira that Tomoko's pregnancy was a promise he had made to Cora for her sacrifices. "Tomoko has been trying to be hopeful, but the uncertainty and Cora's absence are taking a toll on her. We all hope and pray that Cora survived and will make her way safely back to us."

Keira knew well what that double whammy of not seeing someone you loved dearly and not knowing that had happened to them could do to a person's state of mind.

Unable to hold back her curiosity, she asked Michael how Tomoko got pregnant and how it was possible that she was so far along in her pregnancy since she presumably hadn't been pregnant when Keira first met her.

"Ah, those answers will have to wait for another day I'm afraid."

"What did I miss?" Blaise asked as she returned to the conversation.

Meeting Tomoko, Keira thought. She had debated whether to tell Blaise about that experience but certainly didn't feel ready to explain it at the moment.

Keira's time piece rumbled with a message from Squirmy. He wrote, "This is a bull's eye of a video, partner. Glad I wasn't actually abducted by the ninja! Dang. More importantly, are you okay?"

"Yes! Thanks for checking in," she responded. "How are you feeling? You'll never believe where I am!?! I'll explain later. Please cover for me." Then realizing she had no idea when she'd return, she asked Michael.

He wanted Keira and Blaise to spend the night if that was okay with them. He'd return them to San Diego tomorrow. They figured they could keep their bosses at bay for a day and agreed to the plan. Keira asked Squirmy to tell Wozniak that she was sick.

Moments later Squirmy acknowledged he'd cover for her and that he had some pep in his step after getting released from the hospital. He signed off with "Onward."

Onward, she thought, as she gazed at the badlands in front of her and wondered how long they'd stood there, waiting and still, like guards keeping watch over the world.

CHAPTER 27
INTO THE SPHERE

KEIRA'S MIND chatter wouldn't quiet enough to allow her to sleep. She knew it was early in the morning but wasn't sure of the time.

After having toured the compound, the scale of what Michael and his team of Manifestors and Misfits had accomplished was dizzying to process. For starters, they had a viable food and water supply that they were able to regenerate and sustain.

And thanks to Spyder's handiwork, the compound was off the digital grid. Spyder had created a blind spot in the government surveillance system that essentially hid the compound from government satellites and drones. Planes and choppers could still fly overhead and spot activity with the naked eye from above, however, so one person was always on monitoring duty.

Whenever an overhead flight was expected to cross over, the guard alerted the whole compound to go into one of the below-ground rooms out of sight. In fact, most of the compound was built underground. These hiding protocols happened every few days on average. As far as anyone knew according to public records, the compound belonged to Michael, which would make it seem unusual to see more than a few people around at any one time. Everyone had to be extremely careful and not get lulled into a sense of ease.

Currently, seventy-seven people lived at the compound, and each had a job or multiple jobs to do. As Michael showed her earlier that morning, they even had a media department. Its aim was to launch a recording series that would reveal the truth about Green-Y, the Chusei, President Miller, the Russians, and Go Slow. The journalists in the media department were working hard to corroborate sources and locate evidence to prove the connections so that no one could convincingly paint them as kooky conspiracy theorists.

Michael didn't show her everything, however. He said it was for her own good and more would be revealed later as appropriate. He also wouldn't answer her question about whether they had intentionally set the warehouse on fire or if it was an accident.

Now as she stared at the ceiling of the small bedroom she shared with Blaise at the compound, she wondered if this was always how it would be with Michael. He'd know the plan. She wouldn't, except she might be given little bits of information here and there—just enough to keep her from losing her mind in frustration but not enough to fully understand what was happening.

She felt like a rat in a maze trying to find the cheese while Michael stood by watching her. These thoughts bothered her, even though he'd told her multiple times that he would purposefully withhold some information to protect her.

Keira wanted to know what was coming before it landed ready to kill her, like a dragon in a virtual reality game. Her nervous system eventually would not be able to keep up with such ramped up levels of adrenaline and vigilance. That she knew. It was only a matter of time before biology failed her. There had to be another way.

She tried to calm her agitation by zoning out and letting her thoughts drop away. She stared at the light gray walls decorated with a couple of architectural drawings from the 1900s. The room had bunk beds, a sink with a mirror above it, and a dresser. An efficient efficiency, she thought, that formed quite the contrast to the opulence of the compound's communal spaces.

She heard a gentle knock at the door. She rose from bed and noticed that Blaise still slept soundly on the bunk below her. The beds were too small to share, which probably also contributed to Keira's poor sleep.

Keira peered through the door's peephole to see Michael standing there. When she opened the door, he smiled and said quietly, "Some part of you was probably hoping to talk to me, my dear. I have good tidings and a plan."

Thinking she'd believe it when she saw it, but nonetheless tripped out by his timing, she stepped out of the room and closed the door. He gestured for her to walk by his side and then tapped her shoulder reassuringly. They walked in silence down the windowless hallway.

After several minutes they came upon an imposing wood door with carvings of oak trees and druids etched into its center with beautiful artistry.

Michael beamed and said, "Nothing can quite prepare you for this, but let's take a few deep breaths anyway." He asked her to face him and to breathe with him, inhaling to a count of seven and exhaling to seven. She found Michael's request strange but couldn't find a compelling enough reason not to comply with it.

Then Michael placed his fingers on a keypad, and the wood door swung open.

⁓

KEIRA ENTERED A MASTERPIECE.

She stepped into a glass sphere with views below to the desert valley, as well as up to the sky, and a resplendent light show within.

Sunlight illuminated stained-glass sections of the sphere in swaths of uplifting colors that burst forth like a delightful summer garden. As light and color washed over Keira, she felt as though she floated over the earth. The effect was mesmerizing.

She and Michael stood on a bamboo platform that served as the walkway through the sphere. It traversed the space in a swirling pattern. In front of her feet, painted on the bamboo in tight cursive, was a William Blake quote: "If the doors of perception were cleansed everything would appear to man as it is, Infinite. For man has closed himself up, till he sees all things through narrow chinks of his cavern."

Keira wondered if her own perceptions had been like a dim cavern. Had she been closing herself off—unable to see the extent of the possibilities around her?

It occurred to her that this sphere was intended to literally open the "doors of perception" in order to witness beauty and inspire awe. The world was not small or uninspiring, she thought, but our approach to it could be.

"Are you ready to be cleansed, Keira?" Michael asked, gesturing to the Blake quote and the magnificence all around them. "It does not happen all at once, and it requires constant upkeep. We harbor deep inside ourselves so much judgment, fear, doubt, regret, and other forms of negativity. These self-limiting perspectives haunt us and separate us from others as well as from ourselves."

He paused as joy and sadness crossed over his face. "As I told you before, I could not reach you until you became vulnerable. That happened as a result of your love for Blaise. Now I need you to begin to love and trust yourself, Keira. That is the only way to fulfill your higher purpose. To love yourself you have to allow your authentic self to shine through—the you that wants to be you! It starts with self-acceptance and is guided by determination."

Michael gripped her shoulders and laughed, his eyes shining with white light and his demeanor confident. "This must be strange for you to hear, Keira! It's also strange for me to say because we've been conditioned to shape ourselves to the world rather than shaping the world to ourselves."

The melding and infusing of color in the sphere was so magnificent, so delicate, and so inspiring that Keira felt in that moment that anything was possible.

"Now for a bit of fun." Michael dropped his grip, stepped two paces in front of her, and swung his arms around and around in circles. During one revolution, as his right hand stretched in front of his shoulder, he seemingly released from his fingertips two hummingbirds. They flitted forward, turned around, and flew back toward Michael and Keira, hovering just in front of her with their pink and green plumage—their tiny wings beating so fast that they sounded like small motors revving to go.

Michael swept his arm aside with the motion of a symphony conductor, and the hummingbirds disappeared. Then he swung his arm back and created in its path a trail of little clouds that drifted toward Keira. She reached into a passing cloud and felt its cool air on her skin. Next Michael produced light rainfall, which fell in warm drops upon them, followed by a rainbow.

Keira beamed with a smile as broad as Michael's.

"That's the spirit!" he exclaimed. "Yes, yes! You can see this because you believe in yourself and in me right now. We are co-creators of our reality, unshackled and unbounded!" Michael hugged Keira with vigor and then quickly released her.

His eyes sparkled. "All things are possible, Keira, when you dispel doubt and look for the deeper connections within"—touching his head and then his heart—"and without!" Michael swept his hands in front of him, causing the rainbow color in the air to undulate as if it were made of water.

Keira moved her own hands into the medium, wanting to see a wave. Next thing she knew, the rainbow water gathered into swell formation and surged in waves that crashed beyond, sending up a sea spray of vibrant colors against the sphere.

She laughed, delighted by what she'd created, and then looked down. Through the clear glass, the expanse of desert sand and plants glowed in the warm hues of dawn. Keira wondered what life forms stirred below as she felt joy and conviction stirring within.

∿

END OF BOOK ONE

ACKNOWLEDGMENTS

I would like to thank Michelle Dombrowski for her awesome cover design, which visually brought to life the world swirling in my head and unfurling on the page. Thanks as well, Michelle, for being an amazing (and patient) sounding board!

I would also like to express my gratitude to Danielle Dyal for her insightful feedback as a developmental editor. Danielle's review of an earlier draft helped me to see the manuscript with fresh eyes and to subsequently forge ahead on the path to improving it.

To Lucy Zhang, thanks for the valuable reminders to stay true to myself and to meet fear with courage.

ABOUT THE AUTHOR

CAREY BLAKELY is a freelance writer, editor, and author of both fiction and nonfiction. Her novel *Crossed Odds* launched the Crystal Dystopia series in May 2022, with more books to come (stay tuned for release dates!). Carey has also co-authored two books of nonfiction: *Crazy Like a Fox: One Principal's Triumph in the Inner City* (by Dr. Ben Chavis with Carey Blakely) and *Next! A Matchmaker's Guide to Finding Mr. Right, Ditching Mr. Wrong, and Everything In Between* (by Barbara Summers with Carey Blakely). She lives in San Diego.

Find out more about Carey and follow her blog, Flourish, at careyblakely.com. Thanks for reading!

Printed in Great Britain
by Amazon

22955711R00128